PRAISE FOR *Worth Forgiving*

"Janet K. Brown touches hearts and lives of those with addictive personalities. Exposing the core of problems in her characters, she leads her reader to do their own soul-searching, offering encouragement as her characters find their way through trials and personal crises. I highly recommend Brown's *Worth Forgiving*."
– BONNE LANTHRIPE, playwright, award winning actress, and author of *The Ringleader*

"*Worth Forgiving*: The title of this hard-hitting story says it all. Is Katie, a recently released convict imprisoned for her drug connections and allowing her daughter to be kidnapped, worthy of mercy? This question haunts both Katie and Larry Pullman, a police officer and seminary graduate seeking a pastorate. The theology of unconditional love runs in Larry's veins, especially with his own checkered past, but he must answer another query: Does his attraction to Katie form a reliable basis for marriage?

"It's hard to say who entertains the most doubts, or which one suffers the most setbacks in this story. But suffice it to say, Janet Brown has mastered the art of raining down troubles on her hero and heroine, and keeping the reader wondering about the outcome."
– GAIL KITTLESON, author of *In Times Like These* and *In This Together?*

"*Worth Forgiving* is a page turning follow-up to Brown's first book, *Worth Her Weight*. If I had only one word to describe it, I would call it 'riveting.' Ms. Brown delves deeply into the reasons for addictions and she also offers the solution to addiction problems. Caution: once you start reading, you may not be able to put it down until you finish this well-written book."
– BLANCHE DAY MANOS, author of the Darcy and Flora and Ned McNeil series

"An engaging emotional novel depicting the redemptive power and love of God. This novel is filled with emotion and drama that will engage you from start to finish. The book depicts the struggles—both internal and ex ternal—that Katie Smith faces based on a rocky past that ended up in a prison sentence. It's more than a novel however. This Christian-based work is filled with life's realities and decisions that are made every day. When Katie gets out of prison she is inwardly imprisoned by her regrets and the emotional distance she feels toward her sister Lacey. Though Lacey would rid herself of emotional issues related to eating and lose 100 pounds, Katie's struggles would be a work in progress . . . Throughout this book will be the struggle to follow one's heart and love despite contrary conflicting circumstances. With plenty of twists and turns it brings the reader to a transparent conclusion that no one is beyond the grasp of God's saving hand. Learn how 'baby Katie,' not biological, comes into Katie's life based on unusual circumstances.

"This book will shares a theme we all face sometime in our own lives—will we forgive others and even ourselves? The reader will be headlong thrown in the internal struggle to find peace, clarity . . . and true love.

"Author Janet K Brown masterfully weaves this page-turning plot into scenarios and challenges that many will relate to: sibling rivalry /envy, unforgiveness, deception, food and drug addictions, self blame and shame, and the quest to find true love.

". . . I give it a five-star rating without hesitation."
– VALERIE CARAOTTA, book reviewer

"*Worth Forgiving* by Janet K. Brown is a Christian novel about second chances and God's amazing grace . . . There are many themes in the novel and over them all is God. 'God gave you a second chance. He's got a plan for you.' No one has ever messed up so badly that they are out of reach of God. God longs for us all to be in a relationship with Him.

"People believe words spoken over them. Katie believes she is 'Alone. Unwanted. Unloved.' In Jesus she will find herself loved. We all need to hear Jesus' words of affirmation to us rather than our own words of condemnation.

"I thoroughly enjoyed *Worth Forgiving* as I journeyed with Katie from despair into the future. [It] was packed full of godly themes and is a compulsive read. I read it in just two sittings . . . pausing only to sleep! I am looking forward to more from Janet K Brown."
– JULIA WILSON, "Christian Bookaholic"

WORTH
Forgiving

BOOKS BY JANET K. BROWN

THE WHARTON ROCK SERIES:
Worth Her Weight
Worth Forgiving

*Divine Dining: 365 Devotions to Guide You to
Healthier Weight and Abundant Wellness*

Victoria and the Ghost

REVIEWS FOR *WORTH HER WEIGHT,*
BOOK 1 IN THE WHARTON ROCK SERIES

This book is a hidden gem—one of those reads that is not easy to forget
and will hit the reader in the heart at certain points. There is an immediate
connection with and sympathy for Lacey and the feeling of wanting her
to succeed in everything she puts her effort to. It's one of those books that
will have the reader screaming at the top of their lungs in the hopes that
the characters can hear.

Moving at an even pace, it has a great little mystery in it too, and
a male character that isn't seen all too often—he's a normal everyday guy
doing his job which is refreshing. This book is an emotional roller coaster
that will stay with the reader for a long while after it's read!

–LYNN-ALEXANDRIA MCKENDRICK, IND'TALE MAGAZINE

The book was great! And true to the way a food addict deals with their
struggles. I know first-hand. Love the book.

–DEELYNN LOPEZ, PROGRAM DIRECTOR OF BEHAVIORAL HEALTH
GROUP AND CO-LEADER FOR CELEBRATE RECOVERY

AN INSPIRATIONAL AND RELATABLE STORY.

Lacey Chandler has always been there for everyone else. However, she believes she is unworthy of love due to her weight issues. She cares for her mother, Betty, who is handicapped. Betty feels useless and often takes it out on Lacey. Her sister and niece come to stay, and Lacey soon finds herself caring for them as well. Local police chief Toby Wheeler has been fond of Lacey for years. He hates that she views herself in such a negative light. He hopes to use his faith to show her that she means more to him, and God, then just a number on the scale.

Millions of people struggle with weight issues, particularly using food for emotional healing. Lacey is one of the most relatable characters I have encountered in some time. Her longing for love and acceptance, as well as her spiritual growth journey, is realistic and identifiable. There are a number of heartbreaking scenes as Lacey tries to learn to love herself.

Appropriate Bible verses are interspersed throughout the story, reminding the reader of God's faithfulness. The characters also demonstrate that hurting people hurt people, which is a good reminder for everyone. Overall, this is an inspirational story, which even includes a few recipes. This book is the perfect companion to Brown's devotional, *Divine Dining: 365 Devotions to Guide You to Healthier Weight and Abundant Wellness.*

–LESLIE McKEE

Janet Brown has truly written her heart into *Worth Her Weight*. Exposing areas that those struggling with food addiction and obesity, she takes the reader into the heart of her character and leads the reader through the journey to redemption. A good read, highly recommended.

–BONNIE LANTHRIPE, AUTHOR OF *THE RINGLEADER*

I dedicate this story to all those who feel unforgiven, unworthy, or beyond reach.

Where there is life, there is hope.

ISBN: 978-1-68313-039-0

First Edition
Printed and bound in the USA

Cover photo: RolandStollner
Cover and interior design by Kelsey Rice

~BOOK II IN THE WHARTON ROCK SERIES~

WORTH *Forgiving*

JANET K. BROWN

P
Pen-L Publishing
Fayetteville, Arkansas
Pen-L.com

CHAPTER *One*

Twin doors swung open to the outside world, and Katie Smith stepped out. *Thunk!* The heavy doors slammed. Sweet honeysuckle along the outside wall smelled like freedom. The sounds of passing traffic were foreign to her ears.

She smiled and glanced up at the sign giving the bus schedule. Two hours. Dropping on the park bench to the right of the exit, she prepared to wait, twisting the coins for bus fare in her hands.

A dove sang a mournful melody. A cold wind howled. If only she had asked Mom to send her a jacket. Three years ago when she went into prison, it had been hot Texas summertime. Add that to lessons learned the hard way.

She reached into her pocket and retrieved a now wrinkled picture of a girl with two front teeth missing. Katie blinked back tears, jutted her chin, and sat taller. All she had to do was stay clean, get her own place, and move her daughter back in with her.

A red Hyundai Santa Fe pulled to the curb. A tall, shapely brunette climbed out of the driver's seat. "Care for a ride?"

Katie blinked. She barely recognized her older sister, Lacey, since she'd lost so much weight. "Mom said she couldn't pick me up."

"She couldn't, but Toby agreed that I should."

"Humph." Katie should've known Mr. Police Chief would keep tabs on her. "Thanks, but I'll wait for the bus."

"Your choice." Lacey shrugged but waited.

Katie walked toward the strange car and glanced at the backseat.

"Rachel isn't with me."

"Why not?"

Lacey shifted to the other hip and planted her hand there. "Do you really want your daughter to see you coming out of prison?"

Katie's face was on fire. She tried to outstare her sister, but it was no use.

"My coming wasn't my idea, you know. Mom insisted."

"How is she?"

"Feeling rough. I had to get Joanne to keep Rachel." Lacey's fingers drummed the top of her car.

Only the drumming and wind sounds interfered with Katie's tumbling thoughts.

Lacey climbed in her car, started the motor and yelled out the window. "Where to?"

How dare she? Katie's back turned into a stiff rod. She would not be manipulated by family. This was her fresh start. "Blast it all, it won't be Wharton Rock."

"Surprise. Surprise."

"I don't need your sarcasm."

"Then where to? The prison system approved Mom's house as your home."

"They also agreed to the halfway house in Apache Falls after Mom explained you hate me."

"I . . ."

"Picking me up was Mom's idea, not yours." Katie glared, daring her sister to disagree.

Lacey scowled.

Strains of heavy metal music pierced the quiet, bass notes rocking the ground. A black Ford F-150 pickup pulled behind Lacey's car. The shaved head of Katie's old boyfriend Collin stuck out the driver's side window.

"Going my way, sweet stuff?"

He came. Katie had written him, giving him the date, but with their rocky history, she had expected no favors. His mischievous grin still made her heart go pitter-pat.

He revved his engine.

"See you round, sis. Looks like I have a ride after all."

Katie's blonde hair whipped across her mouth. She winked, gave a sexy shake of her upper torso, and sashayed toward the truck. She climbed in moments before Collin gunned the engine, leaving Lacey in his dust.

A sense of foreboding strangled Katie the moment her bottom hit the seat. *Bad choice number one on my second chance?* A hand-rolled cigarette lay under Collin's open beer can. The truck wove between cars at a heart-pumping speed. Garbage in the truck's back floor sent such a stench she covered her nose with the curve of her hand.

She gripped an arm rest. "Slow down. The cops will be after us."

The angry tone to her words won her a Collin glare. "They've got bigger criminals to go after. Like you, my sweet." His grin turned wicked. He didn't slow.

Katie held on and kept her mouth shut.

The hundred and fifty mile trip was made in record time with no cop stops. When they entered Apache Falls, Collin made his way to an old apartment building near the baseball complex.

"Where are you going?" Katie asked.

"I have a place here." The truck ran over speed bumps and came to a halt near iron and concrete stairs. He leaned over and kissed her cheek. "Thought you'd need a place to stay."

His breath stunk of mouthwash and whiskey. Good thing he hadn't lit the cigarette.

"I've got a place in the halfway house on Lucille Street. I told you that."

Collin jumped out and slammed the door. He stomped up the stairs.

What could she do now? She was at least fifteen miles from her new home. "But not far from my old roommate, Beth," she whispered. Maybe Collin had a phone. "Hey, wait up."

Before she went through his front door, he was adding to his booze buzz. Inside, he draped across her and smothered her with wet kisses. She'd been away from this too long. The smells and untamed passion made her feel nauseous.

"Got a phone? I need to make a call." She giggled in his ear.

His eyes flashed with lechery. From his back pocket, he withdrew a cell phone and threw it her way. Just as she punched in the last digit, Collin tugged her to the sofa. The phone was answered and disconnected before Katie could free her arms.

She pushed against Collin's chest and dashed to the kitchen. "I'm dying for a Pepsi. All we got in prison was weak tea." In the fridge were beer, mustard, and a bowl of corn. Her stomach lurched. She ran for the bathroom and locked the door.

Collin tried the lock and beat the door. His yells escalated. Katie lost her breakfast and washed her face. What a great way to begin her new life. She'd lost Wayne, and she sure wasn't calling Lacey when she'd just made a four-hour drive to pick up her sister for nothing.

Collin's knocking stopped. All was quiet.

Wanting to cry, Katie slid to the floor. She blinked and stiffened. She needed something to take off the edge. Maybe she should ask Collin for some of his stash. What did it matter now? Crazy to think she could stay clean.

She punched Beth's number again.

"Yeah." The voice was female but fierce. "Who is this?"

"Katie Smith." She wiped her lips with the back of her hand and tasted something like rotten eggs. "I just got out today."

"Katie? I can't believe it. I thought you had ten years."

"I know, but I got out early. Hey, I need a ride."

"From Seagoville? You've got to be kidding. I ain't a taxi service."

"I'm in Apache Falls. At Collin's. I need to get to a halfway house on Lucille."

Heavy breathing ensued. "Meet me at home plate, field one, in fifteen minutes. And be ready, you hear?"

The line went dead.

How would Katie get out of the apartment? One small window was over the bathtub, but it was too small. Time ticked by. She stood and edged toward the door.

Crash! The door splintered. Collin rushed through the shattered wood and lunged toward her. Plunging under his arm, Katie ran for the door.

Collin dropped his baseball bat to grab her arm. She scooped up the bat. "Thanks." She ran down the steps with him on her tail. The ballpark was across the street, and yet, so far away.

No one was there. Her heart pounded. Her stomach rolled. Perspiration broke out over her upper lip. She was too early, and Collin was crossing the outfield. She was doomed.

CHAPTER *Two*

"Hey, Katie." A huge, fleshy arm spread over the window ledge of a white Suburban.

Katie couldn't tell at first whether it was male or female. The blonde hair was short and shaggy, shoulders like a linebacker—voice, rough and rugged—but the eye twinkle was that of a caring female. Katie and Beth had parted on a strained note, but hey, she came.

"Whose car?"

"Mom's. Get in."

One glance at Collin looming large at the pitcher's mound was enough incentive. Katie jumped in and held on as the Suburban skidded away from the park and wound through city streets toward the interstate.

No one spoke until the vehicle stopped before a big, white house with homes on the left side and condos on the right. Two young women sat on a lopsided porch swing. An orange sofa with stuffing exposed from a hole in the middle stretched across the opposite porch wall. A pillar that used to be white separated the sofa and swing.

"Thanks, Beth. I won't forget it." Katie got out.

Without a word, Beth barreled off in a cloud of dust from the dirt washed into the street.

An older version of Beth came out of the house and down the steps. She towered over Katie, accusation springing from her eyes like a knife.

"You must be Katie Smith."

What was it with these giant women?

"That's right."

With shoulders bigger than her hips and legs as tall as Katie's legs and torso combined, the woman clutched Katie's arms and turned her toward the house.

"You're late. Come on in. I've saved a bed for you."

A nudge sent Katie sprawling into the red dirt before the woman strode off. No one made a move to help her, so she picked herself up, dusted off the legs of her jeans, and jutted her chin. She wouldn't stay even a week if she could help it.

The mistress of the halfway house marched across the shabby living area, upstairs, and down a hall—three rooms on one side, two on the other. She stopped at the last one on the right.

"You'll share this with Nicole. She's off working now. My name is Wanda Early." She pierced Katie again with those laser brown eyes. "You'll do what I say, or get out."

"You betcha." *I'll get out.* A cold bath of perspiration soaked her underarms. If she didn't follow the rules, she'd be back in prison. The chill of prison walls and bathroom abuse made Katie change her answer. "I'll be good." She gritted her teeth. Being out of control put her on edge.

"Fine. Dinner is at six. Be downstairs to help by five." Wanda left.

The bare twin mattress mocked Katie's need for comfort and rest. She closed her mind to everything but how she could afford her own place and move her daughter home. Better than living with a goody-goody sister who resented her and a mom that stayed as angry as a disturbed rattlesnake.

A wavy wall mirror showed off her curves and made her smile. She hadn't lost her figure in prison. A frown came next. Most of her sister's adult life, she had been a hundred pounds overweight, so how come she'd won a husband who loved her, while Katie went from one loser to the next? Not that she ever wanted for male companionship, but love wasn't in the equation. She'd thought so, but no.

"What are doing in my room?" A black girl with brown-tinged teeth and a rear end that protruded way beyond the rest of her body stood at the door, an ugly glare making her uglier than she would've been.

Without turning around, Katie spoke to the mirror image of what was probably her roommate. "Just admiring the goods." Katie winked as she swiveled. "You must be Nicole."

The girl didn't answer. "Your *goods* aren't wanted here."

Katie blew across her right hand finger tips. "You aren't exactly my type either, sugar." She batted her eyelashes. "But I'm here for now, so deal with it."

The girl moved into her space, snatched Katie's arm, and twisted it behind her back. "Keep everything to yourself and you can live. Got it?"

Pain shot down Katie's arm. Bravado disappeared. She nodded. The girl let go and flounced to her bed just before Wanda appeared and threw a sheet and blanket in the direction of Katie's bed. It missed, but Wanda retreated without a backward glance.

Thirty minutes later, the sound of pots and pans clanging from downstairs interrupted the quiet. Nicole stood and stashed something white under her mattress. She straightened to find Katie staring.

"You didn't see nothin'."

Katie shook her head. Staying clean on the outside was going to be harder than she'd thought.

CHAPTER *Three*

Rain pelted like a never-ending reminder of Katie's failure. Two days in a halfway house was like a disease—fast to come, long to leave—not unlike the three years in prison. It took daily promises to herself. This time she'd do it right, stay clean, and not hang out with losers.

If only she had a nice-looking outfit, but all she had were the jeans and a T-shirt and no money to buy more.

"You look worse than a collie with hot spots." Nicole came in and flopped on her bed.

"What's that?"

"The collie I had as a kid would get so hot in the summer that her hair fell out in bunches. Doc called it hot spots. Sad looking."

"Ah, such kind words." Katie let the sarcasm drip from her mouth.

She left the room. Time to go job-hunting. So far, she'd headed north, south, and west with no luck at finding businesses. East was all that was left for a person on foot. She left word for her parole officer with a hope of help, but the woman hadn't even called her back.

"Hi." A voice as small as its owner came from behind Katie. An across-the-hall resident seemed to have attached herself to Katie, as if looking for a mentor.

"Hi, Madison." She glanced at the girl's bright-turquoise shirt. "You been shopping?"

"Mother said she found it for me."

"Why don't you live with your mother?"

"She don't have no home."

How pitiful. "Where will you go when you leave here?"

Madison shrugged.

"If I can ever get a job, maybe we can get a place together. I'll be moving my daughter back with me by then."

With a quick clap, Madison jumped in place. "I would like that. I love kids. The restaurant where I work needs a server. Denise quit yesterday."

"Really? Where is it?"

"On Grant Street, about a mile east." Madison explained how to get there.

"Thanks, Maddie. I'll go check." Katie fled out the door and braved the rain.

When she arrived at Country Dinner Restaurant, she was soaked. She perched on a barstool, ordered a Coke, and asked for Paul, like Maddie had told her.

Fifteen minutes later, a disappointed Katie braved the wet weather again. According to Miss Plump and Perky, Paul was off, and she would need to come back tomorrow. Another day of defeat. When would she ever get a place where she could bring her daughter and make it up to her for what she'd done? Would Rachel ever forgive her? First, Katie would have to get her away from Mrs. Know-It-All sister Lacey.

Nine women gathered around a pot of spaghetti that Nicole and another woman had cooked. Katie would worry about poison if Nicole didn't plan on eating it too.

"Like it?" Nicole glanced around the table but settled her gaze on Katie, who quickly lowered her head.

Tingles tickled her spine. She shivered. A halfway house was worse than living in Hicksville with an overbearing sister and a patronizing mom.

"Someone's coming up the walk." Madison passed the open window on the way to her seat.

Voices carried. Katie couldn't miss the familiar tone. "Just what do you mean by that crack?" *Mom.*

"Nothing." *Lacey.*

The tendons in Katie's neck tensed and ached.

"I've not seen Katie since last summer, and now she's out. You got to see her. I didn't."

"I know, Mom."

"You should've brought her home, but no. You left her to the city all alone."

"I didn't leave her, Mom. She left me and rode off with that loser Collin."

"She probably did that because she knew you didn't really want to help her."

A knock sounded. Wanda laid down her fork, wiped her mouth with a napkin, and went to answer. Three of the residents, including Nicole, jumped to their feet and circled Wanda.

"Ma'am, we're the family of Katie Smith. I understand she lives here." This voice was masculine. *Toby.*

"Let me help, Mom. We don't need you falling on this gravel driveway."

Oh, no. The whole family in rare form. Perspiration brought new tingles slithering from Katie's arm pit. Maybe that meant Rachel was with them. Katie stood about the time the other three went back to their dinners.

She peeked around a curtain. A flush warmed her heart along with every part of her body. Looking like her sweet Rachel, but older, a young girl with long black hair trailed after Lacey. Katie swayed and snatched the windowsill for balance. The last time she'd see her sweet baby girl, Rachel had been four. This beautiful child would now be seven. Three years without seeing her mother. Would she scream? Or run? Or turn her head?

Katie's heart stilled then set off at a gallop. She wasn't ready to face her yet. This was supposed to come when she already had a home and could invite her to come live with her and decorate her new room. It was too soon. She was still a failure. She glanced up the stairs, considering a run for it.

"I'm Wanda Early. I prefer a call before my guests have visitors."

Maybe Wanda would send them away.

"Katie's parole officer gave us the address but not a phone number. We'll be happy to call next time, but we drove all the way from Wharton Rock so her mother could see her." The male voice, obviously Mr. Policeman Toby, took the lead. *Not surprising.*

Wanda hesitated. "It's dinner time. She can't visit until she finishes eating and does her turn at dishes."

"I came to see my child." Mom's voice was adamant with a bit of insult.

"Please, ma'am, is there somewhere my mother can rest until Katie is finished?"

That would be pushy Lacey. How could Katie get out of this mess?

Wanda's shoulders slumped. She was really human. "Of course, she can come in." She opened the door wider and motioned toward the overstuffed flowered sofa. "I'll send Katie in when she's finished." Wanda darted back to the dining table.

Her gaze zeroed in on Katie, who lowered her head and scooped up spaghetti like a ditch digger.

"You heard. Eat. Wash dishes. See to your family."

How could Katie get out of this? How dare Lacey bring her mother and her daughter to this place? This was as bad as being seen in prison.

"I'm tired, and I want to see my daughter. Now." Mom's voice escalated. The sofa and chair where she sat were out of Katie's sight, but Mom's words were not out of her hearing.

A wisp of black hair swung around the door. Two childlike brown eyes peered into the dining room. Katie's heart melted faster than the butter on her roll. She gulped and stooped down where no one could see her but Rachel.

"Hi, baby."

The child's eyes widened but didn't hold fear.

"Do you remember me?" Katie whispered.

Rachel nodded.

"Next time you come to see me, I'll have a place of my own. You won't have to come to this icky place." Katie held her hand out, ready for a shake.

A wee hand slipped out and touched Katie's, igniting an electric spark. Could her baby have forgiven her?

"I'll have a bedroom just for you to decorate like you wish."

Rachel pulled back her hand. "I have a room of my own at my house."

Kathie's mouth went dry. "But this way you could be with me."

"What are you doing, Rachel? Come back here." A trace of anger darkened Lacey's tone.

Before Katie could get off her knees, Lacey appeared.

"What are you doing?" The question was posed to Katie while Lacey enveloped the child in her arms. "Come out here and visit with Mom."

Katie stood. Her throat closed off and would allow her no words.

Then everything spun out of control. Lacey grabbed Katie's arm and tugged her into the next room. Toby gathered Rachel up in his arms. Mom let out a yell.

"Katie? My Katie?" She pushed herself up with her cane and clutched Katie tight against her bosom.

Lacey dropped hold of her sister and plopped her arms on her hips, still ample despite her weight loss. "What do you mean by trying to talk to Rachel without our knowledge?"

"I'll take her outside with me, hon."

Drat that interfering Toby.

"She's my daughter," Katie squealed. "I have rights."

Wanda walked into the room. Her voice rose over the uproar. "Out! All of you out!" She pointed to the front door, then turned to Katie. "You can leave too, but only after you do the dishes."

"Oh, yes." Mom clung to her baby girl. "Come with us. You don't belong here. You should be with your family."

Katie forced a calm she didn't feel. In times past, a little boost from speed would help, but today, she must handle problems without chemical enhancement. She clamped her teeth together and stiffened her spine. Her arms slipped around her mother as she rubbed her mom's back.

"But I must be up early in the morning for a job interview. It's so exciting, Mom. Rachel and I will soon have our own place, and you can visit us anytime you want." A twinkle crept into her tone as she planned. "Everything will be okay now. Just wait and see."

"But . . ." Mom slumped.

Lacey towered over the two, her words menacing. "You try to take Rachel, and you'll have a fight on your hands, a fight you will not win, baby sister."

"I said leave." Wanda moved to the door and motioned them out.

When her family closed the front door, Katie's bravado vanished. She wilted like a rose in summertime. Was there no hope for her after prison?

CHAPTER *Four*

The clock ticked. The secretary tapped blue-and-green striped nails on her desk. Larry squirmed and cracked his knuckles, a habit his mother said he did when he was nervous. To still the action, he tucked each hand under the opposite arm. He was beginning to hate job interviews. Perhaps that was because he came in with a big disadvantage.

From the hall came a tall, stooped man, his head bald except for grey-black fringe around the edges.

"Reverend Pullman?"

Larry jumped to his feet and stretched out his hand. "Yes, sir."

"I'm Reverend Schumacher. Sorry you had to wait. Would you follow me to my office?"

His smile seemed genuine. That was a good start. Wasn't it? Or was the wait on purpose?

"No problem."

Larry limped behind the pastor of Apache Falls Covenant Life Church. He passed several offices where various people were preoccupied. The two turned to the right, passing an empty office. Would that be the one he would occupy if he got the job? What a big *if*. Rejection had become his middle name since graduation from seminary.

The pastor moved into a larger office with plusher furniture and motioned Larry to have a seat before he turned his attention to some papers.

Larry was embarrassed by a loud pop from his knuckles. He sat on his trembling hands. When the man looked up, Larry tried for a nonchalant smile but didn't quite pull it off.

Reverend Schumacher bent over his desk. "Have you ever worked with teenagers?"

He had been a teenage thief. Did that count? "No, sir. Why?"

"We need a part-time youth director. Teens are an active, rowdy bunch. Not everyone has the patience, and . . ." he cleared his throat and straightened, "even in that ministry, your single status can be a handicap. You would have to be extremely careful and never be alone with any one child."

Larry couldn't keep his hands penned down any longer. His pulse galloped. He took a deep breath, trying to squelch his irritation.

"But the letter spoke of a full-time associate minister opening."

The brown executive chair squeaked when the pastor leaned back. He steepled his hands. His smile turned patronizing.

"Let's admit facts, Reverend Pullman. A single man can't fill a pastorate. As I said, we would take a risk even with teens." He glanced down again at Larry's resume.

The sound of outside voices and the squeal of a car filled the quiet room. Larry swallowed. So, there it was again. Why did a loving God call him to the ministry and then desert him? Was this punishment for years of running from God?

"Your seminary grades were outstanding, and the director highly recommends you. I would like to give you a chance." Once again, he cleared his throat.

Pop! There went Larry's knuckles again. He crossed his arms.

"If you're willing, I'm prepared to try you out on a temporary basis for the part-time position. You would be in the office all day Wednesday, with youth group that night, and be here for Sunday. That's all, except activities you might plan for Friday night or Saturday. Teens need to be kept busy."

Larry swallowed the sour taste of disappointment. He needed money to pay the school loan and living expenses. His mother charged very little rent, but at thirty-one years old, he should be paying his way, not relying on her. He still did some work with the Wharton Rock Police Department. With both jobs, he might survive until . . .

"Thank you, sir. I won't let you down." He stood, shook hands, and tried to hide his limp when he walked out of the office.

When his hand touched the doorknob, Reverend Schumacher stood.

"How did you hurt your leg?"

Larry paused but didn't turn. "I was injured in a gun fight while I was a Wharton Rock deputy."

His tone was soft. He left before it dawned on the pastor that Larry had two handicaps holding him back from ministry.

Outside, gray clouds resembled his mood.

Be thankful, Pullman. God gave you a second chance. He's got a plan for you.

One sun ray pierced the clouds like an answer from the Lord. Larry picked up his step, soon climbing into his Dodge Ram truck. The famous Hemi engine roared when he pushed on the accelerator. Monday morning had flown. He could use some lunch and besides, looking around this neighborhood of the city might give him some indication of what the teens, whom he was expected to teach, were like.

The chipped paint and junkyard lawns brought back memories of his childhood, when he and his parents lived in Apache Falls. His old neighborhood was now home to meth houses and massage parlors. The last tidbits of a bad attitude evaporated.

He steeled his resolve to love other lost souls with the same love God had extended to him. Maybe some of the teens in his new youth group would escape the troubled teen years he had experienced.

On the corner of Beverly and Hawthorne, he spotted Country Dinner Restaurant. Looked welcoming. Lots of cars parked there. He pulled into the last space, climbed out, and went in.

In his rush, he bumped into a server. *Crash!* Dirty dishes shattered, and the server fell on her back.

"I'm so sorry."

He stretched forth his hand to assist the young lady and was met with sky-blue eyes with cobalt circles at the edge of each pupil. His mouth opened. His eyes widened. He couldn't speak, move, or stop staring. She was the most gorgeous creature he'd ever beheld.

"Well, sugar, are you going to help me up or stand there gawking?"

The darker part of her eyes seemed to cover the lighter shade. A smile lit up her face.

He gulped. "I'm so sorry."

With one hard tug, the blue-eyed blonde collided with his chest. His heartbeat blended with hers in a fast sprint. Sweat trickled down his spine.

"I'm so sorry."

She giggled. "Sugar, is that all you can say? Because I've got customers to handle."

A young busboy hurried to pick up the dirty, broken dishes at their feet.

Larry took a deep breath. He should help, but his feet wouldn't move. Had she hit him with a tranquilizer dart? Sure felt like it.

She pushed away from his hot, sweaty body and motioned to a table. "Sit there. I'll be right with you."

She dashed to the kitchen while he finally bent to help clean up the mess he caused. When they finished, the busboy thanked him for the help, and Larry took a seat at the table the beautiful creature had pointed to. Two menus balanced between the sugar and the salt shaker. He glanced through one of them.

Butterflies swarmed his stomach. He knew without looking that she was behind him.

"What will it be, good-looking?"

"Chicken-fried steak."

"You betcha. You want the cream gravy?"

"Naturally."

Her smile could light up his world.

"Naturally."

Within twenty-five minutes, she'd brought his steak, he'd eaten it, and paid for it.

She turned.

He caught her hand. "When do you get off?"

She sighed and shifted to the other hip. "Look, sugar, you're probably a nice guy and all, but I need this job. I shouldn't get involved with anyone right now."

"I wouldn't cause you problems."

A scowl spread across her face, but her brightness quickly returned. "Ah, you're sweet." She cupped his jaw. "If I didn't have to worry about a place to live for me and my daughter right now, I'd give you a tumble." She grinned and patted his cheek. "See you another time, big guy."

He watched her walk away, her words echoing in his mind: "... worry about a place to live for me and my daughter ..." Did she not have a home? If he could help, he would. That was a silent promise. Maybe even a prayer.

CHAPTER *Five*

After Larry left the restaurant, he headed home to Wharton Rock but couldn't stop thinking about the blue-eyed waitress. He turned around and returned, spending two hours in the truck, waiting for her to clock out. His bottom hurt. Would she never leave, or would she work all day?

Another server left. Only two cars were left in the parking lot, and one of them was his. Oh, well, he had nothing to do this afternoon but wait.

He rested his head. She had indicated needing a place to live. If she was sleeping in her car, he would think of something to help. How could he be a minister and not care for the homeless? Her beauty didn't hurt his resolve, either, he had to admit. The sun warmed the truck. His eyes grew heavy and finally closed.

If the screech of brakes at the corner hadn't woken him, he would've missed her. The sun came in at an angle that almost blinded him. The lunch shift had ended. The blonde server came out the back door and headed off on foot.

He was expert at stakeouts. Before seminary, as the newest cop on the Wharton Rock force, the dreaded stakeouts often fell to him and an older guy looking for easy shifts. He bided his time until she turned out of sight. Then he eased up to the next cross street.

Continuing in this way until she turned in to a sprawling, white two-story about a block and a half away, he watched over her path. Since she remained there, he gunned the Hemi and left Apache Falls. Because of his nosiness, he had only forty-five minutes to get to the Wharton Rock

Police Station to work the night shift. He should've slept, not stalked.

❦

Two days later, Larry arrived at Covenant Life Church for his first day as a youth minister. The day sped by. The pastor chose the lunch place, but Larry had dinner at Country Dinner Restaurant.

"You again." The blonde held her menu pad. "I'm ready when you are."

"Burger and fries."

She waved her hand in the air. "You can't ever go wrong with that. My favorite meal ever. I had really missed that. Couldn't wait to get one. This place does them up right too."

"Why did you miss it?"

Her mouth twisted to one side. "I just hadn't had one in a while." She rushed away.

When she brought his meal, she stood waiting. "Go ahead. Try it. You're going to like it."

Stacked with a big patty, two tomato slices, pickles, onions, and lots of lettuce, he opened his mouth wide to get it around the whole thing. "Mmmm. Delicious."

"Isn't it? When I had my first one, I thought I'd died and gone to heaven." She snickered. "And those fries are perfect."

"It's good, but I like the one at Willie's Restaurant in Wharton Rock. You ever been there?"

Her body stiffened. Her face turned red. "Nope." She dashed away.

What had he done?

She rushed back and forth without ever stopping. When it was time for him to get to church for the evening, she had never stopped to even leave a ticket. He motioned. She dropped it off on the way to another table.

"Goodbye," he said over her shoulder when he left.

She shivered, as if chilled by his breath.

Whatever he'd done, it was bad.

Back at the church, Larry flipped the light switch to the youth room and laid his notes on a podium. His fingers shook. He was the last one to inspire a young mind. If God had given him what he deserved, he wouldn't have qualified to be policeman or minister.

At ten until seven, the first student entered. A girl with a plump body and obvious Mexican heritage went to the back row and sat.

He swallowed and reminded himself he was a child of the King. He was forgiven and made worthy through Jesus' blood. That thought intimidated him. That thought excited him. That thought motivated him. He headed the girl's way with an outstretched hand.

"Hi, I'm Larry, the new youth minister, and you are . . . ?"

"Kinsley." Her words were directed at the floor. She didn't lift her hand.

Three girls, probably junior high age, came in, chatting among themselves. Larry met them before they took a seat and got names fired at him faster than a bullet. His memory couldn't take them all in, but he knew Kimmi was the leader.

A tall bean pole boy of maybe sixteen came next. No bashfulness with him. At probably six foot one or two, he met Larry eye to eye.

"Shawn," he said and stuck out his hand to Larry. "You must be the new guy."

A laugh threatened to erupt, but Larry scrunched his lips tight until he gained control. "I must be." He shook Shawn's hand and reached for the next boy, who was everything opposite from Shawn in stature.

Muscles rippled in this boy's arms. Larry would guess he had a six-pack abdomen, but he stood at about Larry's chest in height. His chin tipped. He shook the extended hand.

"I'm Ryan Russell. We're thankful to have you."

"Hello, Ryan."

"Ryan taught us last week," Shawn said.

"How nice." Larry studied Ryan in a new light. *A leader. Nice to know.* "Do you lead the music?"

"No, sir."

"That would be Cody," Shawn said.

"What are you saying about me?" Another boy entered. He was not a match for Shawn in height nor Ryan in build, but he carried a guitar, a telltale sign of his identity.

Shawn ran for the back and threw a football forward toward Ryan, who caught it and kept it.

Larry turned to the newest boy. "I take it you're Cody, and you lead our music, and I, as Shawn put it, am the new guy."

From Larry's right, Kimmi said. "I hope you stay for a while. We're getting tired of breaking in new guys."

Cody gave a quick, overstated bow, got his instrument out of its case, and started playing.

"I agree. We need someone to stay."

What had Larry gotten himself into? No wonder Reverend Schumacher was anxious to push him into youth ministry.

He assumed I had no options, which I don't.

"Hope you stay more than a month." Cody strummed a few chords for emphasis.

"Let's strive for three months this time," Kimmi said.

Larry shifted to one hip. "Let me get this right. Your last youth minister only stayed a month?"

Cody's fingers halted. "And the one before that stayed two months."

"Yikes, when did you last have one that stayed a while?" Larry glanced from one young face to the next.

By now, about twenty more kids had filled the room.

Ryan stepped to within inches of Larry's chest and tilted his head up. "When I was fifteen, our youth minister that had been here for years left. Since then, we've had several. None lasted long." He paused for breath, or maybe a few encouraging nods from friends. "You're our fourth since Christmas. We're kind of weary of *new guys*. Nothing against you personally, but that's just the way it is."

Several voiced their agreement to Ryan's comment.

"Were they all fired, or did they quit?"

Ryan shrugged. "The last guy got fired. Some quit."

"Nobody loves us," Kimmi said.

Larry put an arm around both Ryan and Kimmi and turned them to face all of the class.

"My name is Larry Pullman. I'm your new youth minister. I'm so sorry to hear that you've been through a series of new ones, but I want you to know, I'm a stayer. Also, I want each of you to write down my cell number."

He waited until the ones at the front took a seat, and everyone held up their phones at the ready. Then he gave his number.

"I want you all to keep that. If you have any temptation, any time you feel down or just need to talk, call me. I will answer unless someone's shooting at me." He chuckled.

Twenty-something pairs of eyes widened.

He gave them a gotcha smirk. "I'm a part-time policeman."

One combined loud gasp emitted from the group.

Larry motioned to Cody. "How about you lead us in worship?"

Cody stood and played and sang, "In Your Presence."

After they'd sung several songs, Larry taught them about Joseph. "God meant all the bad things that happened to Joseph for good. When you go through rough times, God can bring good out of it too."

They listened. No one made trouble. Some, like Kinsley, said nothing. Some, like Ryan, answered every question.

By the time the service ended and the kids filed out of the room, Larry's hands no longer shook. God had anointed his words. He had fallen in love with a group of teenagers.

CHAPTER *Six*

After leaving the church, Larry was charged up and didn't want to head home. He decided to stop by Country Dinner Restaurant and see if he could find out what mess he'd stepped into with that blue-eyed server.

The light was off on the sign, but several people moved around inside. Betting the door was locked, Larry backed out, but a floodlight illuminated the blonde server leaving the restaurant.

He pulled alongside her. "May I drive you home?"

Loose gravel scattered across the pavement. She kicked a bit toward his truck. "Stay away from me, you hear?"

"I'm not a stalker, I'm—"

"Leave me alone. I don't need your help." She strode away.

He gunned the truck. "Wait, I know you don't know me, but look, I'm a cop. You can trust me."

The blonde slumped. "I'm too tired to fight. If you're a cop, I'm Snow White." She slowed her speech and emphasized each word. "Leave me alone."

His breath came like a deflated tire. "Okay. I won't bother you anymore."

He left, but the man that he hoped he was wouldn't let a defenseless woman walk through this neighborhood alone at night. Since he knew where she was headed, he drove there and waited to see that she arrived home okay. He gave it twenty minutes.

In fifteen, there had been no sign. He went to the cross street parallel to Lucille and drove down the path she should be walking, but he saw no sign of anyone. This part of her route had few outside lights. He parked and walked.

When he passed a closed-up station on the corner, he caught the sound of rustling gravel and running feet. He halted but then heard nothing. He moved again. A squeal came from behind the station. This time, he was assured that he wasn't imagining things.

His 9mm was in his glove compartment, so his only weapon was the element of surprise. A thief wouldn't expect a cop. Wharton Rock's police chief, Toby Wheeler, taught Larry to "walk soft, like an Indian," which was hard with his size thirteen loafers. But he had to try.

The area was dark. One porch light across the street caused his huge shadow to show up on a side wall. Larry moved closer to the building, and his shadow disappeared.

From the station's back, grunts and whispers suggested there was more than one person. Larry didn't sign up for suicide.

He turned back toward the truck to get his gun.

"Help." A female voice. A scream stopped him in his tracks and sent him plunging into the situation.

Two figures struggled from one glimpse of light to the next. Larry couldn't make out much except one was bigger and male.

From the other figure came more shrieks and then a low mumble. "No. Not again."

Larry tugged the man off the woman and landed a punch to his jaw.

Keeping hold of the woman, the attacker punched Larry in the gut. "Stay out of it, man."

Larry doubled over. Before the pain lessened, he threw his weight against the man until he let the woman go. Off balance, she fell to the ground.

Fire sparked from the man's eyes in the light of the nearby street light. He yanked up his pants and lashed out at Larry, who was on him like a bear disturbed from hibernation.

"Hey, man, we're just having a bit of fun. Stay out of it."

Larry kicked the man in the spot where he was aiming his fun. The man squealed and backed away.

"Okay, I'm gone. Okay? You're welcome to her." He turned and ran.

By that time, the woman had crawled to her feet. Larry put a hand on each of her upper arms to steady her.

"You're safe now."

Struggling against him, slapping at his arms, spitting at him, she screamed over and over. "No, not again. No! No!"

Even though he outweighed her by a good hundred and thirty pounds, he battled to gain control. "It's okay. You're okay." He must've said that a dozen times, but still she fought. He braced his legs to keep from falling. Finally, her cries diminished. Her body melted against him, a wet mop with no resistance.

"It's okay. You're safe now," he said one more time.

Her gaze lifted. The street light illuminated her face. It was the blonde from the restaurant, the one who had refused his offer of a ride.

An I-told-you-so rose to the tip of his tongue, but he swallowed it like castor oil. His hand brushed back the wiry wisps that curled across her forehead.

"I won't hurt you. I would never hurt you. I'm a cop and, I hope, a gentleman."

With one last ounce of stamina or maybe it was stubbornness, she pulled away, studied what she could make out of his face, then laid her head against his chest.

They remained there a few minutes with Larry afraid, if he moved, she'd fight again.

"Thanks for your help. My name is Katie Smith." Her voice was shaky but no longer hysterical.

"I'm Larry Pullman. You kept yelling 'not again.' I wanted to make sure you knew you could trust me." He held her away from him. "He didn't hurt you before I arrived, did he?"

She straightened. "Naw. I'm good."

"What did you mean by . . . ?"

"Not again?" She dropped her head. "Forget about it."

"Okay."

Katie Smith. Why did that name ring a bell?

Her glance roved over him. "You really are one of the good guys. Huh?"

He chuckled. "I've been trying to tell you that all this time." He put an arm around her shoulders. "Now, let's get out of here before we attract the attention of more guys than I can handle."

"Okay. But I'd say that body could handle a lot."

A smile turned up one corner of his mouth. She'd noticed the new biceps he'd been working on. His ears burned. Good thing she couldn't see that in the near dark.

They walked around the station to his truck. He opened the passenger door.

"Your momma really did teach you to act like a gentleman."

He dipped his head. "Yes, ma'am." He closed the door and circled to the driver's seat.

The motor roared and skidded down the street.

She broke into laughter and pulled a wad of money from her pocket. "He didn't even steal my tip money. Idiot." A few blocks down, she pointed, "Turn—"

The truck was already moving to the cross street before she said anything. She wrinkled her nose. "You know where I live?" She paused. "Did you have a cop friend check on me?" Her tone was angry.

He drove on to where she lived and stopped before he answered. She wasn't going to like it.

"So you stalked me?"

"I watched over you."

"No, you stalked me."

"Tonight, it's a good thing I did."

She huffed and opened her door. "I've been taking care of myself for a long time, Mr. Pullman."

"I know. So forgiven?"

"I'll have to think about it." She climbed out and didn't look back.

Katie Smith. Before seminary, he was rookie cop. During that time, he worked a kidnapping case. One of the perps was the child's mother, Katie Smith. Could that connection be what made her mad when he mentioned Wharton Rock? He shook his head to dislodge such thoughts.

CHAPTER *Seven*

"Hi." A wee voice came from the sofa when Katie walked inside. Madison sat in the corner with a book. "I was worried. You're later than usual."

Katie plopped beside her. "I'm fine. Hey, what did you do with your evening off?"

Madison gnawed her lip and clutched her book to her chest.

Angry voices descended the stairs. Trouble brewed.

"Get the **** out of my face!" *Nicole.*

Wanda's tone was soft and silencing. "This, my dear friend, will get you thrown out of *my* house."

Scuffling and banging reverberated through the house. Katie glanced at Madison.

She whispered, "Drug search."

"Why?"

Madison shrugged.

"You better watch it, girl. I'll get you next time." Wanda stormed down the stairs and into the kitchen.

Katie's muscles didn't relax. After what she'd seen the day she arrived, the surprise was that Wanda didn't find drugs in Nicole's things. Katie rubbed the back of her neck and looked at her watch, then dragged a weary body across the room to the group phone. She had an urge to talk to her mother. Besides, she didn't want a repeat of that night's attack.

"Hello."

"Hi, Mom. It's Katie."

"Hi, baby. How are you?" The change to softness helped.

"Okay. Say, Mom, would you ask Lacey and Toby if they'd drive my Honda here. I need a car."

Silence greeted Katie's request.

"Mom?"

She huffed. "Lacey's asleep. She isn't going to like this. I don't know if that car even runs anymore."

"I need a car, Mom. It's not safe for me to walk home from work so late."

"You got a job? That's swell." Mom's voice grew louder. "I'll see what I can do tomorrow. I wish you had let us know to bring it when we came last week."

"I didn't know you were coming. Remember?"

"Oh, yeah. Okay, I'll try."

"Thanks, Mom. See you." Katie hung up.

Madison stood. "Mother picks me up. She might come get you, too, or we could ask Paul if we can always work the same shifts."

"Thanks, sugar." Katie hugged her new friend.

"Your lip is cut, and your right eye is puffy. Are you okay?"

"I'm just swell, as Mom would say." With fists clenched, Katie turned to head up the stairs.

That same wee voice stopped Katie's forward progress. "Nicole did have drugs. She got them from your boyfriend."

"What?" Moving closer to Madison, Katie shifted her hips and positioned her crooked arms at her waist. "What did you say?"

Wanda swept past them and locked the front door. "Get to bed, you two."

While they tiptoed up the stairs, Madison kept her voice low. "A guy stopped by looking for you. He said he was your boyfriend. He talked with Nicole. Before he left, I spotted him handing her a small packet of white powder."

A sensory sting slithered up Katie's spine. She didn't want to ask. Her mouth opened, but nothing came out. Feeling like she might pass out, she swallowed a nasty taste and tried again. "What . . . ?"

"Bald head, mischievous manner, drove a black truck."

Collin. He was going to get her busted yet. "Thanks." Katie veered into her room.

Nicole sat up and winked. "Thanks for hooking me up."

Perspiration trickled along the curve of Katie's jaw, though she shivered with the chill of the A/C blast of air. She bounced her curls with a shake of her head.

"I don't know what you mean."

Nicole swayed a path into Katie's personal space. "Don't give me that, my new friend. Collin stopped by looking for you just when I needed something to take off the edge." She winked and shook her shoulders. "I said thanks. You say you're welcome. Got it?"

The space closed further. The snarl in her voice sent a new chill down Katie's arms.

"You're welcome, but I didn't send him." Katie swept the girl aside and dropped to her bed. "I ran away from him, so don't pin your problems on me. I'm clean."

"Humph." Nicole lay on the bed. "For how long? This is real life, baby. You got enough money to move out yet?"

"No, but—"

"And you won't. Odds are stacked against us ex-cons. Got it?"

Katie pulled the covers up to her neck and feigned sleep until the girl shut up. She had to get out of this place, but how? Madison had saved four hundred. She, one hundred. How long would it take to afford two month's rent and a deposit? Too long.

Silence finally settled on the room, and the light went out. Nicole must have run out of steam, or else the drug effect wore off and left her unconscious.

Katie opened one eye then the other. Wrong move.

"Anyway, I look forward to your Collin returning tomorrow."

Scrunching her eyes together, Katie prayed she hadn't heard her roommate right. Collin returning was the last thing she needed.

"More coffee?" Katie held up the pot.

"No, I think I've had enough. Thank you," Larry said.

That was probably true. Katie glanced at the huge wall clock over the soda machine. Two hours. Larry had finished his dinner in thirty minutes, so he'd drunk lots of coffee since then.

Warmth flooded her heart and gave her a haughty smile. She had never been much of a talker, preferring instead to act, but talking to this man felt good—felt calming, felt right.

"I have a solution for you," he said.

"What?" She couldn't believe she'd told him about trying to get her sister to bring her car. The cook's bell dinged to tell her food was up. "Excuse me," she said and dashed to pick up two chicken fries for table five.

Larry sat at a corner booth, staring at the cottonwood tree banging against the window. His fingers traced his black mustache. In his sport coat and slacks, he was so tall and dignified, and nothing like any man she'd liked before now—but like him, she did.

She hurried back to his table. "Okay, what's your solution?"

"I will take you to pick up your car."

His mischievous grin set her heart to galloping.

"I can't ask you to do that." She fidgeted with her order pad.

When she turned, he grabbed her wrist. A slight flush spread up the sides of his neck. He rubbed the hot spot and stared at the table.

"When I leave here, I'll head to Wharton Rock. It's perfect."

She dropped her pen, reached to pick it up, and tried to stifle the wild thoughts that teased her mind. How could she have forgotten? He was a policeman. He worked for Toby. "Oh, my word." Did she say that out loud? Her hands shook so badly, she reinforced her hold before she dropped her order pad. She'd tried so hard to get away from Wharton Rock's small-town gossip. How could she like a man from there?

He made eye contact. "The last time I mentioned Wharton Rock, you seemed mad."

"You're a policeman there?"

"Yes."

"What are you doing here?"

"I've got a life outside of police work."

"I know, but—"

"So, shall I drive you to pick up your car? You really don't need to be walking to your house after work, especially at night."

Saved by the bell, again. She grabbed a meal to go and rushed to the man waiting at the register. Her hands kept busy, but her mind was frozen on the picture of walking into Lacey's house, saying "hi," and asking for her car keys. That visual turned her stomach.

One pass again near Larry's booth made up her mind. If she planned on staying away from Lacey, Mom, and Toby for good, what alternative did she have? She needed transportation. She could do this. With an exhale that rid her mind of ugly pictures, she plopped one hand on a hip.

"Okay, here's the deal, sugar. You can take me to my car, and I'll be appreciative, but our relationship ends there. I'm working for money to start over, to pick up my daughter, and move into my own place *in Apache Falls*. Got it?"

Larry nodded. "Got it. When do you get off?"

"Not till eight."

He threw down some bills and stood. His expression made her tummy churn even worse.

"Then I'll be waiting in the car outside when you come out." He strode out before she could respond.

CHAPTER  Eight

Country Dinner Restaurant was barely out of sight before Larry got the conversation going. No radio interfered, and he seemed an open book. Katie hoped he didn't expect her to return the confidences.

"That Shawn sounds like a mess," she said. "I think I'd like him. The whole youth group sounds like a handful."

Larry raised his eyebrows. "I think so."

"I can't believe a policeman is doing volunteer work in Apache Falls." She cocked her head to the left. "Are you on probation or something?"

A chuckle rumbled from Larry, but his hands gripped the steering wheel tighter. "Good one, Miss Katie. I doubt I'd stay a cop for long if I were."

"True."

His knuckles were turning white. He grew silent and withdrawn. Katie stole a glance sideways every little while. His body was so tense he resembled a board. Was the cop hiding secrets?

She gnawed her lip. "I was rude back there. At the restaurant. When you offered to, you know, take me to my car."

"Yes, you were."

"I'm sorry."

"You're forgiven." The muscles in his biceps visibly slackened. His shoulders relaxed.

She wasn't telling her life story, but maybe he deserved a little info. "You see, I hate Wharton Rock. I dread walking into my sister's house and asking for my car keys. I know I have no choice, but I still hate it."

"Why? It's a nice town. I'm sure your family loves you."

"They do, in a way."

"You never did tell me why they have your car."

She studied him. If he'd been a cop in Wharton Rock long, he had to have been in on her daughter Rachel's rescue.

"How long have you worked for the Wharton Rock police?"

"Two months. Before that, I was in school."

His black eyebrows drew together. Something troubled him. Maybe he didn't know. She'd caught a break.

"You didn't answer my question." Larry sped up and passed a slow-moving car.

"I was in prison. Okay?"

He tensed again. His expression turned grim. "Thanks for being honest with me. You see, I recently remembered where I knew you from. I was a rookie on Toby's force when they took you away. I quit shortly after and went back to school."

"Oh, well, thanks, sugar, for being upfront and open." She laced her words with tons of sarcasm. He could have explained that before she spilled her guts.

"I'm honored by your honesty. You didn't have to tell me."

"Humph." She faced the window.

His large hand enveloped hers on top of the console between them. "Would you like for me to go into your sister's house with you?"

Her head jerked up. "Would you?"

"Sure." He glanced at her. "To be *upfront* with you," he added on a layer of mockery, "Toby and I are good friends."

Great. She hit the jackpot with this guy. Something her mother used to say all the time about "jumping from the frying pan into the fire" popped into Katie's mind.

On the side of the highway was a white sign: *City of Wharton Rock, Population 2,891.* She had promised herself she wouldn't return until she had a home and some money and could pick up her daughter to live with her. Yet, here she was.

Rachel! If Larry went in with her, he'd see Rachel. What would he think? What did he already know? Jitters set her body to tingling until the Dodge

Ram parked in front of the old home place. Lacey, the good daughter, took care of their mother, her daughter, and a husband. Katie tensed. And the bad daughter returned to grovel.

Katie grabbed the armrest and held on, as if it would keep her from proceeding.

Larry opened the passenger door.

There was no escape.

"What kind of car do you have?"

"A little red Honda coupe with a dent on the side."

"Maybe it's in their garage."

Katie cringed. "They wouldn't sell it, would they?"

"Did you call your sister to tell her you were coming for it?"

"I told Mom." Katie stood on wobbly legs. Mom would've told her if Lacey sold it. Wouldn't she? Katie took a deep breath, shook out the kinks, and sashayed to the porch.

When the door opened, Katie's gaze slid lower and made eye contact with her daughter. Katie squatted.

"Hi, baby, how are you tonight?"

"Okay." Rachel seemed poised for trouble.

"You remember me, don't you, baby?"

While holding the door almost closed, Rachel nodded.

Lacey's voice came from behind the child. "Who is it?" The door widened. "Oh, hi." She motioned. "Come on in."

Without consent, Larry followed her.

After the door closed, he stepped to Katie's side. "Hi, Lacey, Mrs. Chandler."

"Hi, Larry. Toby's in the back," Lacey said.

About that time, Toby walked in. Ignoring his sister-in-law, he aimed his words at Larry. "Thanks for bringing her to Wharton Rock, man. Saved us a trip. Car's in the garage." With a key in his hand, he went out the door, holding it for Larry to come with him. "We'll get the car out and make sure it's okay, Katie. Be right back."

Mom was leaning back in her recliner. "You got a kiss for your mother?" She held her cheek toward Katie, who obliged.

Lacey perched on the sofa. Rachel crawled up on her lap.

"Have a seat," Lacey said as she scooted to one side.

Katie was on fire. She waved her hand like a fan. "No, I'll just get my car and be done."

"You hot?" Lacey's tone sounded mocking. "I'll turn on the fan." She slid the child to the sofa and rushed across the room.

"No problem." Katie snickered. "You were always hot when you were fat." And Katie would be fine once she was out of this house.

Lacey scowled, turned on the fan, and took her seat.

"You moved to your own place yet?" Mom had to open a sore spot.

Katie's temple pounded. Beads of sweat dotted her upper lip. "No, I've only been working ten days, Mom, and only had one payday. I'm saving up." Katie licked her lips and moved to stand in front of the fan.

"How much money have you saved?" Lacey asked.

That's none of your business, nosy. "Some of us like to party, not work all the time." As if she was having a grand old time.

Lacey stiffened. "I don't work all the time, and it seems to me that partying is what got you in trouble."

Mom harrumphed. "You should be living here with family, not off with strangers. Should've been part of your parole, seems to me."

A motor outside roared to life.

"I'll check and see if my car is out and ready." Katie turned to the door.

"Always running away," Lacey said.

Katie plopped hands on her hips and heaved a deep sigh. "As if you need to know, I'm not running away. I'm planning for a home for Rachel and me."

Lacey hugged Rachel to her side. "Rachel isn't going anywhere."

"She's my daughter."

"You gave her . . ." Lacey clamped a hand over her mouth. Her face reddened. "I'm sorry." She swallowed. "Rachel is blessed with two mothers." Her voice softened.

Katie squatted before her daughter once again. "May I have a hug before I go?"

Rachel glanced at Lacey, who nodded.

Soft, looking-for-love arms circled Katie's neck. "Goodbye, Mother."

"Oh, baby." Katie nuzzled her face in Rachel's dark tresses. Tears seeped from her eyes, despite her effort at control. "I love you. I would never hurt you." Her words rushed out like an unkinked water hose. "Never. You hear?" She pulled back. *But I did.*

"I know," the child whispered.

The door swung open. Toby clomped in. "Larry helped me hot shot the Honda. It should be okay, but you may need a new battery."

Katie stood and patted the top of Rachel's head. She turned to Toby. "Thanks, brother-in-law." She stomped past him and out to the car.

She didn't realize anyone was with her until she sensed Larry's presence behind her. She twisted, holding her arms behind her. "Thanks for bringing me." She gave him a sideways grin. "Guess you've saved me again."

"I'm glad I could help. I'll be praying for everything to work out for you."

Katie dropped behind the wheel. "Everything will work out better if I stay away from Wharton Rock." She revved the engine and backed away, leaving him standing like a protective sentinel.

CHAPTER *Nine*

Looking across the twenty or so teenagers, Larry's knees threaten to buckle, causing him to grasp the podium. He would rather face down a criminal with a gun than these kids. What did he have to offer them but failure and defeat?

Though he was assured of God's calling him to preach, he didn't remember anything about teenagers. He swallowed his case of jitters and turned to his Bible text from I Samuel and began his talk.

"Jonathan was a faithful friend to King David when he was a nobody. What does being a faithful friend mean?"

Kimmi raised her hand. "To stick with them if someone talks bad about them."

Larry nodded.

Ryan cleared his throat before he spoke. "I think it's being kind to someone just because of who they really are, not because they're popular or smart or whatever."

"Good, Ryan. When Jonathan befriended David, he wasn't King David. He was his dad's sworn enemy."

"A true friend wouldn't steal his friend's girl." The sentence came in a low tone from the second row. The boy's mouth clenched. He stared at his shaking foot crossed over the knee of his other leg.

"Ah, thank you, young man. Last week was my first time here, but I didn't see you. Are you new?"

"Yeah."

"Yeah, what?"

The head of a freckled-face boy with reddish-brown hair popped up. "Yes, I'm new. This is my first time." He glanced over at Shawn. "And it may be my last if *he* comes all the time."

One of the three girls led my Kimmi reached over to pat the speaker's hand. Perhaps, she was the one who invited him.

Larry searched his mind for what to say. To correct or not to correct? To welcome or go on with the lesson? His underarms were soaked by now. He swallowed a lump forming in his throat. The first time he went to church in his late teens at the invitation of a kind friend, everyone made him feel as if he'd come home. His heart broke for this boy. The hurt and pain showed in the creases across his forehead and the tightness of his jaw.

"I was just thinking the proper answer would be 'yes, sir,' but right now, I would like to say thank you for coming and for entering into our class. What's your name?"

The boy scowled. "Brady."

"Nice to meet you, Brady." Larry stepped from behind the podium and reached across the empty first row.

Brady remained silent but shook his hand.

"Does anyone else have a comment?" *Please, Lord, get me out of this awkward moment.*

Brady stood and stormed to the door.

While his hand hovered over the knob, Larry rushed after him.

"Don't leave. If you're hurt, this is the place to be. These are the people to pray with you." He waved his hand across the room.

Brady stopped, swiveled, and stared at Shawn. "I have no desire to be in a class with that jerk." The boy was panting by this time. "He stole my girl on purpose." His nostrils flared. "He's an example of not being a friend."

Shawn stood with fists clenched at his sides. "That's not true, and you know it." He stomped toward the two standing by the door. "You treated her awful. I was only trying to be kind to her."

Both boys' voices escalated. An usher opened the door, peeked in, and closed it again. Brady stepped nose to nose with Shawn. Before blows were struck, Larry stepped between them, his voice booming as best he could. At times like this, a soft tone wouldn't get their attention.

"Shawn, take your seat. Cody, come play a song. Brady, sit there. I'll sit beside you." He motioned to the front row.

Cody's guitar calmed the building tension. While he played "How He Loves Me," many started singing. Music did soothe the anger monster. When he stopped the song, Larry stood.

"Let us pray." He nodded Cody to keep playing.

The boy softened the tune. The more Larry prayed, the more he sensed God's presence in the room. When he lifted his head, he noticed tears in Kinsley's eyes.

After the end of the prayer, conversations began across the room. With piercing eyes and a frown, Kimmi's friend talked with Brady.

Larry moved toward Kinsley and placed his hand on her shoulder. He longed to pull her into his arms as her tears increased, but with abuse so rampant, he dared not take such liberties.

"Is there something I might pray with you about?"

She nodded, all the while wiping her eyes with her tissue.

"Call me anytime. I can see you're upset."

"I can't." She hiccupped. "Not now." She rushed from the room.

Brady broke free of the girl who invited him. Moving with speed, he was next out the door.

Larry heaved a deep breath, feeling a failure after only a week. Being a youth minister was hazardous duty.

Reverend Schumacher stepped inside and motioned for him. Pressure pushed on Larry's chest, making his breathing harder. He moved toward the pastor.

"Hello, sir."

"Hello, Reverend Pullman. Please stop by my office first thing in the morning. Shall we say eight thirty?" His brows rose.

"Okay, sir, I'll see you then." He took out his handkerchief once again for wiping up sweat.

Kimmi passed him. "You need a wife." She winked.

"I know." Larry rubbed his neck with the hanky. "Believe me, I know, but it's not easy."

"You want us to pray for you, Pastor Larry?" Ryan stepped behind Kimmi.

"Yeah, we'll pray," Kimmi said.

"Thanks, guys." *And I'll pray tonight about that meeting in the morning.* He may already be without a job.

❧

At eight thirty sharp, Larry entered Reverend Schumacher's office and took his seat. He rubbed his cheek with shaky fingers.

Reverend Schumacher nodded to his secretary to close the door.

"I hear you had some difficulty in the youth service last night." His words seemed matter-of-fact, but his tone was judgmental.

Larry scooted to the edge of his chair. "Yes. A visiting boy decided it was a good time to confront one of our teens."

"The argument got rather loud, I understand."

"Joe looked in about the time I took charge and told each of the boys to be seated. We ended with a calming hymn and everything was okay."

The pastor steepled his fingers. "I understand one of your young ladies is with child."

Larry examined the face of the man across from him.

The pastor didn't flinch.

Kinsley's tears came to Larry's mind, along with her refusal to discuss her need.

"I don't know anything about that. Who is it?"

"I realize this was only your second Wednesday night, but a good youth minister would find out such things. The girl would probably talk with another woman. I was hoping not having a wife wouldn't hinder your youth ministry, but I see it's a handicap in any ministry."

Larry's jaw tightened. His shoulders tensed. "I know, sir, but I can't very well manufacture one, now can I?" He shouldn't have spoken so harshly.

Reverend Schumacher leaned back in his chair. "That youth group has problems. I expect you to be their mentor as well as their minister."

"But—"

The pastor halted him with his hand in the air. "I know this is only your second meeting with the kids."

"Yes, sir."

"I want you to know those kids and control those meetings or I'll need to find someone who can." The man stood.

Larry's legs quivered as he put weight on them. He paused to make eye contact. "Please, sir, give me time. They're good kids. They need someone to stick with them. I don't know why, but I feel God wants me to be that one."

Reverend Schumacher's mouth eased into a smile. He stretched out his hand. "I'll give you a month. Don't let me down."

"I won't, sir."

CHAPTER Ten

Katie's pockets brimmed with money. From under her bed, she pulled out a metal box. She had found it at the restaurant and asked Paul if she could have it. He hadn't said anything. To her, that meant "yes." In it, she kept her meager savings. With a closed door, alone in her room, she poured her money out on her bed. Though her stash was growing, she was a long way from independence.

Nicole crashed into the room, spilling some of the drink she carried in a Styrofoam cup. Her eyes widened. "Wow, you have lots of money."

Katie scooped it up, stuffed it into the pockets of her black jeans on the floor, and hid the box behind her back.

"Tips were good yesterday." Her voice was shaky.

"So?" Nicole plopped onto her bed.

"So, lots of days aren't that good. I might need to live on it for a while."

Nicole shrugged and bent over to untie her athletic shoes.

Katie pushed the metal box back under her bed and sat. Her heart was racing. Did Nicole notice? Should she ask Madison to keep her savings? Or Wanda? Katie's head swam. In this place, she trusted no one.

"When's your boyfriend coming back?"

"You mean Collin?"

"Yeah." Nicole sipped from her cup, sat on the bed, and stared at the ceiling. A moment later, she jumped up and paced.

"I don't think Collin is my boyfriend anymore. He's still doing drugs. I have to stay away from him if I'm going to stay out of jail."

Nicole raked her fingers through her frizzy hair. "It's hot in here. Doesn't Wanda know the meaning of air conditioning?"

"She keeps it higher to save money."

Katie snatched her black shirt and shimmied into her black jeans. That had been her one clothes purchase. Paul demanded the servers wear black. All Katie's clothes were pink or some shade of red.

Nicole's Styrofoam cup flew across the room. Crushed ice and some liquid splashed on Katie, followed by silence, then three heads peeping through the door to their room.

Hands on hips, Wanda glared from Nicole to Katie.

Katie shrugged. "Hey, guys, I've got to go to work."

Wanda's gaze went from Katie to the cup on the floor and back to Nicole. "Clean it up, now."

"Why me?" Nicole met her glare for glare. "Why not Katie?"

"I didn't—" Katie started.

"I saw you enter with that cup in your hand. You think I'm stupid?" Wanda took two steps closer.

The other two girls disappeared.

Madison appeared behind Wanda. "Katie, you have a visitor downstairs."

"Who is it?"

Madison dipped her head and lowered her voice. "That same handsome guy who came last week and told me he was your boyfriend." She took a quick glance at Nicole.

Visitors meant trouble, but Katie wanted out of that room. "I'm on my way to work anyway. I'll check it out. Collin isn't my boyfriend anymore, if that's who you mean."

Madison rolled her eyes.

Katie skipped down the stairs, through the kitchen, and into the living room, but no one was there. He surprised her from behind. Damp kisses trailed round her neck. She swiveled.

"Collin. What are you doing here?"

"I came to see you, sweet stuff." He rocked in front of her, his face inches away from hers. "I missed you. Didn't you miss me?"

"I've got to go."

He raced around to get back in front of her. "I'm clean, baby. Honest. I've quit the stuff."

She plopped her hands on her hips. "Then how come Nicole seemed to have stuff after your last visit?"

"I don't know what you're talking about. Who's Nicole? I came to see you, baby."

She huffed. "I'm late for work."

Before she got through the door, he snatched her arm. "I'll drive you."

"I have my own wheels. Thank you."

"When will you be home?"

"Late." She stepped off the porch.

He circled her body, pulling her to his chest. "You don't need this place. Come live with me again."

"I'm saving for a place of my own." She turned her head to miss his lips. "I want to get my daughter back with me."

"Little Rachel lived with us once before. Remember? I love kids. We'll be a real family."

A real family with drugs in the house. "I need to be careful or I'll go back inside. You have a record too. I can't live with you."

"Nobody will know."

She rolled her eyes. "Like only my parole officer. They have to approve where I live, and you ain't it."

He stepped back. She raced forward. When she reached her Honda, she got behind the wheel.

"I'll think about it."

She closed the door and backed out. Collin's place was better than here. She could say she was living with a friend. Maybe they wouldn't check out his record. Despair reared its ugly head and slapped her in the face. Being in prison was so much easier. Three squares and no bills. Ex-cons could never catch a break.

Maybe she should take Collin up on his offer, go get Rachel, and find a job closer to his house.

Who was she kidding? She was lucky to have the job she had, and she didn't trust Collin to keep Rachel when she was at work.

When she pulled into the Country Dinner Restaurant, she recognized the white Dodge Ram in the parking lot. Her heart skipped a beat when a tall, dignified man with black hair and mustache climbed out. He waved.

She got out of her car. "Hi, Larry. You here for dinner?"

"Yep. Dinner and to ask you a favor."

She paused. "What's that?" She had nothing to offer him except her body. Had she read him wrong?

"Let's go in. You get settled, then order me the chicken-fried steak special. We'll talk after dinner. I'm hungry."

"Okay."

By the time Larry finished eating his dinner and the rush died down, she stopped by his table to refresh his tea.

"So what's the favor?"

"I told you I was helping with youth at a nearby church?"

"Yeah."

"I need a wife."

"Excuse me?" Her brows jumped and so did her voice.

"Everyone keeps telling me you can't work in ministry without a wife. It's really holding me back."

"So you want me to marry you?" Her voice raised another decimal.

He looked around and whispered, "No, I just need female help with these teens right now, or I'm going to lose my job."

"I thought this was just something you were helping out with."

Her heart hammered against her ribs. Had she not only hooked up with a policeman but also a preacher? Before he could answer, she dashed for the kitchen and went out through the back door. She gulped a lung full of fresh air, trying to decipher what this man was asking of her. By the time her heart and breathing slowed, she went back inside and over to his table.

His face was the color of watermelon. He fingered his tea glass. "Sorry, I'm not telling this very well."

"Seemed like you're telling it too well." Katie lowered her voice. "Look, Larry, in case you didn't know, I'm not a nice person. I'm an ex-con. I'm not wife material, and I'm sure not a youth minister's wife material."

"You're kind and friendly and caring. Your down-to-earth sense of gab just might get to these kids. If I don't get a certain young lady to confess her problems to me within the next week, I've lost my ..." He paused. "My first opportunity to help people." He looked up at Katie, his brown eyes soft and sincere. "I'm desperate for a woman's point of view. Could you just go roller-skating with the group tomorrow night? If it's awful, you don't have to come anymore. Deal?"

Her stomach let off a swarm of butterflies. She'd never felt so inadequate before, but she'd also never felt so needed, and that was wonderful.

"You don't know what you're asking but . . ." She stuck out her hand. "Deal."

CHAPTER *Eleven*

Gliding around a skating rink on wheels reminded Katie of the rush of freedom when she left prison bars behind. She hadn't roller-skated since she was twelve and went with the Wharton Rock youth group. A time of innocence when she'd been happy. She didn't remember being happy since.

While lost in her memories, Larry came up on her, making her jump. He tapped her shoulder as he slid past. His skating took as little effort as it took a robin to fly. Her ambitious nature made her speed up to catch him. Larry caught her hand, sending sparks up her arm and straight into her heart.

"How you doing?"

His eyes, like chocolate pudding, drew her.

"I'm just fine, sugar. You said be myself. Well, here I am." She winked.

His ears flamed. "That's good."

A couple of girls bumped into each other. Larry skated away to help them off the floor.

All this skating and talking left Katie parched. She aimed for the exit to get a cola. She skated by the fat girl in Larry's group, who sat beside one of the parents helping chaperone, and overheard the mother's words.

"You shouldn't have come. Don't you have any pride?"

The fat girl's head dropped, but not before Katie spotted a tear.

Katie skidded to a stop and spoke to the girl. "You remind me of my big sister." Skating was the one place Katie outshone her sister. Already heavy, even in her teens, Lacey was awkward at any sports, but Katie did it well. *That and attracting boys.* "How about getting a cola with me?"

The girl sniffed. "Okay." She tried to stand, but with her skates still on, her feet went out from under her.

Katie grabbed her just in time to steady her. "Yep, my sister never could skate either." Talking as she went, she guided the girl to the counter to order drinks. "She always hated sports stuff, but she was always ..." *fat.* Katie swallowed. She'd almost said the word. Lacey used to yell that she hated her when Katie did that.

Katie grasped both the girl's arms and faced her. "You know what? My sister was heavy all her life until recently. She lost all her extra weight and looks good." Katie had never admitted that to Lacey before. Maybe she should. Oh, dear, was Larry bringing out good in her. She hadn't thought there was any left.

Katie ordered two sodas and led the girl to a nearby table. "What's your name?"

"Kinsley." The girl's head remained bowed. Her Mexican heritage was evident, another thing that reminded Katie of Lacey, who'd picked up their paternal grandmother's genes.

"I wasn't calling you fat," Katie said. "I was just telling you about my sister." And she was calling her fat. *Me and my big mouth. Larry should've known better than to ask me to be a confidante to these kids.* "My sister was fat ... or ... heavy. And she was sad a lot." Funny, Katie had never remembered that until now. All she knew was that Lacey was Miss Do-Gooder, while Katie was the wild child, and the more good Lacey did, the more Katie wanted to be bad. Why was that? Where were all these crazy feelings coming from all of a sudden?

"It's okay. I know I'm fat." Kinsley spoke with a soft tone, but now she stared straight at Katie, almost belligerent. "You don't have to tell me that. Fat and going to get fatter." The dam to her tears opened, and the flood streamed down her cheeks.

Careful to block the view of those nasty chaperones that were mean to the girl, Katie embraced Kinsley. She patted her back, spoke tender, baby-sounding words like "there, there, it can't be all that bad," and tousled the girl's full, black hair that also reminded Katie of Lacey. When the tears slowed, Katie eased away and smiled.

"Thank you," Kinsley moved back in her chair and regained her composure. "Ryan's mom was right. I shouldn't have come."

Katie stood. She shifted to one hip and crossed her arms in front. "And just why not?"

"I can't skate."

"Well, they're not skating either. Neither was one of the boys. He didn't even put any skates on. At least you tried."

"But I'm fat."

"Is that a disease?"

"And I'm pregnant."

Katie had no comeback. She'd succeeded in finding out a secret that Larry probably needed to know, but she felt like an idiot. She had told him she was the wrong person for this job. What advice could she give?

Oh, well, no problem, just get on drugs and end up in prison like I did.

"I . . . don't . . ."

"It's okay." Kinsley wiped away a few new tears. "I thought no one knew, but obviously, Ryan's mom knows." She put her hand on her forehead with her elbow on the table.

"How far along are you?"

"About six months. I can hide it well, the benefits of being fat in the first place." Her laugh was hollow.

"Have you seen a doctor?"

Kinsley shook her head. "Just took a test."

"Does the father know?"

"Yes, but he and his parents are moving to Missouri this summer."

"How old is he?"

"Seventeen."

"How old are you?"

"Fifteen."

"I was seventeen when I had my daughter."

Kinsley's head jerked up. "You have a daughter?"

"Yeah." Katie grinned, but the grin soon disappeared. "But I messed up, so she's living with my sister."

"The fat one?"

"Yeah. Well, she's not fat anymore."

"How old is your daughter?"

"Seven."

"What did you do when you found out you were going to have her?"

"I guess I was lucky." *In a way.* "Her dad married me."

"That was good."

"Yeah." Katie dropped her head. This was like true confession time. What had Larry got her into? "Only he moved me to Colorado and then dumped me when I was eight months along."

"Rough."

"Yeah. Anyway, that's not you." Katie brightened her tone. The conversation was scraping the bottom. Denial always worked best for her. "My life is good. Yours will be too."

"Thank you. Ah, Katie?"

"Yeah."

"Can I call you sometime?"

This girl was making it hard to stay in the denial zone. "I don't have a phone."

Kinsley's eyes widened. "I couldn't live without a phone."

Katie shrugged. "It's no big thing. If you want to reach me, just call Larry, or call Country Dinner Restaurant." She laughed. "I spend most of my time there. I intend to buy a phone next week, and they'll have my number."

"Okay. Thanks." Kinsley downed the rest of her soda.

"How about we give skating another try?"

"If you'll help me."

"I will." Katie led her new friend to the rink.

Larry eased by them. "Way to go, Kinsley. We'll have you skating yet."

Kinsley slipped. Both Katie and Larry gripped one of her arms, holding her steady.

A group of boys rushed by en masse. Katie remembered one played the guitar. Wayne had played guitar. The memories threatened to crush her again. She stiffened and swallowed and tried to forget.

Larry's smile warmed her heart. Could she ever live up to his belief in her? For the first time in ages, she wanted to.

Larry was having fun. He'd never expected that. This was a job, but having Katie with him, made it nice. He hadn't roller-skated since he turned his back on his church group at the ripe old age of fourteen, right after his dad died. He'd forgotten how much he enjoyed it. Maybe teaching teens wasn't so bad.

Without a wife, however, he might lose the job and a chance to do some good.

The kids needed help. If he'd had a youth minister who'd really cared, would it have made a difference in his life? If he'd grown up without regrets, he might not have gone into law enforcement. Funny how things worked out when God was involved.

By the time he and Katie had eased Kinsley around the rink a couple of times, they needed to head back to the church.

"Everyone, time to go," he called.

"One more lap," several kids yelled back.

"One more lap, then skates off." He nodded and motioned to the sidelines while skidding to a halt beside a chair.

Katie was helping Kinsley to her seat. All three began to unlace.

After a couple of minutes, Larry called to an employee, who stopped the music and asked for everyone to head off the floor.

Mr. and Mrs. Russell, Ryan's parents, rose with a huff, looking puffed up and impatient. "May we head on home with Ryan now?" Mrs. Russell asked.

It was time for Larry's cop voice. "No, ma'am. You agreed to chaperone this outing. I'll be driving the van. What if there's trouble? Besides, I need Mr. Russell to drive the other van, not these kids."

"I guess I forgot," she said.

How Ryan got to be so nice with parents like he had was a mystery to Larry. Youth ministry was as much about praying for parents as for teens.

"I want you to know I so appreciate your help tonight."

Mr. Russell straightened, smiled, and tipped his chin up. "Thank you, young man. We were happy to do so."

Mrs. Russell appeared contrite. She bit her lip but kept her thoughts to herself.

Kids with their own cars scattered. The group with no transportation headed out and loaded in the vans.

Once they were back at the church, an hour went by before the last teen was picked up. When Larry and Katie were the last two left, he opened his passenger door for her to get in. The trip to the halfway house was quiet.

When they arrived, he got out and rushed around his truck.

Katie flung open the door, almost hitting his arm.

"Are you trying to not wait for me to be a gentleman?" He strove for a teasing tone.

A street light caught Katie's widened blue eyes. She patted his cheek. "I'm not used to that kind of treatment."

He held the door while she slipped out. "Do you want me to stop?"

Her lips quivered. She caught his arm. A strange expression came across her face, as if she was really thinking hard about his question. Maybe she liked to be treated roughly. If so, he had the wrong girl. He could never treat a woman without respect.

"I don't know." Her voice quivered as much as her lips. "I've never been around a guy like you." She rubbed a hand up and down his bicep. "You're more muscled than I thought."

A flush swept up his neck. Thankful that a street light couldn't highlight red skin, he cleared his throat to regain control. "I guess that's good."

"I'd say so."

She winked but dropped her arm. He could no more move than if he was glued to the ground. She also seemed immobile. His pulse went into gear, like the take-off of a race car. She just stood there, studying him, her eyes glistening in the moonlight. Shaking like one of his teens on prom night, he willed his gaze to look up at the sky. He began to breathe again.

"Beautiful moon, almost full."

"Yes." She stepped toward the house. "I should be getting in before Wanda locks the door."

He gathered her hand in his and walked with her. They'd had a moment there, and he was still struggling to recover.

When they reached the porch, she faced him but didn't look up. "I had a nice time being your wife tonight." She giggled.

He clasped both her hands. Though his weren't huge, hers were so small they were lost in his grasp. The lump in his throat choked him. He merely dipped her hands up and down, bowed halfway, and left. It was all he could manage.

CHAPTER *Twelve*

The halfway house was quiet. The clock struck eleven. Wanda hadn't locked the door. No one met Katie. A mouse rushed across the hardwood floor and disappeared under the big shelving unit to the side. *Eerie!*

With gentle movement, Katie went up the stairs. All the second floor doors were closed. Seldom did she come home without hearing voices, usually angry ones. Did Nicole beat her home? *Doubtful.* Katie opened the door.

"It's about time." Wanda perched on the edge of Katie's bed.

On the other bed, Nicole lay motionless with eyes closed. Beside Wanda lay five packets of white powder. Sweat broke out on Katie's forehead. Her stomach churned and heaved.

"What's that?" *Stupid comment.*

Wanda stood. "That's what I want to know."

"Look, I'm clean," said Katie, but who would believe an ex-dope head. Her knees shook so badly she feared she would fall. Easing down to her bed, she hoped to stem the nausea.

"The police are on the way."

"Oh, no, please." She grabbed hold of Wanda's arm. "Don't turn me in. I'm clean. Honest."

"We'll see about that."

Heavy boots clumped up the stairs. Wanda went to the door. "Over here, officers."

A woman Katie had seen only twice—Pat Kelley, her parole officer—rushed past the policeman and entered the room. She loomed over Katie. Her quizzical gaze probed her parolee before she spoke.

"I understand this was found on your bed." She indicated the drugs.

"Did Wanda also tell you that I've been gone all evening?"

"Yes, as a matter of fact, she did."

Katie relaxed a little. Maybe Wanda wasn't unreasonable. With all the commotion, Nicole hadn't moved. Katie had a sneaking suspicion who might have put those drugs there.

"When did you find these here?" A police sergeant addressed Wanda.

"About an hour ago."

"When was the last time you checked this room?" he asked.

Wanda heaved a sigh. "Not since this morning."

"Ma'am." The sergeant tapped Nicole. "When did you come in and go to bed?"

She opened her eyes and yawned. "Oh, hi. Sure is lots of activity going on in this room tonight. What was the question, officer?"

Katie cringed. Nicole playing Miss Innocent was worse than acting like a youth minister herself.

"When did you come to your room tonight?" he repeated.

"Oh, I got here just before Wanda came, didn't I?" She turned guiltless eyes toward their halfway house manager. "Oh, yes, I came in, laid my bag on my bed, and had begun to undress when Wanda peeked in. We both noticed the bags about the same time. Isn't that right?" Again, she looked at Wanda.

"I have no idea when you came in, Nicole. I know you claimed to notice the drugs when I did. Though I think they would've been hard not to see immediately." Wanda's tone shut up the innocent act.

Katie sent off a silent cheer.

With Katie's parole officer going along with them, the policemen took statements from everyone in the house. They took away the drugs and left the house.

"Follow me to the living room," Pat said to Katie.

The two went downstairs.

Before Katie took a seat, Pat turned on her. "Who's Collin?"

"A guy that used to be my boyfriend before I went to prison. He's not anymore." Katie could forget hanging out at his place.

"Then why does he keep visiting you?"

Katie grimaced. "Because he won't take no for an answer. He's been here twice. I'm saving for a place of my own. I'm not with him anymore and don't intend to be. I told him that."

"Yet he came again tonight."

"He did?"

"Before you left."

"That's not true."

"When did you leave?"

"About six thirty."

"I understand it was another guy who picked you up. Is he a drug dealer too?"

Katie chuckled. "No. He's a policeman who works with teens."

"Not exactly your type."

"That's what I told him."

"Name and number?" Pat pulled out a note pad.

Katie gave her the information. Her cheeks heated. Larry wouldn't like facing interrogation every time he came around her. Hadn't she told him she was bad news? Why had she forgotten that and gotten lost in his gentlemanly ways?

Pat glared at her until she blinked. "Everything will be checked out. If we can't prove you're innocent very soon, you'll be asked to leave here. If that happens, let me know where you go." She flipped the note pad closed and dropped it into a purse that fit her tremendous size.

"Like where could I go? I don't have enough to rent a place yet." Not that the state of Texas or Pat Kelley cared.

"You could room with your family. That was what we preferred anyway. Remember?"

Another wave of nausea hit Katie. Life was closing in like a coffin. All she could do was nod.

Her parole officer walked out. Wanda descended the stairs, went over to lock the front door, and stopped in front of Katie.

"You can sleep here tonight, but that's it until this is cleared up."

Katie ran for the bathroom and vomited up that night's hamburger.

CHAPTER *Thirteen*

Lacey lay across her bed. She held a book to read, but her thoughts wandered. At the day's end, she was alone, again.

Toby often worked late. Mom shut out the world with her usual TV programs, and Rachel, hopefully, slept.

Four years ago, Lacey would have been stuffing food in her mouth. That was before the Lord had healed her emotionally and delivered her from food addiction, but the old temptations plagued her at times like this. Loneliness and anger stripped her of peace.

She craved sweets. Lacey had bought Mom a new bag of Snickers. Mom kept them in her room. The sweet, gooey nougat flavor tormented Lacey. She healed daily, sometimes one moment at a time, but the memory lingered.

Shuffling into the kitchen, she flipped on the light and pulled out a stash of protein bars she'd bought in a weak moment two days ago. She peeled off the wrapper and bit into the luscious peanut butter flavoring. If she closed her eyes, she could imagine peanut butter fudge.

She stuffed the rest of the bar into her mouth and took the box to bed. By the time she finished all six bars, her turmoil was sedated, but her tummy was tight and miserable. Her thoughts turned to Katie. That did nothing to help Lacey relax.

Mom suffered because of Katie's rejection. A vile taste rose in Lacey's mouth. When Katie went to prison, Lacey was beginning to trust God for her own food addiction. With her sister out of the picture, Lacey raised her niece without interference and settled into married life with her best friend. Even she and Mom had reached a kind of truce. But Katie would always be Mom's favorite. Life wasn't fair. Whenever Katie was involved, Lacey's anger mounted, and that was wrong. *Lord, help me.*

One day at a time, she reminded herself. *This too shall pass.* She ran through all the sayings that had helped her lose a hundred pounds.

God had been faithful. He had healed her emotionally. Along with her weight loss, He had given her the love of her life as a husband and a sweet niece to mother.

"Lacey." Mom's voice penetrated the silence.

Lacey went running to her mother's bedroom. "What's wrong?"

"This TV is screwy. It went blank."

"We've lost the satellite. Might be the weather."

"I need my TV to go to sleep."

"Well, I'm sorry, Mom. I can't make a miracle." Lacey's huff showed her frustration, but she couldn't stop it. "How about I bring my old CD player in here? Wouldn't music help?"

"I guess."

The TV popped back on.

"There, all fixed," Lacey said. "I'll get the CD player and set it beside your bed, just in case."

The man on the TV held Mom's attention. Lacey was an interruption. She turned to leave.

Rachel appeared at the door, still holding her old doll, Margaret Rose. Lacey had a hard time getting it from the child to wash it.

"I'm thirsty."

Lacey hugged her sweet girl. "Let's get you back in bed, then I'll get you a glass of water."

She glanced back at Mom, wishing she'd think before she yelled and woke up the child.

With everyone back in bed, Lacey climbed into hers. Her alarm would go off in seven hours. Toby would be home in one. She turned out the light and closed her eyes. *Sleep comes to the trusting.* Lacey tended to worry more, trust less.

She dropped off shortly before a warm kiss dropped to her brow, and she woke to hear about her husband's day. Her eyes burned. Fatigue clawed at her muscles. She would sleep in on Saturday. Toby was more important than rest.

By two in the morning, Toby drifted to sleep. Lying awake, Lacey repeated the 23rd Psalm, looking for peace. The next time she saw the clock, it was five and a ringing phone roused her. She opened one eye to see the number.

It was Larry Pullman's number. Why was one of Toby's cops calling on her phone? "Hello?" Her voice sounded weak. She was so tired.

"Lacey. It's Katie."

Adrenaline pumped through Lacey's veins. She sat up, now wide awake. "What's wrong?"

"Can I come to your house?"

A spot of déjà`vu. Katie, stuck in Colorado, pregnant, with her husband gone. Katie, with Rachel, leaving Collin and needing a place to crash for a while. A wilted orchid left in the sun too long would've been stronger than Lacey at that moment. A pain struck her temple like a knife. She dropped the phone with one word, "Katie."

Toby wrapped her in his arms and picked up her phone. "Katie, what is it you want?" His eyes widened and then he sighed. "Oh, Larry, why did she call you?" Holding the phone aside, he spoke to Lacey. "It's Larry on the phone now. Katie has been thrown out of the halfway house. He says it's not her fault."

"Why did he get involved?" Lacey rolled up her pillow.

Toby shrugged. "The police needed him to corroborate her story."

"And she was with him?" Lacey's voice escalated. "Just how close is he to Katie?"

Toby went back to the phone.

Lacey caught some of the other side of the conversation, something about Katie helping Larry with a youth group. Lacey gasped. Her ears were obviously playing tricks on her. Katie wouldn't have anything to do with church.

Toby chuckled. "Katie doesn't have a very good reputation in Wharton Rock, but you do." He glanced at Lacey.

She shook her head. "I can't take Katie right now."

"Tell her to come on." Toby disconnected.

"I can't. I just can't."

Lacey beat her fists against Toby's chest before she slumped in submission. Katie still made the messes, and Lacey cleaned them up. She cried until the moisture dried, she was exhausted, and it was time to get ready for work.

CHAPTER *Fourteen*

A chill shifted through Katie's veins. Drained of all emotion, she moved into numb. All of it piled on top of her like so much trash. She moved one foot and then another. *Follow the list.*

Call Lacey.

Go to her house.

Sleep a few hours.

Take a shower.

Go to work at three forty-five.

Work hard.

She hadn't worked out the next step yet. The police could have her behind bars by then. She clutched her money box to her chest like a life vest.

"Do you feel like driving?" Larry asked.

Katie's gaze rose up, up to the height of the man. "What?"

"Do you feel like driving?"

"Sure."

Larry picked up one of the boxes that Wanda had dropped at their feet when the police had called her. He took it to Katie's Honda and returned and gathered the clothes, scattered where they'd been thrown.

Standing immobile, Katie watched, her gaze following the man's movements. "I'm going to Lacey's?"

"Yeah, just to sleep and shower."

"You're sure she gave her okay?"

"Toby did."

"My sister hates me." Katie's voice was monotone.

Larry took her arm and led her to her car.

She sat behind the steering wheel, glaring at it, as if it were a snake ready to pounce.

"Listen." Larry slammed the door and talked through the open window. "Let me check with Wanda to see if we can get your car tomorrow. I'll drive you. You're in no condition to drive."

"I can drive."

"No, you can't." His tone was an exclamation point.

She clutched the front of his shirt. "Don't let them tow my car away."

"I'll make sure." He led her to the passenger side of his truck. "Stay here. I'll check with Wanda."

Wanda? Why? There was no evidence the drugs were Katie's. But there was no evidence that they weren't either. Wanda claimed to have an eyewitness that the drugs were on the bed before Katie left and Nicole arrived. Any eyewitness meant one of her halfway house comrades. Who hated her that much?

Katie's energy level peaked like a power surge. Her face flamed, and her mind fired off a to-do list. She popped out of Larry's truck and ran to her Honda.

When he came back out of the house, he yelled, "Stop."

She was behind the wheel and backing up.

He revved up his truck and followed her all the way to Wharton Rock. He parked behind her in front of Lacey's house and stormed around the vehicles before she could get out.

"What do you think you're doing? You could've been killed in your state of mind."

"But I wasn't, was I?"

His fists curled. His jaw clenched.

"Look," she said with a sigh. "I'm better. Okay? Really. I just need to prove my innocence. I appreciate you confirming my nighttime alibi, but if Wanda has an eyewitness that said the drugs were there before I left?" She grimaced. "I've got to get a place in Apache Falls to keep my job. And I must find the eyewitness."

"I'll help."

Katie's shoulders slumped. "Larry, you're a good guy. Don't get involved with my trouble. It could ruin you."

"I can take care of myself."

"You don't know people like those women."

"I know you."

She sniffed. "Guess you have me there. You don't really know me, though." *I wish I was worthy, but I'll never be again.*

"Katie, I'm a policeman. I've dealt with everything."

"Then you know better than to be caught with me."

Toby called from the front porch. "Hey, you guys, you're going to wake up the neighborhood. Come on in, Katie. Lacey just woke up Rachel and has breakfast on the table."

Katie didn't have time for breakfast. She needed a phone and a shower, then she'd head back to Apache Falls.

Larry waved to his friends. "I'll be heading home. Get some sleep."

Katie shifted the box in her hands. "I can't sleep."

"If you want your wits about you, you better try."

"Okay." She plodded across the yard, past Toby and into the house that shouted "failure."

Lacey's feet yanked along imaginary leg weights while she set the milk on the table and took a seat. A sleepy Rachel nibbled her fruit-flavored cereal. Toby had not joined them yet. Before he headed toward the table, they heard Katie drive up. The voices outside grew in volume. Toby ran toward the noise.

Needing sustenance to face her sister, Lacey took a bite of boiled egg. A car motor started and roared away. The front door opened and closed. Shivers snaked up her spine, sending prickles across her neck. The kitchen closed in around her. The egg tasted like cardboard. She didn't have to turn.

"So what happened?"

"I don't know." Katie moved to face her sister. "I went with Larry to a skating rink with his youth group. When I returned, cocaine was on my bed, and Wanda had called the police."

"Have a seat. Knowing you, I assumed you'd just want toast."

"I'm not hungry."

"You need to eat."

Lacey put bread in the toaster. Toby took the other seat and started eating his cereal. Staring at her mother, Rachel's eyes were as big as baseballs.

"Hi, baby," Katie said.

"Hi."

"Eat your cereal, Rachel." Lacey's tone was brusque.

Rachel took a few more mouthfuls. Lacey set the toast on a plate in front of Katie.

"Are you taking me to school?" Rachel asked her birth mom.

Katie had a caught-in-the-headlights look. "I can." The words drug out an extra two syllables.

"I'll take you when I head to work. You know that." Lacey laid a strawberry beside Rachel's plate.

The child ate it while nodding. Sounds of crunching toast and slurping milk echoed across the room. The tension at the table was as real as a fifth person. Toby pushed away his empty bowl and sipped his coffee.

"If you need me to, I could take her to give you more time this morning."

"How generous. You get to go back to sleep when I leave." Lacey's tone was less sweet, more sour. She needed to scrap this stinking thinking before she faced patients or her boss.

The cords in Toby's neck strained. He was hurt by her attitude. "You didn't have to stay awake for me last night. You knew I'd be late."

"I can't sleep until you get home."

"That's not my fault. You should try."

"You think I didn't?" Lacey almost screamed. Tears burned her eyes, but it wasn't Toby she wanted to fight with.

Katie got up for a cup of coffee. "Glad to see they keep this around now that you're here, Toby. Mom and Lacey never used to buy coffee."

A lump bigger than her egg formed in Lacey's throat.

"You okay, hon?" Toby stood and dropped a kiss on her forehead. "You're so flushed."

The room was a furnace, and air was in short supply. She swallowed again, this time dislodging the lump.

"Go get your clothes on, Rachel. I'll be ready to leave in fifteen minutes."

"Okay." She turned to Katie. "Goodbye."

"May I have a kiss?"

Rachel kissed Katie's cheek and left.

Lacey scurried around, picking up bowls and plates and putting away leftover food and milk. She wiped the table and counter and went toward her bedroom to finish preparing for her work day.

"Can I use your cell phone, Lacey? Just while you're getting ready. Two calls."

Lacey snatched her phone, threw it at Katie, and closed her bedroom door.

Toby slipped in.

"Don't let her get to you like this. She's not staying. You can bet on that. Not if she can make other arrangements. She doesn't like being here anymore than you like it."

"I know." Lacey added some light makeup and brushed her hair. She found her shoes.

Toby hugged her. "I still wonder at how small you are and marvel at God's goodness. I love you, Lacey Kay."

Thankful there was no tension now in the bedroom, Lacey brightened the day with her best smile. "I love you too."

"I'll go in at noon, so I should be earlier tonight."

"Good."

"Make sure Katie's gone by that time." Toby winked.

"She needs sleep. Put her in Rachel's bed after we leave."

He saluted. "Yes, ma'am."

"Katie." Mom's voice rose like thunder, even with the door closed. "So you've moved back home."

Lacey rolled her eyes. "Good luck." She opened the door.

Mom greeted Lacey with a smile for the first time since Katie went off to prison. "Isn't it wonderful to get our Katie home? She can bed with Rachel. Sure glad you traded her twin bed for a queen-size."

"I'm not staying, Mom." Katie got off the phone.

"And why not?" Mom tried to put her hands on her hips, but she dropped her cane. "You're staying, and that's settled."

"I can't, Mom. I have a job in Apache Falls."

"Joanne said Willie is needing another server. You can work here."

"No, I can't."

Voices escalated. Tension was back. Lacey picked up her purse, caught Rachel's hand, and kissed Toby, again. "Sorry, babe."

He grinned. "I'm going to bed."

"Good luck with that one."

"Toby," Mom called "move these boxes into Rachel's room."

Lacey drove off, carrying the weight of a new burden and the turbulence of a hateful mindset. Self-pity had returned with a vengeance, until she remembered something said in her twelve step meeting last week. *When someone makes you mad, they control you.*

CHAPTER *Fifteen*

Wharton Rock's police station on Saturday bustled like an ant farm. With the break-ins at two stores in town, an assignment was designated to every cop on duty. Feet marched back and forth across the black-and-white tile floor, the only thing that added character to the gray metal desks—one for Amber, the receptionist, and two for the patrolmen on duty. Two more desks hid behind partitions where the detectives worked, and one more desk for Ruby, the combination dispatcher and bookkeeper for the department.

With pencil clicking against a patrolman's desk, Larry's job was to watch the computer screen. A vagrant sleeping behind McCoy's Furniture Store had spotted a man in the alley the night of the last break-in. Armed with his description, Larry loaded the rendering by an artist from Apache Falls into the database. Larry's monitor flashed repeated faces while he watched.

"Hey, Larry," Toby called from the one and only real office. With the door open, his walnut-colored desk faced the lobby. "Go with Willie. There's some trouble up at Hamburger Heaven."

"Sure."

Larry stopped the flicking images, donned his policeman hat, and chased after the detective. Willie's long legs and head start caused him to reach the patrol car first. The motor roared to life. The car backed out and stopped to pick up Larry just turning the corner of the station.

"What's going on?" he asked.

"Well, preacher, looks like we might have us a hostage situation."

The wide brim of Willie's Stetson almost hid his eyes, but Larry didn't have to see them to know they were dancing. That positive attitude despite the odds was something Larry loved about the detective. He just wished he and Toby could win him for Christ. A grin curved Larry's mouth. Willie was weakening on that score. He'd been to church the last two Sundays.

The two pulled into Hamburger Haven's parking lot. In groups, people watched the place, standing way back from the door. Willie skidded to a stop, leaped out, and strode toward Sonny Joiner. Larry shut his car door and straightened about the time Willie marched back that way.

"Go cover the back. From what I hear, the only ones in there are Tammy, the manager, and the thief. I'll initiate communication with him if I can."

"Yes, sir."

Larry flipped his hat up and down by way of acknowledgment and then headed to the alley, out of sight. He readied his weapon and aimed it at the back door.

Since he had a hostage, Larry doubted the criminal would come that way, but he held steady. No one ever knew what a criminal might do. An image of Katie floated across his view. Could he know what she might do? She'd done drugs in the past. She'd lived with Collin. My goodness, she'd done terrible things. Just because she said she wanted to go straight didn't mean she would. He wanted to believe. He wanted to trust. He cared.

A rattle sounded from inside. Larry shook his head to clear his blurring eyes. He steadied his gun hand. His heart hammered against his ribs.

The door opened, showing a frightened Tammy. "Don't shoot," she said.

He lowered the gun. The huge black man behind her focused an angry eye on Larry. Tammy moved to the right. The man jerked her back in front of him. His shirt rose and fell with labored breathing.

"Lay your gun on the ground, or I'll shoot her."

Larry glanced around. It was just him and them.

"Do it, now." The voice escalated.

With care, Larry placed his gun on the gravel.

"Kick it away." The man's voice was more like a bear's growl. He resembled one too.

Larry nudged the gun with his foot until he could no longer reach it without moving. His eyes squinted, the two men locked in a visual duel. The thief had a hundred pounds on Larry, but their height was the same.

With one quick movement, the thief shoved Tammy out of the way and dashed for the tree cover behind them. Larry snatched his gun and sprinted through the trees. A speck of blue showed to his left. He swerved that way. The man crossed the next street and went to the back of a house.

Larry rounded the corner of the house in time to see the man jump from a dog house. Larry doubled back the other side of the house, gaining him a little edge. The man ran down the alley. Larry gained on him, getting closer by the next block, where his prey ducked into a drainage ditch.

Larry leaped onto the culvert. The man scrambled up the ledge. Larry dove and missed, but he caught the man's leg and refused to let go. The man turned and kicked with his other foot. Tires squealed from behind them.

"Hands up." Willie leveled a gun on the thief.

Larry released the captive. With heaving breaths, he struggled to stand while whipping out his handcuffs.

"Turn around."

He put the cuffs on the thief and tugged him toward the patrol car. Willie holstered his gun and got in behind the wheel. Larry mopped his face with a tissue in the front seat.

"Sure was good to hear you on that ledge."

White teeth sparkled against Willie's black skin. "You had it under control, preach. I trust you."

"Yeah, well, next time don't trust me so long."

Willie guffawed. "You've come a long way from that rookie that got his leg shot up."

"Not something I care to remember, detective."

A slap across the steering wheel proved Willie was still holding in the laughter. Larry leaned back and tried to remember to breathe again.

When they got back to the station, Willie jumped out first.

"You cuffed him. You bring him in."

"Yes, sir."

After the criminal was locked up to await transport to the county jail, Larry went back to his computer search. The flicking images lulled him to sleep.

"Wake up, preacher. It's time to go home." Willie's voice carried across the room.

Larry jerked awake. His monitor had stopped moving. He had a match. "Yeah, I will in a minute."

Rubbing his eyes, he stood, stretched, and strode into the police chief's office.

The brim of the white Stetson rose. Toby pushed it to the back of his head. "Hey, Larry. How's it going?"

"We've got it, chief. Come see." He turned, knowing that Toby would be right behind him.

Overlooking Larry's monitor, Toby whistled. "Good work." He turned to another patrolman. Jinks signed on with the department only a few months before Larry's first days as a cop. "Put out an alert on Cameron Bennett. Call Doss over in Knox County. Our break-in boy hails from Benjamin, it seems."

"Why, Chief Wheeler, I'll just be happy to do that." Jinks drew out *happy* from two to three syllables with his country twang.

Toby retreated to his office and picked up his phone.

Before leaving, Larry used his computer for research on Collin Plummer, Katie's alleged drug dealer. He also searched out the ladies at the halfway house—everyone, including the manager.

By the time he left, he was armed with everything he needed to make a visit to Wanda and Collin. *Three o'clock. Plenty of day left.*

CHAPTER *Sixteen*

Katie scanned the restaurant. The place was rocking on a Saturday evening. Only two tables were empty, and neither of them were hers. Driving from Wharton Rock to work that day had taken lots of time and gas, but she promised herself that living with Lacey was only for last night. Katie needed her job to gain independence.

Paul, the owner of Country Dinner Restaurant, couldn't wipe the grin off his face.

She winked as she went by. "Our Saturday business sure has jumped with the opening of the car detail shop down the street and the beauty shop next door."

He leaned against the counter, giving his head a flirtatious wobble. "Doesn't hurt that people like my new server either."

"Why, sugar, whatever do you mean?"

Katie touched her forehead to her boss' shoulder. Her hips swayed more than usual as she headed to the corner booth. It was always best to keep men on a line in case she needed something. Katie's straight as an arrow sister would cringe at that kind of thinking, but when you'd been as low as Katie had, you did whatever you had to do to survive. The circular booth held four men from the car detail shop, regulars every day now.

"Ah, my favorite server. Glad you saved us a place in the corner." The shortest guy, and also the boss of the others, stood and put an arm around Katie.

She gave him a gentle shove, leaving him to fall back in the seat, laughing with all his might.

"What will it be today, sirs?"

"What's good on Saturday?" the biggest and youngest asked.

Her tone softened. The boy couldn't be over sixteen. "Everything." She offered her sweetest smile.

"Well, I want chicken-fried chicken breast, anyway," the boy said.

"Sounds good to me," the boss said amid two other assents.

"Four chicken-fried chicken breasts coming up. Along with four sweet teas."

The men nodded.

She leaned toward the boss and winked, then turned just in time to face Larry. Her heart skipped a beat. Her face flushed. Suddenly, she felt untrue.

That was crazy. She wasn't dating Larry. He was nothing more than, like the four men behind her, one who came in the restaurant a lot, and sometimes, he was convenient for a ride. A lump wedged in her throat. *Or saving her from an attack.*

"Hello, Katie. How are you?"

She had to swallow twice to dislodge that lump. She took a deep breath. "Why, I'm just marvelous." She strung out her Texas twang a bit more than usual, then dashed to the kitchen to place orders, gather her wits, and cool her cheeks. She was acting like a sixteen-year-old, the last year of her childhood.

Making up four salads gave her heart time to return to regular rhythm.

Madison inched toward her. "Would you make up a couple salads for me while you're at it?"

"You betcha."

Madison picked up dinner plates and disappeared into the dining room.

Katie and Madison rarely worked the same shift, Paul obviously liking to have one of them there all the time, but Saturday night was different.

While Katie loaded her salads on a tray to take out, Madison returned to get hers.

"Thanks for the help."

Katie bit her lip. "How's things at the house without me?"

Madison paused. "I miss you."

"But no one else?"

"You didn't expect Nicole to mind you being gone?"

"No."

Madison loaded four drinks to her tray. "Wanda is, well, she's Wanda. What can I say?"

"Yeah." A wave of sadness crept over Katie. Surviving on the outside was a hundred times harder than prison.

"Where are you staying?"

Katie shrugged.

"Your sister's?"

"No." *Except for last night.* Katie's voice escalated. "I can't. That would be real failure."

"You don't have enough for an apartment yet, do you?"

Katie shook her head. Her jaw tensed. "If I could get my hands on whoever put those drugs on my bed, I'd . . ."

"I'm sure it was Nicole. I know she got drugs from your boyfriend two weeks ago." Madison scurried back to the dining room.

Collin's place. Why hadn't Katie thought of that? She didn't believe for a minute that he was totally clean, but he did have a warm, dry place for her to sleep and a shower that worked. That had to be better than sleeping in the Honda as she had planned for that night.

She served the four men in the corner their salads, dropped off two of the waters at one table, and one in front of Larry.

"What can I get you today, sugar?" She may have found her voice, but perkiness came harder with the too-good-looking-to-be-real lawman.

He scanned the menu, then lay it aside. "Why am I kidding myself? I look over everything but still choose the burger and onion rings. I just can't top that."

She giggled. "I'm with you."

"Yeah?" He looked up. "Something else we have in common."

Her cheeks flamed. She stiffened. "I don't see as we have anything in common, Mr. Pullman."

He glared and counted out on his fingers. "Wharton Rock. Love of teens. Loners."

Her posture steeled. Her fingers tightened on the side of the table. "I'm not a loner. I like lots of friends around."

"Where have they been?"

She shifted her hips and lowered her voice. "I've been kind of out of contact for three years."

"Yeah, there's that."

"And I hate Wharton Rock. You love it. And who said I like teens?"

"I could tell. Would you be available as chaperone again next weekend?"

"No."

"Please."

"I'll go order your burger."

"It would be Friday, not Saturday."

"Why would you want me?" Talk about bad influence. He had to be insane.

"You're good."

"Humph."

"By the way, you saved my job with what you learned from Kinsley."

"Job?" She rolled her eyes. "You could do without that volunteer thing, couldn't you? Teens are trouble. Believe me, I know." *Especially teen boys.*

His knuckles cracked twice before he weighted his hands down with his thighs. His voice held a wistful tone.

"I want to help them. Teens need a friend, especially teen boys. Believe me, I know." He emphasized the repetition.

Katie's shoulders slumped. She let out a breath. "But how can we help, especially with Kinsley? It is what it is."

"I went with her to tell her parents."

Katie's fingers tightened over the writing pad in her pocket.

"She asked for you to come with her."

Katie's eyes widened. "Really?"

Larry nodded.

"What did you tell her?"

"Told her you were busy moving, but I'd go with her."

Katie snickered.

"Well, you are moving. I wasn't lying."

"Not really."

He caught her hand and pulled it from her pocket. "You helped that girl, Katie."

"How did her parents take it?"

"Her dad, not so well, but her mom is seeing that Kinsley gets the helps she needs. That's all on you."

No words came from Katie. Her body felt numb, her mind reeling.

"So, will you help me again?"

"Ask me in a couple days." *After I move back in with Collin.* "I doubt you'll still want me."

"Yes, I will."

She pivoted and walked to the kitchen to turn in his order. She'd love to hide there for the rest of the night.

The next hour swept by so fast, she didn't even know when Larry left, but she noticed an emptiness about the time she saw him through the window.

Larry interrogated Wanda at the halfway house first. She was hiding something, but he didn't know what. He caught several of the women at home. A girl by the name of Madison was at work. Two others were interviewing for jobs, and one was visiting friends.

All the women had prison records, and many had a history of drugs. Nicole, who had been Katie's roommate, talked fast and bragged a lot. From the looks of enlarged pupils, he would guess she was back on drugs since she got out of prison, but did she hide them in plain sight on Katie's bed, or did Katie buy her own?

Talking with the women did nothing to bring him peace. Though they offered up ideas that made him trust Katie, they also hinted that the drugs could have easily been hers. He couldn't prove they were, but he couldn't prove they weren't. He had one more stop to make.

Collin Plummer's apartment was in an old part of town near the city baseball diamonds. Paint peeled. Steps crumbled. Old cars abounded.

Still, the place was better than lots he'd seen. It didn't house only drug dealers and one night stands.

When he knocked, a bald head peeked through the door.

Larry showed his ID.

Collin laughed. "I've never been to Wharton Rock."

"I just had a question about Katie Smith, and she lives here in town."

A frown replaced the laughter. "I told the Apache Falls police. I didn't sell Katie any drugs. I'm clean, man."

"Did you sell to anyone else in the halfway house?"

"None of your business. This isn't your jurisdiction. Now leave me alone." Collin slammed the door.

Squat! For all Larry's efforts, he got squat. He still couldn't prove Katie's innocence. Was that because she was guilty? He kicked at pebbles on the apartment steps. Could a drug addict change? Was he being crazy trying to help Katie?

She had warned him to stay away. He should've listened. He knew what she had been, what she had done, and the probability that she might return to the same actions. Her saucy smile and genuine-seeming compassion had pricked his heart. Did it also make him a fool?

She swore to no more drugs–desiring, instead, to get a place of her own and move her daughter in with her–but once upon a time, she'd given her daughter's dad permission to kidnap the girl and hold her for ransom. Could a person like that be redeemed?

He stomped his foot, believing that Katie was telling the truth. He saw firsthand how much she had cared for Kinsley. Katie put up a hard front, but he couldn't believe she was all bad, even though she continued to remind him of her corrupting influence.

Perched in his car, he prayed for Katie, for his youth group kids, and for himself. He started the motor to leave. While he sat there, two girls had come and gone from Collin's door. The boy was surely dealing drugs. Larry so wanted to believe that Katie wasn't buying.

CHAPTER *Seventeen*

By the time the restaurant closed, Katie's legs felt as if they carried five-pound weights. Fatigue pulled at every muscle, and her brain could no longer focus on anything.

"See you, probably next Saturday," Madison called.

Katie searched through her brain fog to catch up. "Oh, yeah, Paul will put us on the same shift."

"Get out of here, you two." Paul turned off the grill and checked the deep fat fryer.

"Don't have to tell me twice." Madison went out the door.

Katie dropped to a chair. She had finally gotten a cell phone, but she couldn't remember Collin's number. Refusing to return to Lacey's, Katie glanced toward her car and shivered at the thought of sleeping in that small backseat. After heaving her frame out of the chair, she called a good-bye and left for the drive to Collin's apartment. Choices were slim.

Upon turning the corner, she ran smack into a gun barrel held by her old friend, Beth. Katie's heart jumped into her throat.

"What are you doing?"

"What does it look like?"

A man came in behind Beth. His stomach drooped over his beltline. His pudgy face was pink. "Who's this?"

"Shut up, Reso. It's an old friend." Beth surveyed Katie. "Get out of here, and keep your mouth shut." She pointed to the side with her gun hand.

"Don't do this. Paul is good people." Katie stood her ground.

Beth spoke through gritted teeth. "I said leave."

"Katie," Paul's voice sounded from the front. "You left your car keys, I think."

The streetlamp highlighted Beth's tense jaw. A nightmare vision of Paul's bloodied body worried Katie.

"I'll get rid of him. Trust me." She kept her voice low.

"Okay. Go."

Beth's overweight friend closed the gap and whispered in her ear. "You sure?"

She nodded. "Go," she said again to Katie. Her voice was shaky.

At that moment, a police car pulled into the lot.

"You okay?" one of them called to Paul.

Beth jerked Katie into the shadows.

"Just closing," Paul answered.

"There's been a rash of thefts around here this last week. We'll wait until you're ready to leave."

"Appreciate it," Paul called.

Beth's fingers released Katie's shirt. Katie stepped around the restaurant.

"Who are you?" the patrolman asked.

Paul moved between them. "She's one of my servers, officer. A good one." He smiled and turned to Katie. "Here, you left your keys on the counter."

"Thanks."

When she reached the driver's side of the Honda, she felt the touch of a hand and looked toward the ground. Hunched over, Beth winked.

"We're leaving. Not a good time. Thanks for keeping your mouth shut."

"Okay, you helped me out with a ride when I got out of prison. This makes us even."

"Wait until I'm gone before you move your car."

"One last favor then. Leave this place alone."

"You got it." Beth vanished into the darkness.

The Honda started on the first try. Something to be thankful for. She took a deep breath and massaged her right shoulder, sore from heaving big trays all day. She aimed her car to the north side of town and Collin's apartment, hoping for a soft bed and no hassle.

With the fatigue of the day's events weighing her down, she shuffled to building five, apartment two hundred forty three, and knocked.

"Hey, sweet stuff." Collin embraced her. "I wondered when you'd come back."

She hefted a box of her belongings to the bed in the front bedroom.

"You're sleeping with me, babe."

Survival, she reminded herself. *Do what you must.* She picked up the box again and trudged toward the back bedroom, dropping it on his dresser.

Willie plopped across his bed. "Care for a bit of dessert before my guests arrive?"

With Collin, dessert probably meant speed. Right now, it sounded like a good idea. "Maybe. What you got?"

"Speed. Cocaine. Ecstasy."

She could sure use some energy. "Speed, maybe." In her mind, prison doors closed, Rachel's face glimmered, tears formed in Larry's eyes. Three years of being clean. Did she really want to throw that away? "No, wait, I just need to sleep."

"Now, you're talking." With lust in his eyes, he turned down the bed and began to undress.

She blew out a breath. "I'm exhausted, Collin. I'm going to sleep, not make-out."

"Hey, it's Saturday night. Party time."

"Then party without me." Katie unloaded her box into a half-empty drawer at the bottom of the chest.

He bounded up and into her face. "Let's get things straight here. You don't live here for free."

"I'm broke until payday."

"I don't want your money."

"Then what do ...?" She stopped and released a breath. "I'm your party prize."

A smile slithered across his lips like a threat.

She patted his cheeks and turned on the charm. "I will, sugar, I will. Just not tonight. Okay?" She gave him a long, lingering kiss to remind him of good times.

It was him that broke the contact with a push. Speaking volumes with his eyes, his gaze rove from her face to other body parts.

Filthy-tasting bile crept into her mouth. She hadn't been with a man in over three years, and she enjoyed the clean feeling. She would never be a straight arrow like her sister, but could she not be worthy of her daughter's love?

"Now, get dressed." Collin winked.

She nudged up to him and used her sexiest ploy. "You're the only one I want, big boy." Filth covered her soul.

Survive. I need to survive.

A knock sounded at his door. He clasped both her hands in his. "Get dressed. And do something with your hair." He stormed from the room.

Out of her box, she yanked the only dress she owned. She hadn't worn it since she was last with Collin. The plunging neckline and short skirt would be his choice, not her black jeans and tops for work. Tears pooled in the corners of her eyes. She went to the sink to wash her face and fluff her hair.

More voices filtered through the closed bedroom door. She tipped her chin, squared her shoulders, and entered the room.

"Who do we have here?" one man ambled toward her.

Collin dropped his arm around her shoulders. "She's mine."

"You sure?" The man's leer undressed her and covered her in slime.

"Well ..." Collin acted as if he were thinking it over. "We have business first."

The man nodded.

"Katie, haven't seen you in ages," said a girl to the right.

Katie remembered the face, not the name. It was one of Collin's regulars back when she lived here. Katie flashed a smile that didn't reach past her lips.

More people entered, giving less room to move. A tall man with a mustache reminded her of Larry. How she wished it was him. He would rescue her and be kind, but it wasn't Larry. The room closed in. She couldn't breathe, couldn't think, and couldn't escape. Or could she?

After blowing him a wispy kiss, she said, "I need to freshen up," and she slipped back to the bedroom. A couple followed. They headed to the bed, not giving her a second look.

Her box of belongings brought her back to reality. She wouldn't leave without taking everything she owned. She gathered her stuff, went through the door, and inched around the living area. Collin was nowhere to be seen.

She was moving out the front door when a solid grip tightened around her wrist. "I don't think so. Put down that box."

She did.

Collin pointed to the middle of the room. "Now get out there unless you want me to tell the cops I sold you the drugs they found at the halfway house." His smile was so evil that she expected a pointed tongue to slip between his lips.

In the corner behind a table, she slid to the floor and cried. A new guy sat beside her. He handed her a tissue.

"What's wrong, princess?"

"I need to leave here."

"So, leave."

"Collin won't let me."

"What?" The man frowned and picked up her hand. "You're not his slave."

Her body shook with sobs, but his words were kind. Her gaze slipped toward her box. The man glanced there.

"That your stuff?"

She nodded.

He took her hands and assisted her to her feet. "How about I take out your stuff, and you come with me?"

She swiped at her tears. "Collin's watching me. Would you slip out of the door with my box? I'll wait until he's not looking and run after you."

"I'm happy to help, lady, but I'm in a hurry. Do you want me to set your stuff at the bottom of the steps?" He brushed the wiry curls from her forehead. His touch was gentle. "If you'll give me your car keys, I'll set the box in the backseat and leave the keys on the driver's seat. How about that?"

Kindness and gentleness had been rare and a long time coming. She wilted like a rose in July.

"That would be super."

She'd be sleeping in her car, after all, but anything was better than this. After tugging her keys from her coin purse, she handed them to the man.

His smile seemed real. "It was nice meeting you."

"Thanks."

"See you at Collin's next Saturday?"

She licked her lips. "I don't think so."

"You're smart. Frankly, I doubt I'll come anymore. It's really not my style."

Collin was headed her way. It wasn't working. She looked at her new friend.

"I thought you were in a hurry."

"I am. See you around."

He clutched her keys and lifted the box and was out the door before she could turn back to the party and act nonchalant.

Another man trapped Collin, blocking Katie's view, which meant he couldn't see her. *Great timing.* She hurried out the door and down the steps, nearly tripping over her box of belongings at the bottom. She gasped. Her gaze followed a screech.

The red Honda barreled out of the parking lot without her.

CHAPTER *Eighteen*

A phone call blasted Lacey awake for the second time in two days. Her heart hammered. She recognized the number—Katie's new cell. With fingers tightening around the screen, Lacey blinked and breathed.

"Aren't you going to answer that?" Toby's voice was groggy.

"Fine." Lacey touched it to answer. "What is it now?"

Katie was crying.

Lacey winced. She loved Katie. Without question. A long exhale erupted, transforming her into a nicer person.

"Katie. You okay?" *She wouldn't be calling if she was okay.* Adrenaline pulsed through Lacey. She sat erect. "Katie, answer me."

Gulps could be heard over the line.

"Katie, what's the problem? It's one in the morning." Lacey had opened her house to Katie the day before, and she'd quickly vanished.

"My car was stolen." Katie's voice was hoarse with emotion and could barely be heard. "Can you come and get me?" She gave some quick directions to the location.

With Katie's first words, Lacey was donning the jeans and shirt she'd taken off a couple hours earlier. A vision sparked in her mind of a little blonde girl who followed her big sister everywhere and thought she walked on water. *When did all that change? The teen years? Yeah, late teens.*

Toby leaned on his elbow. "Where are you going?"

Lacey bent to see in the mirror. Her hair stuck out at odd angles, so she ran a brush through the tangles. "Katie needs a ride."

He grinned. "What happened to 'I never want to hear from her again'?"

"She makes me so mad." Lacey dashed into the bathroom. When she came out, Toby was dressed.

"Let's go." He picked up the keys. "I'll drive."

That was probably best. Her whole body trembled. She wrote out a note for Mom and Rachel, in case they woke up.

The ride to the city was quiet.

In Lacey's mind, Katie as a child vied with Katie as a criminal. A cold sweat replaced a warm spot and then reversed. Fear of losing Rachel dimmed in light of letting her sister get hurt. A woman alone on the streets at this hour was fair game. Yet how many times had Katie put herself in exactly that position with her irresponsible attitude?

A shiver slid down Lacey's spine. It was best not to know all the trouble her little sis had faced. Katie had turned away from what she'd been taught. She had turned her back on Mom, Lacey, and God. Had anything really changed?

At the apartment complex, a small figure emerged from the shadows. Lacey leaped from the car.

"What in the world are you doing clear across town?"

Katie stopped.

"Is this where your car was stolen? Huh?" Lacey wasn't about to make it easy. Not when she'd had to make a trip in the middle of the night because of a wayward sister. "Who took it? Your latest conquest?" A sharp edge clipped each syllable.

Katie did an about-face.

"Lacey." Toby spoke gently from beside the car.

Heaving from labored breathing, Lacey held a hand over her mouth. *Forgive me, Lord, for angry words.* She softened her tone and limited the critique.

"Come on, Katie, get in the car."

Without comment, Katie pivoted, went to the car, and sat in the backseat.

Lacey climbed back in, and so did Toby. They took off and were soon entering the highway leading west toward Wharton Rock. On the trip, Lacey opened her mouth to ask questions three times, but she used her hand once again to stifle the interrogation. Katie didn't want to talk, well, Lacey didn't want to listen.

By the time they walked into their house, her muscles hurt and her jaw ached because of the tightness. She bit back any questions.

"I don't want to wake up Rachel or Mom, so you can sleep on the sofa the rest of the night." She marched to a cabinet and pitched Katie a sheet, a pillow, and a blanket. "See you in the morning."

Toby trudged after his wife to their bedroom and kept his mouth shut, until he closed the door.

"She's the victim, babe. Her car was stolen. What else could she do?"

"Don't start with me. I'm tired." She lay in the bed, pulled up the covers, and closed her eyes, but she knew sleep wouldn't come for hours. She distrusted Katie but was appalled by her own angry behavior.

Katie curled into a fetal position on the lumpy sofa. How many nights had she spent on this thing over the last eight years since she'd left home, hoping to never return? Despite any resolution she made, she still boomeranged.

Tick. Tock. Mom's favorite clock hanging over the door into the kitchen ticked louder than a time bomb. And made her just as uneasy. Sweat formed on her forehead. The sofa's velveteen finish created so much heat, she wondered if the air conditioning was working. It was only May but already hot in North Texas.

After flipping to her back, her short legs stuck out over the arm rest. Outside, trees waved in the moonlight, casting eerie shadows on the wall.

Katie didn't blame Lacey for being mad. Katie shouldn't have trusted Collin. She knew, or should've known. It was Wanda's fault, or Nicole's, for putting drugs on her bed. Though hoping to stay out of Wharton Rock, Katie was out of options.

Pain throbbed over her eyebrows. She closed her eyes. That helped some, but sleep was impossible with an aching head and a mind full of torment. She counted the clock's ticks.

Questions and problems compounded the longer she lay there.

No car insurance.

Paul. She needed to call him. There was no way she could work that day. Probably never again.

Did Nicole steal her money?

Katie got up, slipped her hand to the bottom of her box, and found the metal money container. She didn't know why she hadn't checked there before. Maybe she just assumed the money was gone. When she felt around the inside, her fingers closed over two bills. There had been five twenties and one fifty. She had been robbed, which made her mad, but there was something left behind, and that calmed her anger.

Upon awakening a few hours later, her first sight was Toby and Lacey kissing in the lighted kitchen. Lacey's words were muffled. Katie hated them both.

What right did Miss Prim and Perfect have to a loving husband just because she lost weight? Big deal! Katie had given up everything for love, and what was her reward? A hundredth return to her mother's house with no money, no car, and no one to love. Tears streamed down the sides of her face and tickled her ears. Her sheet became a tissue.

Toby swatted Lacey on the behind when she started across the dining room. She eased open Rachel's bedroom door and went in.

"Come on, sweetie, time to get up."

The child moaned. "I don't want to wake up."

"Breakfast is ready. You'll feel better after you eat."

"Mmmm."

Lacey stepped out but looked back. "Don't make me come back and get you. You'll be late for school if you don't get out of that bed." The insistent tone was less stern, more wheedle.

Oh, brother. Katie yawned and stretched.

Lacey took two steps her way. "You want some breakfast?"

"I want some coffee."

"You know where it is."

Lacey went back to the kitchen. Winnie the Pooh fuzzy slippers shuffled Katie's way. She opened one eye.

"Rachel?"

The child bent over her. "Hi. I didn't know you were here."

"Came while you were asleep."

"Oh. Will you be here when I get home from school?"

"Probably."

Rachel turned and skipped into the kitchen, obviously now wide awake.

The family bantering and teasing did nothing to lessen Katie's headache. Thank God, her brother-in-law kept coffee around there now. She followed Rachel.

By the time Katie entered the bright lights, Toby said "Amen," and the three dropped hands.

Just forget that I'm here.

Katie poured a cup of coffee and drank it like a needed antidote. The pain lessened. Her vision quit blurring.

"I should be home by four," Toby said.

"Well, you know it's a certain someone's birthday today." Lacey winked at Rachel.

Toby's face crinkled. "I didn't know that. Who is it?"

"Me!" Rachel shouted, bouncing up and down on the plastic cushion, her face aglow.

And I have no gift.

"Well." Toby put his elbow on the table and rested his chin in his hand. "I guess I'll have to take my girls out to celebrate tonight."

His girls? Don't mind me. I'm just the one who gave birth to her eight years ago.

Katie's pain resumed its pounding. She gritted her teeth, missed, bit her tongue, and yelped.

"You okay?" Lacey asked.

Katie straightened to as tall as her five foot two could reach. "No, I'm not okay. Did you ever think I might have special plans for my daughter's birthday?"

"But how were we to know you'd be here?"

Lacey took her last bite of banana and scooted back her chair. With a few steps forward, Katie got in her sister's space and made eye contact.

"Well, I'm here now, aren't I?"

"Look, sis. You left your daughter with me nearly four years ago. She's been part of our home since before Toby and I married."

"And so now I'm home, and I want her to live with me."

Katie shook her head inches in front of her sister's face. Rachel moved over and clung to Lacey.

When Toby stood, he loomed taller than either sister. He crossed his arms and puffed out his chest.

"Ain't gonna happen, Katie. I'm sorry, but that child is ours, emotionally and legally."

The blood drained from Katie's face. She couldn't breathe. She lay down her trembling coffee cup and slapped her sweaty palms against her pajama-clad thighs.

"As soon as I have enough money, I'll fight you on that."

The girl in question burst into tears and ran from the room, bumping into her grandmother on the way. Mom lifted questioning eyes. A huge grin spread over her face.

"Oh, praise God, Katie, you finally came to your senses and came home." She threw up her arms and hugged her baby girl.

Katie's heart dropped to her toes. She'd made her daughter cry and landed in her mom's clutches again.

CHAPTER *Nineteen*

After Mom came in, Lacey dashed to Rachel's room. Toby went to their back bedroom, and Katie squirmed in Mom's trap. Her cane tapped against the hardwood floors while she dropped bread into the toaster and ordered Katie around.

"Get me the jelly out of the fridge, will you?" She sat at the table. "I'm so excited you've finally listened to reason."

Katie sat in the chair across from her mother.

"Look, someone stole my car. I had no choice but to come here. Also, I was robbed when they threw me out of the halfway house. I've been saving for a place of my own."

The toast popped up.

"Would you get that for me, sweetie?"

Mom never listened. Katie sighed and got the toast.

"I'll be out of here soon. I need another job. I should be able to save fast living here."

"Of course you can." Mom bit off the tip of the toast. "And I told you, Willie needs servers. Go check with him."

"Too far to walk."

"Marjorie will pick me up in a little while for art lessons. She'll be happy to drop you off and pick you up on our way back."

I just bet she will. "Okay." Katie was back in it again, letting Mom plan her life, but she could do nothing else. "I'll be ready."

"I'll call Willie before we leave. Can't hurt to pave the way."

Katie's temperature was rising and probably her blood pressure. She gritted her teeth and headed off to dress. The rest of the family had gone. Katie hadn't even been allowed to speak with Rachel after hurting her feelings.

Maybe while she was waiting for Marjorie to pick her back up, she could find somewhere to buy something for Katie's birthday. What did eight year olds like?

Oh, she'd forgotten. What bills were in her box? She checked. Two twenties. Well, she was forty dollars ahead of what she thought she had, but not quite up to the one hundred fifty she had saved over almost three weeks of work. Her fists tightened, causing her to drop her jeans. She picked them up but dropped them again. She wanted to scream.

The morning was over before Mom and Katie were out the door. Marjorie waited in the driveway. Mom spoke to her friend but nodded toward her daughter.

"You remember Katie, don't you?"

Marjorie frowned. "I remember."

So much for Marjorie being happy to take her.

"Some bad person stole Katie's car. Can you believe it? She needs a job. Willie is hiring, so I thought we could drop her off. It's just a few blocks from class," Mom said.

"Sure," Marjorie said.

Wharton Rock was such a small town that everything could be reached within five minutes. That was one of the things Katie hated. Everyone knew everyone else's business, and gossip ran rampant. Lacey and Toby loved this town, but Wharton Rock, Texas, had given Katie nothing but grief.

The car stopped and let her out. A slightly sagging sign over double doors said "Willie's Restaurant." Beside it was a life-sized wood carving of an Indian brave. In the window, someone had taped a hand printed sign reading "Chicken-Fried Steak special today $6.99." Larry and Toby and an older man sat in plain view.

Katie missed her Apache Falls job already.

Willie's Restaurant door opened, and Larry Pullman stood before her like a childhood dare. Her heart skipped a beat. Perspiration formed under her curls on the nape of her neck.

"Katie?"

He played the gentleman, holding the door for her, but his brow furrowed. She wasn't sure if his expression showed worry, questions, or excitement, and she didn't care. Pulling back her shoulders to increase her height, she lifted her chin and swept past him without comment.

When she marched across the room, Toby called out, "Hey, Katie, you remember Pastor Lloyd, don't you?"

She turned. Her gaze fell on the older man. "Oh, yes," she stretched out her hand, "Nice to see you again, preacher."

"Little Katie." Merry eyes glowed amidst all the wrinkles. "I haven't seen you in ages. How are you?"

She shifted her hips. "I'm wonderful. Haven't seen you either. Of course, I've been in prison the last three years, so I haven't seen anybody except other inmates." She laughed and continued on her quest.

Willie hadn't changed. The cigar he bit between his teeth was the same length. His apron could've been the same one he wore when she, as a teenager, had bussed tables. The lack of change symbolized Wharton Rock. Time stood still. Everyone in town was considered family, and gossip ran wild when something bounced them out of their self-made utopia.

"So, little Katie, what will you have for lunch?"

She hated to spend her meager resources, but she was hungry. "A burger and onion rings."

Willie barked out the order. Then he took a quick glance at her before returning to his paperwork.

"I hear you're needing a job."

"I am. I'm good at serving. Done it for years."

"So I hear," Willie said.

Tingles tickled her back. She would bet Larry's stare was focused on the spot. Well, he was kind to her, and she liked his looks. A flush crept across her cheeks, but this was her business, not his.

"Do you have an application?"

Willie plopped down her order. "Can you work tomorrow?"

Did she hear right? "Am I hired?"

"You want to work or not?" He lifted his head while his eyes pinned her to the spot.

"Yes."

"Then can you work tomorrow? I need you at three."

"I can be here." At least she hoped so.

"Okay." He returned to his paperwork.

"Okay."

She finished her food, paid Willie, and turned to leave, making sure her hips swayed in her wake. Larry jumped to reopen the door. She yanked on her short skirt, as if that would make it longer.

"Thank you, Larry."

After a slight bow, he trailed after her. "You're welcome. So what's the deal? I saw Marjorie Joiner and your mother drop you off."

"They're going to their art class."

"Look, your mom will probably be another half-hour anyway." He plopped on a bench beside the Indian statue and patted the seat next to him. "Have a seat and tell me what you're doing in Wharton Rock."

She sat. "I've decided to move back, coming home to my roots and all that, you know." She spoke to the wind and waved her hand in confirmation. "So I need a job here."

"But why? You hate this town."

"Well, if you must know, Mr. Nosy, I took up Collin's offer to let me stay there. It wasn't what I expected. I trusted some guy who offered to sneak my belongings out of the apartment and put them in my car. When I escaped," she raised her open palms to the sky, "my car was gone."

"Oh, no, Katie." He clasped her upper arms. "I'm so sorry."

An aroma of spice mixed with viral male sparked shock waves through her brain. She moved away, causing his arms to drop, so she could breathe. *Ah, for pity's sake.* Tears stung her eyes. Romance wasn't in her forecast. "I'm okay." She blinked.

Her gaze took in the up and down rhythm of his chest. She longed to take refuge by leaning into his strength. *Wow, what a wake-up call.*

She stood, stiffened her spine, and tugged her skirt again. A policeman wasn't her type. He didn't need a criminal to turn his life into a trash heap.

"If there's anything I can do," Larry said.

She swiped her eyes. "Oh, I'm fine. Just fantastic. I have a job, a place to live, and a family that cares."

Mom cared because she wanted to straighten her out. Lacey, now, maybe not.

Marjorie drove up as Toby and Pastor Lloyd came out of the restaurant. Katie went to get in her escape hatch and closed her eyes and her mind to reality. It was easier that way.

CHAPTER  Twenty

When Katie got to Lacey's, a banner flew over the dining table, party favors were spread out, and a big cake with "Happy Birthday, Rachel" on it took center place on the table top. Lacey smiled at her sister. "Think she'll be surprised?"

"What are you doing home from work?" Katie frowned.

"I asked off for the occasion. I wanted to get everything ready before Rachel and her friends got home from school."

Katie winced. With the run in with Larry, she forgot to look for a store to buy something for her daughter. Now she would be at the party empty-handed. An ache settled between her shoulder blades. She tried to rub the spot, but her hands wouldn't reach.

Like an explosion, seven girls along with Rachel burst through the door with Toby bringing up the rear.

"These girls are ready to party, Miss Lacey," he said with a chuckle.

Lacey patted her hands together. Upon seeing the table, Rachel squealed. Another girl whistled.

"Wow," she said. "May I have one of these?" Holding a candy lipstick and a mock manicure set, she looked up at Lacey.

"Of course you can. There's one for each of you." Lacey beamed like birthday candles.

When did she get to be mother of the year? Katie retreated to one corner and took a seat. Her back throbbed. So did her head. She shouldn't be there. Never had she felt such a failure other than when she told Rachel goodbye before prison. They should've kept her there. Fitting in and getting ahead on the outside was hard. So hard.

"Here's one from your birth mother." Lacey handed Rachel a present wrapped in pink paper with a purple bow.

Katie's ears perked. What was Lacey up to? The heat in Katie's cheeks rushed up her neck, setting her ears on fire. The desert had nothing on her mouth for dryness. She couldn't drum up enough spit to swallow. Lacey was never nice to Katie, and she knew Katie couldn't pay her back.

When Rachel opened the present, she squealed and passed her creative package of crayons, posters, and stickers to the friend beside her. She jumped from her seat, ran for Katie, and engulfed her in a big hug.

"Oh, thank you, Mother. How did you know that was what I wanted?"

"I ... ah ..." Katie glanced at Lacey, who nodded. "A little birdie told me."

The warmth of the child's embrace did strange things to Katie's insides. She'd missed those hugs. At ages three and four, she had been Rachel's world. *Until I ruined everything.*

Rachel dashed back to her friends. When she opened the package from Lacey and Toby, they also got a hug.

They deserve it.

Katie sat in quiet reverie. The party swirled around her like a parade before an audience. Presents, more squeals, games, pizza, many laughs, then cake and ice cream before parents began picking up daughters. The festivities were over.

"That's the last girl." Lacey turned to Rachel. "Happy birthday, baby. I think we had a nice party, don't you?"

"Yes, it was the best, Mom. Thank you, thank you, thank you."

Toby dropped big hands on his wife's shoulders. "You get Rachel ready for bed. I'll do cleanup."

"I'll do the cleanup." Did Katie just say that? What brought that on? She stood to follow through with her words.

"Are you sure?" Toby stroked his chin. "The girls left a big mess."

"I'm sure." Katie went to the kitchen. "Where's the trash sacks?"

Toby showed her, while Rachel and Lacey headed to the bathtub.

With her cane tapping, Mom hobbled toward her room. "I'm going to bed."

Katie picked up all the trash around the party table and cut the cake to fit under a cake dome.

Toby sighed. "If it's okay then, I think I'll head to bed. I've got a long day tomorrow."

"Sure." Katie scowled.

"Katie, if you don't want to do it, tell me."

"I said I'd do cleanup, didn't I?"

Katie gripped the counter. She wanted to tell him to get out of there and leave her alone or she'd throw the rest of the punch in his face.

"Okay. Goodnight." He left.

As if she were back bussing tables, Katie moved fast and was putting on the last strokes when Lacey came back through. Katie hung up the dish towel and plopped onto the step stool.

"Why did you do it?"

"Do what?" Lacey stopped for a drink of water.

"The gift. I don't have any money." Well, technically she had forty dollars, but that was savings.

"I knew you wanted to give Rachel a present."

Katie chewed on that along with a second piece of cake.

"Why did you do it?" Lacey sat and nibbled a banana.

"What?"

"Why did you offer to cleanup?"

"I'm not useless."

"I didn't say you were."

"You implied it. You never think I'm worth anything. I might've gone to prison, but I can do things." Katie tightened her jaw.

Lacey's voice softened. "Ssh." She put a finger across her lips. "I know you're not worthless, but it was an unusually kind thing to do. That's all."

The nice words melted Katie's anger like chocolate in summer heat.

"Larry says I'm a good girl. He doesn't know me well, of course, but I guess I wanted to prove him right, at least this once."

"Larry, huh?" Lacey hesitated. "Sis, leave him alone. He's a really good guy and doesn't need—"

"I'm not going to corrupt your precious little policeman." Katie's jaw again grew taut, and her muscles clenched. "I'm going to bed."

She marched to the couch. See if she did something good for Lacey again.

❧

Lacey's eyes opened. While brushing back wisps of hair caught on her cheek, Toby grinned.

"How's my girl this morning?"

"Mmmm. Dreading the day."

"I just know you'll get good news."

"What if I don't?" She flopped to her back.

Under the covers, he caught her hand. "God's in charge, babe."

"I know, but it's hard. What if I do have cancer?" She turned back to him, as if his assurance would make the difference.

"Then we'll deal with it. You'll get treatment, and the Lord will do the healing."

"But what happens to Rachel and Mom while I have treatments? Will I lose my job? What about—"

He tucked her head under his arm. "Enough already. We'll face each thing as it comes. You sure you don't want me to go to the surgeon with you?"

"No. He won't do anything today. Just tell me if I require a biopsy or not."

"Come by the station as soon as you get through." He caught her chin and made eye contact. "Okay?"

She nodded.

"That sure was nice of Katie to clean up last night, wasn't it?" He squeezed Lacey.

"I think she did it to impress Larry." Lacey pulled away. "I'm worried about Larry. If Katie has her sights on him, he'll never know what hit him. Tell him to stay away."

Toby chuckled. "I can't do that, babe. Larry's a grown man. I don't think he'd take kindly to me telling him what to do. Besides, he's tougher than you think. Don't dismiss his ability to read people. Remember, he's not only a policeman, he's a preacher."

"That's what worries me. He's too doggone naïve for the likes of Katie."

"Maybe Katie has changed."

"Don't count on it."

"Then why did you spend money on a gift for her to give Rachel?"

"God told me to."

"Good reason."

"Yeah."

"Then why the worry?"

Despite her misgivings, a smirk broke out on her face. "I'm not trusting God, am I?"

"No."

"I'll do better. God has my day."

"And He's got your sister."

CHAPTER *Twenty-One*

When Larry was a block away, a red Pontiac GTO burst from the Dairy-land parking lot. He sped up and chased the red blur until it crossed the bridge over a dry creek bed and entered the highway heading to Apache Falls. Larry's patrol car slipped in a puddle of leftover rainwater and swerved toward the bridge.

His wheels squealed. His heart raced faster than the culprit that was outrunning him.

Bam!

The explosion halted his vehicle.

He clambered out and kicked the flat tire that failed him when he needed peak performance. He gritted his teeth and repeated "BH8 V562" until he could pull out the notepad from the glove compartment. His mind churned worse than his stomach, but it wasn't the Pontiac driver that tormented him.

She'd gone home with Collin. *Why didn't she call me? I wouldn't take advantage of her.*

A vision of Katie and Collin alone in his bedroom haunted Larry's nighttime dreams and daytime activities. She'd slept with Collin before. Why not now? She didn't owe Larry anything. What did she mean, "It wasn't what I expected."

You're stupid, Pullman. She told you to stay away.

He just couldn't. She was basically good. Down deep. He was sure of it. She wanted love and acceptance. That didn't make her a bad person.

He kicked the tire three more times and collapsed against the side of the car. Tears came to his eyes. He swiped. It was ridiculous. He was a grown man—a minister, no less. He didn't need a woman to complete him. He only needed the Lord.

Help me be what You want me to be to Katie, and no more.

Time to do his job and not God's. Climbing back into the driver's seat, he clicked to speak on the radio.

"I've got a license plate to check." He gave it to Ruby and explained the situation.

"Get back to you," she said.

"Thanks. Got a flat tire to fix."

"Sorry, preacher." The sound of laughter vanished with the radio's connection.

After yanking out the spare and the jack from the trunk, he squatted beside the source of his present angst. In a few minutes, the tire was changed, and he was on the way back to the station. He passed Willie's Restaurant, and his heart flattened like the tire. He skidded to a stop and swung around the side where one parking space remained. He hadn't seen Katie for over a week. He had asked her to go on the monthly fun trek with the youth department, but she hadn't answered. Tomorrow night was the date.

The absence of a car didn't help since Katie didn't have one. Toby and Lacey took turns bringing her and picking her up from work. He circled the corner and peeked in Willie's window, but he didn't see Katie. She could be in the back. He entered.

Willie threw up his hand. "Hi, there, Larry. Take a seat. What you want to drink?"

Trapped. Now he had to stay, though there was no sign of Katie. "Sweet tea."

"Coming up."

Larry took out his cell. Katie's number was listed as number three. His thumb lingered over it.

No. Don't be a sucker.

Upon jerking back his thumb, he dropped the phone. When he reached to the floor, he grasped the phone and noticed a pair of super-small tennis shoes supporting short, shapely legs. His gaze traveled up sexy curves into a pair of cobalt eyes, brilliant and glistening.

Katie winked. "Hi there, sugar. Here's your tea."

"Hi." His breathless word was barely audible. He cleared his throat. "I didn't think you were here." *Lame, Pullman.*

"As you can see, I am." Her teasing grin matched her tone.

"Yeah." He dropped his phone again.

"Slippery thing." She picked it up and laid it on the table.

"Yeah." Boy, was he a sweet talker.

"What will you have?"

"Nothing. I'm fine." He dipped his chin and tried to regain control.

"You don't want dinner?"

"Oh, yeah." He snatched the menu but then put it back. "Can't beat—"

She chimed in, so they said the words together. "A burger and rings."

They both laughed. Their taste in food was one thing they shared.

"Be right out." She turned toward the kitchen.

Every male eye in the place followed the sway of her hips. He tensed.

Larry's phone rang, showing the station number. He'd told Ruby to catch him on his cell while he had dinner. Good thing he texted before he came inside the restaurant and lost his ability to hold onto the phone.

"Pullman," he answered.

"I contacted the police chief in Woodward. They stopped the guy in the GTO for speeding. Do we need them to hold him?"

"Let me check. I'll call you back."

He called the Dairyland manager. No theft. No assault. *Guess speeding was the only crime.* He dialed Ruby.

Katie sat down his food and went to walk away, but he grabbed her arm and held up a finger while he talked into the phone.

"Hey, Ruby. No reason to hold him. Tell Woodward he's all theirs."

"Will do." She signed off.

Katie jerked against his hold. "I have other customers."

"I know. Just wanted to double-check. You never gave me an answer about tomorrow night's bowling trip."

She glanced at her arm and scowled. "You going to let me go, or am I under arrest?"

He dropped her arm like it was on fire. "It's okay."

When she left, he devoured his dinner. While she scurried around the dining room, his gaze followed her movements.

By the time he took one last bite, she laid down his ticket and winked before she sashayed away.

She could keep her winks and her smiles. He'd tried to be her friend, but she'd made it perfectly clear she wasn't interested. Fine. Neither was he. Standing to stretch his long legs, he strode toward the cash register, pulling out his wallet as he walked. He plopped down the ticket with his cash on top and turned.

"Officer Pullman, I think this was meant as a note for you." Willie handed him back the ticket.

Larry flipped to the other side. It read, "Love to go. See you at five. Katie."

Willie grinned.

Larry's ears flamed. "Thanks." He couldn't get out of there quickly enough.

❧

Ten minutes before Larry left to pick up Katie and go to Apache Falls for the teen bowling trip, his phone rang.

"I need to see you in the office, Reverend Pullman." What did the senior pastor need to see him for on Friday evening?

"The youth group has an activity tonight. We're going bowling. In fact, I was just leaving Wharton Rock to head to the church to meet everyone." Surely, this meeting could wait until morning.

Reverend Schumacher cleared his throat. Though his tone softened, his authority oozed through the phone.

"I have more work to do. I'll wait for you. Be here in half an hour?"

"Yes, sir." Larry's hands shook as he disconnected. What had he done now? He grabbed his bowling ball and dashed out the door, hoping Katie would be ready early.

Katie. The mention of her name awakened feelings he never expected to experience. Since he'd answered the call to preach the Word, his only passion had been to tell others about Christ. Peace at submitting to that call was real and enveloped him with purpose, something he had lacked since his dad died.

Women were nice, but he didn't need one to fulfill him. Christ did that. Why did the mere thought of Katie set his heart to racing? She was all wrong for a preacher's wife. Even she knew that.

Crossing Wharton Rock took all of eight minutes. When he neared Toby's house, he summed up self-talk about winning Katie to Christ and not fostering any romance. The object of his racing heart waited by the curb.

He jumped out. "You're ready early."

She quirked an eyebrow. "You're here early."

An involuntary zip struck the back of his neck. He rubbed. "Yeah, well, I need to get there and meet with the senior pastor first."

"And I need to get away from my sister." A curious, quizzical look crossed her eyes. "Why are you meeting someone? I thought we were going bowling?"

"We are, but this came up at the last minute." Something he didn't appreciate.

"What for?"

"I have no idea."

She chuckled. "You're probably corrupting those kids."

His can't-believe-you-said-that smirk was his only comment. The ride into town was quiet and full of tension.

"Wait here," he said after parking behind the church. "I'll wave when I'm through talking to the pastor. It will be a half-hour before the kids arrive."

"Sure," she said, but something in her expression made him uneasy.

CHAPTER *Twenty-Two*

Wait? No way will I wait in the car. After a couple of minutes, Katie followed Larry.

Without seeing him, she had no idea where to go. The first room was an empty gymnasium with a door that spilled into a hall. She spotted Larry several feet down that way. Following a few feet behind, she stepped through the door. The hall led her through murals of children in bold colors. Footsteps echoed in the empty building. Larry turned right and disappeared.

Pulling off her sandals, she ambled along with as little noise as possible. The hardwood floor chilled her feet. Ten feet past his turning point, carpet stretched toward double doors, his obvious target. She luxuriated in the carpet's soft pile and snuck to one side.

He vanished.

Doors opened to what looked like an office, also deserted. Male voices drifted from farther back. She took one step then another, looking right and left. The voices grew louder. What were Larry and the pastor discussing? His youth group would be here soon. Was Larry quitting? Did he have problems with another kid? Was Kinsley still okay? Katie halted.

"We don't want our young people exposed to someone like her. Never bring her again. Understood?"

Katie stiffened.

"I disagree, sir." *Larry's voice.* "In fact, I brought her tonight to go bowling with us. The girls identify with her. The boys think she's fantastic, and she's a big help to me."

"She's an ex-con," the other voice said.

Katie's blood chilled. Her vision blurred. Her fingers grasped for the wall, seeking an anchor. Would Larry ask her to stay in the car or cancel the youth trip and take her home? His voice was too soft to hear.

The louder voice lowered in volume but held on to control. "You will not take her with you or you will no longer have a job here. Do I make myself clear?"

"Yes, sir."

A job? Katie took off running. She wouldn't wait for him to give her an ultimatum. She had money. She'd get a cab.

"Katie!" Larry called.

She pushed herself harder until she couldn't breathe. Down the short hall. Through the main office. In the middle of the long hallway, she tripped. Her big toe throbbed. She rubbed it, and the pain lessened.

Larry turned the corner, bearing down on her. "Katie, stop. I didn't know. I'm sorry you heard that. Katie. Stop."

Using the wall, she tugged herself to her feet and picked up speed, rushing into the gym where she collided with the muscular boy she'd previously met. Ryan, she thought his name was.

"Sorry."

He caught her arms. "I'm sorry too. Are you okay?"

"I'm fine. Just leaving."

She glanced behind her. Larry was nearly there.

"Aren't you going bowling with us?" Ryan asked.

Katie's forward glance lit on a curvaceous redheaded female, whose glare ran up and down Katie with distrust, maybe even resentment. Before Katie could move, the woman's expression changed to charm.

"Larry, so good to see you. I guess Reverend Schumacher told you I'm your new assistant. I'm so excited." She stepped into Larry's extended arms.

Katie escaped through the back door and hid behind some bushes. More familiar faces arrived. Larry came out the door and called.

"Katie?"

"She was just here. Want me to get in the car and search the area?" Ryan asked.

"That would be good. Thank you."

"Why did she leave?" Ryan asked.

Larry hung his head. "She was hurt and scared."

Scared? She wasn't scared of anything.

"Is Miss Michelle replacing her as your assistant or as your girlfriend or both?" Ryan asked.

Katie cringed. She had been crazy to hope, to think she might belong with a church group—to think a man like Larry could care for a girl like her. She was no good. Hadn't she told him that? Maybe he was beginning to believe her.

Larry rustled Ryan's hair. "Mind your own business, young man." He chuckled, but his voice was deadpan.

"Gotcha. I'll search. Be back in time to leave for bowling."

Remaining on her knees in her hiding place, Katie's legs cramped, but she would not move. Blossoms from late blooming honeysuckle stuffed up her nose, yet the aroma was delightful. Her fingers tightened over her face to keep from sneezing as she watched the unfolding drama in the parking lot.

Kimmi and her two friends circled Larry. Upon discovering Katie's disappearance, their voices filled with potential secrets. He smiled and ushered the girls into the church. More and more teens arrived. Ryan drove around the church and down a side street. After he returned, everyone loaded into vans or cars.

One more time, Larry scanned the lot, but he no longer called her name. He closed the van door and drove away.

She stretched out the kinks from her legs. Tears streamed her cheeks. Prison was better than this, for sure. Life on the outside brought only anguish and heartache.

Though Larry scored well that night, bowling was the last thing on his mind.

"Any word?" Ryan dried his hands on a small towel.

Larry shook his head. "I left word for Katie's brother-in-law. Haven't heard from him yet."

"If she rode with you, how would she get home?"

Larry shrugged. "A cab, I guess, but I can't believe one could've picked her up that fast."

"Pastor Larry." Kinsley's voice wavered as she came up on his left. "Is Miss Michelle taking Katie's place all the time?"

Larry flinched. "I guess."

Ryan cleared his throat and straightened his posture. "Katie came with Pastor Larry, but she disappeared."

Kinsley's eyes widened. "What happened to her?"

"We don't know. I searched all over before we left the church," Larry said.

Kinsley hit a number on her phone. When she got no answer, she dropped her hand and her features fell.

"I hope she's okay. She's the reason I'm still here. I was going to . . . Well, never mind. We must find her."

"I agree." Larry rubbed his chin. "Look, guys, remember, I'm also a cop. After the bowling is over, I'll search. I'll find her."

"We'll help," Ryan said.

"No." All Larry needed to hurt his career was to get his youth group involved in searching the seedy places that Katie might frequent.

"But Pastor Larry." Kinsley's voice sounded more pleading, less confident.

Larry's hands settled on her shoulders. Michelle moved to his side.

"Hey, what's going on here?"

Was she instructed to watch him? Larry's ears heated. A bead of sweat trickled down his temple. Maybe he should quit this job now. But he needed the money, and he loved the kids. *Lord, help me.* He dropped his arms and took one step backward.

"I was encouraging Kinsley over a problem she has."

"You mean besides being pregnant?"

Larry hated Michelle's hateful tone. Kinsley's cheeks pinked. She turned and moved back to the lane where she was bowling.

"Ryan, it's your turn." Larry tipped his head to the boy, who was in Larry's bowling group.

When Ryan went in search of his ball, Larry turned to Michelle. He used his cop tone.

"Michelle, I appreciate your help, but don't ever speak to one of my kids in that way. If it's not uplifting, keep your mouth shut."

Michelle's jaw tightened. "That girl's problem is visible for all to see. I'm not sure she should be allowed to associate with the rest of the group."

"She made a mistake, but God loves her and has forgiven her. Still, she must live with the consequences of her sin. The older teens understand that. I discussed the situation with the junior high kids in private. There's no reason to throw it into her face in public."

"You're the youth pastor." She leaned against him and even batted her green eyes. "A good-looking pastor, at that."

Annoyed, he nudged her aside. "Kimmi is calling you. I think it's your turn."

When bowling was over, they returned to the church where they would go their separate ways. Some loaded in parent's cars. Some went with friends. Kinsley's dad was the last one to pull up. Before she left, she whispered to Pastor Larry, "When you find her, will you let me know?"

He gave her a warm smile but kept his arms at his side. "I will. Promise."

With all the headlights gone, darkness swirled around Larry and Michelle.

"The night is young." She looped an arm through his.

"Not young enough, and I've got lots to do." He moved to her car, waiting for her to climb in. When she did, he closed the door and waved goodbye.

He tried Katie's new cell one more time. Still no answer, so he headed first to the Country Dinner Restaurant.

"Hey, Paul," he called to the manager. "Have you, by any chance, seen Katie tonight or talked with her?"

"No. I think she moved. She quit here a couple of weeks ago."

"And you haven't talked with her since?"

"No."

Larry believed him. "Mind if I ask the servers?"

"Suit yourself. Is Katie okay?"

"Probably. Her sister is anxious, so I need to find her." He wasn't exactly lying.

As if thinking of Lacey precipitated a call, his cell rang. Toby's name showed on the screen.

"Pullman."

"What's this about not being able to find Katie? She went off with you, didn't she?" Toby's baritone was calm, typical of Larry's Wharton Rock boss.

"She did."

Larry explained the situation. Toby let out a long breath.

"Let me ask Lacey. I just got home." After a brief moment, he returned to the phone. "Lacey hasn't heard from her."

"I'm going to search. I'll keep you posted."

"Need some help?"

"Not for now. I'll call if I do."

"Okay. Remember, she's my kin. I can be there in twenty minutes."

"I doubt there's a problem. She probably took a cab to a friend's house. I just feel responsible."

"I understand. Lacey and I will pray."

"Thanks."

Larry disconnected and tried to flag down a female server he didn't recognize. About fifty, carrying an extra thirty or forty pounds on her short torso, the woman bustled toward a table. After she deposited the food from her tray and turned back toward the kitchen, Larry stopped her midway.

"I don't know if you remember me. I used to eat here a lot. Katie Smith was always my server. Have you heard from her since she quit?"

The woman's red face scrunched up like a wilted tomato. "Katie? No, but I barely knew her."

"She didn't call you tonight?"

"No, why would she? What business is it of yours?"

Larry tried to read the woman's body language. She seemed sincere. He dipped his head.

"We're friends, and she's disappeared."

"Oh, no. I hope she's okay. Look, if Katie called anyone, it would be Madison. They were friends before Katie starting working here."

A droplet of hope seeped into his heart. It jump-started his pulse.

"Is Madison here?"

After an intent investigation, the woman must've decided she could trust him.

"She was on duty until about an hour ago. She had an emergency come up and left."

CHAPTER *Twenty-Three*

When the door opened, Larry tried to stomp past Collin. "Where is she?"

Collin blocked the way. "Oh no, not without a warrant you don't. Beside, you have no jurisdiction in Apache Falls." He glared at Larry. "If you don't quit harassing me, I'll have your badge in that hick town where you do work."

Larry swallowed the lump in his throat. He rubbed his temple that had been throbbing since Katie disappeared. Now, at midnight, he'd covered every place he knew without success. Madison was at the halfway house and knew nothing, or so she claimed. The last place he wanted to be searching was Katie's ex-boyfriend's house, but he had to face facts. She would turn to Collin before she turned to him.

Tripping over the doorstop when Collin shoved, Larry caught himself and regained his I'm-a-cop manner.

"When Katie was kicked out of the halfway house, she turned to you. Now, she's vanished. Explain."

His chin lifted to extend his height even greater than the six inch edge he had on the drug dealer. The intimidation seemed to work, or maybe it was just fear. Collin's eyes widened. His mouth opened into an o shape before he released one word.

"When?"

Larry's body was as rigid as the barrel of a shotgun. He glanced at his watch. "About six hours ago."

"What did you do?"

Larry reached toward Collin's throat. "I'm asking you that question. After all, the last time Katie was here, her car was stolen."

"I didn't have anything to do with that."

"Oh, really?" Larry let the sarcasm drip like poison. He dropped his hands and tried to remember his I'm-a-minister air. "Please, I'm worried. May I search your apartment? Perhaps she's hiding and not even you know she's here."

It worked. Collin stepped back and opened the door wider.

"Go ahead. I'll help." He caught Larry's shoulder. "I care, you know."

"Yeah." Larry slipped back into sarcastic mode. "With her gone, you'd miss out on drug sales." He went right into the nearest bedroom.

"Katie's clean."

Larry heard the words behind him and so wanted to believe them. He did believe them, or he wouldn't have invited her to help chaperone the youth group. He couldn't help Reverend Schumacher's attitude. Why did Katie get mad at him? He looked under both beds, in every closet, even out on the small balcony off the living room.

When he strode back to the front door, he turned. "Okay, she's not here. Thanks for letting me look. If you hear from her . . . Forget it. I know you won't call me." He pivoted and started down the outside stairway.

"How about I call the Apache Falls police?" Collin's voice was almost kind.

Larry remembered why he wanted to go into ministry. Everyone deserved a second chance, and God's power was all that could change people. God had healed Larry. Collin needed help, even if Larry didn't like him. Shoot, the main reason he didn't like him was that Katie did, or had. She'd been Collin's for a while, and Larry would never have that blessing. *Blessing.* He was crazy. He needed someone that could be a minister's wife. More than anything, he longed to be a pastor. He needed a wife that would work beside him to lead others to Christ.

Larry took two steps back up the stairs. In the dim light, his gaze probed the other man. His tone was sure.

"You know something, I can tell you care."

Collin stretched for more height. "As I said, you have no jurisdiction here. No right." He closed the door.

He had said he'd tell the Apache Falls police. Larry sorted facts. Did Collin know where Katie was? That wouldn't be anything that interested the cops, but, ah . . . if he knew about the drugs that pushed her out of the halfway house. Larry took the steps two at a time and headed to the police station. A cop always had friends in other departments.

The familiar smells of the halfway house soaked into Katie's pores like a blanket of defeat. She was back at the beginning. She'd been out of prison for forty-five days with nothing to show for it. After the theft and paying for her new phone, she was left with only twenty dollars, no job, and no home.

On the bed across the room, Madison flipped through the pages of a *Glamour* magazine. She and her mom had picked up Katie at the church and brought her there.

"I'm so glad Nicole is gone, and I get to be your roommate."

According to Madison, Nicole had moved out soon after Katie. What had surprised Katie was that Wanda agreed to let her back in.

"Do you know where Nicole moved?" Katie asked.

Madison shrugged. "With a boyfriend, I think. The main thing is that she's gone and can't bring any more drugs into this place." She glanced up from her reading. "You, of all people, should be thankful of that."

"Oh, I am. It's just that . . ." Katie's mind twirled with more questions than answers. "Why did Wanda let me stay? I've not been officially cleared."

Waving a hand in front of her face, Madison settled back to her reading. "Wanda is one of the good guys."

Katie sniffed. That wouldn't be her description of Wanda Early, after she'd kicked her out and threw her stuff in the yard.

"Lights out, ladies. Go to sleep," Wanda called from the door as she flipped the light switch.

Katie's phone rang. Again, Larry's number showed on the screen. When would the man give up? Probably his guilty conscience.

Talking about guilt made her think of her mother and sister. And little Rachel. Would they worry? Lacey had given the child a nice gift that the girl thought came from Katie. Katie owed them a heads-up about her whereabouts.

In the dark room, the phone screen stood out, giving the time as five after eleven. Too late to call, or were they sitting up until she was found? Larry would have called them.

She slipped into the bathroom and dialed.

"Katie, where are you? We've been worried sick." A touch of panic sounded in Lacey's voice.

Katie had done the right thing to call. "I'm fine. Surprise, surprise, Wanda at the halfway house let me back in."

Lacey's voice lowered. "Why, Katie? I mean, it's okay if you move back to Apache Falls, but why did you leave Larry and scare him to death? He's running around the city like a crazy man. Why did you agree to go with him in the first place? Was he just a ride to the city?"

Her sister would never understand. "I did need a ride, sis, and now that Wanda has let me back in, I might get my old job back. It's all good."

"That's hateful."

"It's real life."

"You owe Larry an apology."

"I don't see it that way. He owes me one."

"What does that mean?"

"Ask him. Anyway, I'm hanging up now. I just didn't want you to worry."

"Are you going to call Larry?"

"I am not. I never want to speak to Larry again."

Katie hit disconnect, turned off her phone, and crept back to bed. Madison snored. Sleep could be elusive when a person was angry and hurt, though Katie would have denied both.

The rising sun shone through the eastern window and woke her up about eight. Sometime after five, she must have fallen asleep. Now Madison was gone. Katie's phone showed no missed calls. She clambered to her feet, dressed in black, and arrived in the halfway house dining room before breakfast was over.

Wanda sat at the table, sipping coffee. "Good morning."

"Morning." Katie searched the cabinet for cereal and the fridge for milk. She sat beside Wanda.

In the quiet of the morning, guilt-ridden thoughts crowded Katie's mind. The halfway house manager scanned the *Apache Falls Times*. Katie gulped the last of her cereal.

"Have you talked with the police lately? Did they clear me of that drug charge?"

Wanda's eyes never left the paper. "I have no idea."

With a tighter grasp on her spoon, Katie's knuckles whitened. "Then why did you let me move back in?"

The paper snapped. "You should be thankful."

"I am. I just wondered. Two weeks ago, you said you couldn't take a chance with the police suspicions. Why now?"

Wanda's gaze locked onto Katie's. "If you must know, Madison stood up for you."

What difference did that make? Madison knew nothing. Nicole had been Katie's roommate, and most likely the one who brought in the drugs. Anyway, Madison was out on felony charges. What sway did she have?

Wanda stood. "I'll abide no drugs and no drug-selling boyfriends in this establishment." She stormed from the kitchen, leaving Katie shaking in the quake.

Before Wanda reached the living area, the doorbell rang, and she answered.

A familiar voice brought Katie's spoon to a halt. What was he doing here?

"I don't know if you remember me, Mrs. Early. I'm Katie's brother-in-law."

"Of course, Sheriff, come on in."

"It's Chief, ma'am, but just Toby will do fine. Katie dashed off and left all her things at our house. I thought she'd need them."

"Yes, well, wait a moment." Wanda stuck her head around the corner of the kitchen. "Are you finished eating? I'll show Toby up the stairs. You might want to meet us upstairs and show him where you want your boxes."

Katie choked on the last bite and sputtered out an answer. "Have him plop them on the bed. I'll meet him on the front porch."

After Wanda left, the next sound was that of heavy boots tramping up the stairs and then Wanda's call, "Man on the second floor."

Katie steeled her spine and willed her stomach to digest her breakfast. She lifted her chin and walked to the porch to await whatever message Toby had to give. She had no doubt there was one.

She wandered out into the yard. Hearty weeds pushed against the rocky soil. The only beauty were the dandelions that no one bothered to pull. Gray clouds blocked the morning sun, and to the north, the clouds were black and bulbous.

Heavy footsteps clunked down the two steps from the porch. "Katie." His tone brooked no disagreement. He grabbed her arm and tugged her behind his truck. His expression blended perfectly with the northern clouds. "What's this?" His right hand unfolded, showing a package of cocaine, street value over fifty bucks.

Her strengthened resolve collapsed. Her shoulders slumped. Within a moment, her face chilled like all the blood drained to her toes. "I ... ah ... have no idea. Where did you find it?"

"On your bed."

Not again. Nicole had been the obvious culprit the first time, but she was gone.

"I didn't put it there, Toby. Honest." Ice clunked through her veins. "Did Wanda see it?"

"No. One of the girls called her away about the time she opened your door and told me which bed was yours."

All Katie's pride dissolved. Her heart squeezed. Her legs felt full of water.

"Help me, Toby. Someone's out to get me."

She clasped his collar and lowered her forehead until the crisp cotton of his Western shirt gave her some warmth to the top of her head. His arms reached around her. He gently patted her back. A kitchen curtain was pulled aside. Wanda's face showed in the window. He dropped his arms.

Tears blurred Katie's vision. She had no strength to continue the fight. She held up her wrists, holding them together in front of him.

"Go ahead, arrest me. All the lack of privacy, the boredom, the ugliness of prison would beat this outside harassment."

"I'm not arresting you, Katie." He stepped away, shifting his weight to one hip. "What happened? You owe me an explanation. Without a word, you left, came back here, and worried your family and my friend. What happened?"

"Ask Larry." A tightness in her jaw sent an acrid taste into her mouth. "He was the one searching and worried."

"He was the one who betrayed me."

"He what?" Toby's eyebrows rose. "Larry is the kindest man I know, almost too nice to be a policeman."

And too nice for the likes of her. She had nothing to look forward to. Then she remembered Rachel. Her goal all along had been to get out of prison, work, and get a place for her and her daughter. She had to find a way to make it up to her daughter. *Please, Lord.* Of course, why would God answer her prayers? He hadn't answered any since she was sixteen.

"I want to hear it from you." Toby's tone turned kinder, gentler. His rough palm touched her hand.

"Can we sit in your car? My legs are feeling a bit weak."

"Sure."

He led her around and opened the door. He even started the car and turned on the air conditioning. With ice chunks still breaking up in her body, she didn't need cold air. She settled into her seat and began her story.

When she finished, he remained quiet.

"What happens now?" she asked.

He turned the intimidating packet over in his hand. "I must turn this in as evidence. I'll work with the police here. Going through this same scenario two weeks later is just too coincidental. I doubt they'll believe it's you. I don't." He looked at her. "Why would you try to point a finger at yourself unless you really want to be arrested, and I don't think you do."

"No. Not really."

"You might consider coming home with me."

A flush melted all the ice. "That feels like running away." She stiffened. "And I'm not a quitter."

He tipped her chin. "No, you're not. That was always one thing I liked about little Katie. However big the jam she found herself in, she kept a positive attitude. I'm asking you to do that now."

A tentative smile turned up her mouth. "A compliment from you, Toby? That's weird."

"I guess you'll try to get back your old job?"

"Yeah, but first, I need a twelve-step meeting."

He patted her shoulder. "I'll bet. I'm praying for you."

"It doesn't help."

"Prayer always helps."

"Not for me." She started to climb out. "Oh, and Toby, will you do something for me?"

"I can't not go to the police here."

"I know. Just tell Larry to stay away. Tell him I'm bad news."

He sniffed. "I can do that and mean it."

She appreciated his help, but not his smirk.

CHAPTER *Twenty-Four*

The phone slipped from Lacey's hands. The devil appeared to be dumping on her, just to see if she could take it. "Well, I will!" she shouted to the empty room and threw the phone across her bed.

A knock came on the door. Mom stuck in her head. "You will what?"

"Nothing."

"Excuse me." Mom's voice escalated as she slammed the door.

A sudden craving for peanut butter cups released juice into Lacey's mouth, making her swallow the mere memory of such sweetness. In years past, she would've run to the store, bought a package, and eaten them all in one sitting, but that was before God's emotional healing.

A couple of pain killers might help the physical throbbing she'd endured the last two days. A banana sure sounded good, but she was out. After picking up the phone, she marched out of her room.

"Going to the store," she called to Mom. "I'll pick up Rachel from Joanne's on the way home."

The superstore's bananas were overly ripe, but Lacey grabbed two packages of low fat banana-flavored muffins—one to ease the anxiety over her upcoming chemotherapy, the other to ease the pain of Toby's betrayal. The check-out line was long. When she slid her card, her hands trembled so much, the cashier had to help.

On the two-minute drive to her friend Joanne's house, Lacey nibbled on a muffin. She savored the sweetness while waiting for Joanne to answer the door.

"Come on in," Joanne said. "The girls are swinging in the back."

The two mothers strolled through the house. Before Joanne opened the door leading to the backyard, she faced her friend.

"Are you okay? You look a little pale."

"I'm super, you know." Lacey regretted her harsh tone.

"Excuse me for caring." Joanne's eyes blazed.

"Sorry."

They'd been friends since first grade, Fat Lacey and Skinny Joanne, only Lacey was no longer fat. Joanne claimed a stressful marriage kept her from eating. For sure, she had picked a lemon with her choice of Calvin, but when Lacey's self-esteem was lower than a worm, she envied her friend.

The last three years, Lacey had been thanking God for Toby's love. Their childhood friendship had matured into love, or at least that's what she'd thought until Wanda's call.

Joanne hugged her friend. Lacey winced with the contact and moved back.

"Are you mad at me?" Joanne asked.

Tears began to flow. Lacey's shoulders shook. Joanne dropped her scrawny arms.

"Is it the chemo you're worried about?"

"Partially." Lacey hiccupped.

"What else?"

"Noth ... ing."

"Lacey Wheeler, you're the one who taught me to trust God. Now, it's not 'nothing' that's making you cry, but God's in control. Do you hear me?" She crossed her arms and put her weight on one tiny hip.

"Toby may have shifted his love from me to Katie."

"What?" Joanne's voice rose so loud it brought the girls inside.

Rachel threw herself at her mother. "We're having a contest. Let me stay a little longer. Please, please."

Lacey stiffened. Rachel's probing fingers sent waves of pain around her neck and over one shoulder. What was going on with her? She expected side effects when she began the chemo, but that didn't start until next week.

Beth and Tiffany, Joanne's daughters, added their pleas. "Please, Mrs. Wheeler, let Rachel stay longer."

Joanne made no further attempt to touch her friend, but her gaze wandered from Lacey's head to her feet.

"Go back outside, girls." Joanne's words took charge. "Y'all can play longer while Rachel's mother and I visit."

"Yay," the three squealed as they traipsed back out the door.

Joanne's fingers tapped on opposite arms.

Lacey's head lifted. Physical and mental pain tormented her insides. Her mouth was so dry.

"Can I have a glass of water?"

"Of course you can." Joanne filled a glass and handed it to her friend. "Now, let's figure this all out." She led the way to the sofa.

Lacey crumbled. To keep from filling up with candy and donuts, it was time to bare her soul.

CHAPTER *Twenty-Five*

Katie's life returned to some semblance of normal. Again, she worked for Paul at the Country Dinner Restaurant. She roomed with Madison at the halfway house. So far, nothing had been said about the drugs Toby had found on her bed, but it had only been two days. The police could knock on the door at any time.

Her legs dangled off her bed. She tugged out the box she used for savings. With Nicole gone, her stash might stay a secret. Willie promised to mail her paycheck for days worked in Wharton Rock, so when she received that, her savings for her own place would once more mount.

Did Rachel miss her? Before she'd driven off with Larry, she'd told her daughter she would be in Wharton Rock for a while. The child loved the birthday present Katie had given her, and she didn't know Lacey had bought it. A flush heated Katie's cheeks. She was a lousy mother. What made her think she could undo her sin? She didn't deserve Rachel's love.

But I'm her mother. I tended to her for four years.

But if she admitted the truth, the child had been marched from one man to another, one drug house to the next, been put in danger, and finally kidnapped.

Katie shivered. Pain settled between her eyes. Though Mom was controlling and aggravating, she had found a way to make a home for her two daughters. Lacey had protected Katie's daughter when she was in prison. What had Katie done?

Failed, like always.

Now, when Larry treated her like a lady, she'd failed him too. An ex-con, ex-drug addict for a church worker? What was she thinking?

Her phone rang, and she answered.

"Hey, sweet stuff, how you doing?"

Collin's voice didn't sound like the man who had threatened her two weeks ago. He reminded her of when she fell for him, when he was kind to her, and God knew, she needed some kindness.

"Like you care." She couldn't stop the tenseness in her body. The last time she'd been with Collin, he refused to let her leave, and when she'd gotten help from one of his friends, the man had stolen her car.

"You probably don't want to speak to me."

"Give me two reasons I should."

"One, I talked with the cops. They are going to call you. They found your Honda east of town. I'm so sorry about all that."

A jolt zipped down her spine. Joy in the reality of a red Honda was good news. It would again give her independence and hope.

"Thanks, I'll give them a call."

"And number two," he said.

She waited. Silence drifted through the phone, then heavy breathing.

"I'm not holding on to listen to you breathe, sugar. If I wanted that, I'd seek out a man in person."

His voice came in a whisper. "I'm clean. Honest."

No words came to her mind. Could she believe him?

"I'm attending Narcotics Anonymous meetings."

"The one that meets in the Church of Christ on Grant Street?"

"Yeah. I go on Tuesday nights. Sometimes Mondays too."

"You still selling?" Her tone was harsh, but she'd been down that road before.

"No."

"You going to a meeting tonight?"

"Maybe."

"Good luck with that." She disconnected.

No one knew better than her how hard it was to stay off the stuff, especially for someone like Collin, who'd been strung out for so many years.

The door flew open. Madison rushed in and twirled in front of her. "Guess what?"

"You won the lottery?"

Madison flopped on the bed and clapped her hands. "Mom came into some money. She bought a new car and gave me her old one. And she gave me enough money to put a deposit on an apartment of my own." She rolled over to face Katie and giggled. "Isn't that super wonderful?"

A wave of apprehension blanketed Katie's shoulders and tickled her neck. Was she worried that she wouldn't be in Madison's plans or afraid that she was?

"Well, aren't you the lucky one."

"Will you share an apartment with me? You have your old job back now, and nothing else has been said about the drugs. Why, even Wanda trusts you again."

"I've been meaning to ask you about that." With no chance to hide it, the metal box twisted in Katie's hands. "Wanda said you stood up for me moving back in here. What difference would that make?"

Madison rolled her eyes. "Who knows with Wanda, the fish. Who even cares as long as she let you back?" She jumped up and gathered work clothes. "Got to get ready. You work tonight?"

"Not until tomorrow. I'm going to NA tonight. I need it."

Madison paused. "You're not back into the stuff, are you?"

Katie wasn't, but she sure was tempted. Besides, everyone expected it from her. No, that wasn't true. Toby had seemed to trust her. Who would've expected that?

"No, but I may not be out of trouble with that drug charge yet."

"Believe me, it's all forgotten." Madison waved her hand in dismissal.

"Hey, good news. They found my car."

"Really? Where?"

"Collin told me the cops found it east of town."

"Collin? That's the drug-dealing boyfriend, isn't it? I figured he was hooking up with Nicole. You're not taking him back, are you?"

"He isn't my boyfriend."

"Could've fooled me."

"I may still be in trouble."

"What makes you think so? Collin?" She stretched out his name while batting her eyelashes.

"My brother-in-law, the police chief, brought up my stuff and found drugs on my bed again."

Madison dropped beside Katie and put her arm around her. "Oh, sweetie, I'm so sorry." She straightened and moved her arm. "So, Nicole had a comrade." Her pointer finger tapped her upper lip. "You'll beat this." She stood. "Besides, we'll be in our own place by next month."

"It can't come soon enough for me, but I need two bedrooms myself."

Madison donned drama mode and curtsied with hands waving. "I remember, you wanted an extra one for your daughter." She clasped her hands under her chin. "This will be so exciting. I can hardly wait. You and I make a great team."

Katie had really not wanted to share, but this would be good. At least she'd be out of this ex-con haven.

Her phone rang. For someone who had few friends, her phone was like the DFW airport on Mondays.

"Hello."

"Is this Katie that's friends with Pastor Larry?"

The voice was familiar. That Pastor Larry thing threw her before she remembered the teens called him that. It suited his volunteer job.

"Did you hear me?"

The soft voice grew more urgent. Katie heard a moan.

"I am. Is this Kinsley?" That was definitely a moan Katie heard. Her heart thumped against her chest. "Are you okay?"

Madison twisted her lips and listened. Privacy could be an issue with Katie's future roommate. She cupped a hand over her mouth. Not that the gesture would muffle anything she said, but she had to try.

"I'm in labor. Mom and Dad are at work. What am I going to do?" Kinsley hesitated. A scream came next.

Katie flashed back to her labor pains. She had been seventeen, alone, and frightened.

"Call 911 now. Have them take you to Apache Falls Memorial. I'll meet you there."

"Okay." A shaky reply.

Katie disconnected and glanced up at Madison. If she was going to be her roommate, she might as well start now being a friend.

"Do you have your mom's car now?"

"Sure do."

"Will you drop me off at the hospital on your way to work?"

"Sure will." Madison sat on the bed. "Is it your mom?"

Katie jumped up. "I need to go now."

"Okay." Madison frowned. She sounded mad.

Without regard to Madison seeing Katie's hiding place, she yanked out her one and only twenty, put it in her permanently-prepared tote bag, and walked to the door.

"I'm ready."

"Well, excuse me."

Yep, she was mad.

On the way, Katie chattered like a nervous blackbird.

"Sure have changed these streets since I lived here three years ago. I can't find anything without getting lost. Of course, I didn't have a chance to drive much before my car was stolen."

Madison kept quiet. The car careened down one road and jerked to a stop.

"It's a friend of mine, okay?" Katie bit her lip. She willed herself to calm her heartbeat. "She's in labor."

Madison's fingers drummed against the steering wheel. "You want me to come with you? I could call Paul."

"No, no." She was a friend, and Katie appreciated that. No use throwing a load of aggravation Madison's way. "Look, I'm sorry. Okay?"

"Okay, but I really should go with you."

Her insistent tone worried Katie. "No need. You don't know my friend."

"Where did you meet her? It wasn't the halfway house, was it?"

Her attitude was ridiculous. What was up with Madison? Sometimes she seemed so possessive.

"Look, I appreciate all you've done, paying the deposit on the apartment and all, and I thank you for giving me a ride, but I have a life outside of the halfway house and other ex-cons."

Without another word, Madison looped through the emergency entrance.

"Does this work?"

"Yes, thanks." Katie opened the car door.

"Call if you need a ride home."

"I will." Katie gave the door a shove and hurried to the desk inside. "Has a girl named Kinsley come in by ambulance? She was in labor?" she asked the clerk.

"What is the full name?"

Swell. "I'm sorry. I don't know her last name. She's only seventeen. Mexican background. And in labor. Doesn't that narrow it down?"

Katie's hands tightened over the edge of the counter. The clerk gave her an I-couldn't-care-less expression. Her fingers stilled on the keyboard.

"You're not a relative, I take it."

"No, just a friend."

"You may wait, but I can't give you any information. Sorry. Next." Her gaze turned to the man behind Katie.

Gripping the counter, she shouted. "All I want to know is whether she's here or not. She called me." Katie lowered the top half of her body over the counter to make eye contact from a closer vantage point. "I promised to meet her here. She needs me." A true friend would've been a treasure when Katie was going through the same thing.

"I'm sorry, ma'am. I can't—"

An ambulance siren blasted through an open door to the left. Two men in scrubs wheeled in a stretcher to the side of the counter. A female nurse met them there.

The first man spouted, "Kinsley Martinez, thirty-two weeks, alone, dilated to four, amniotic fluid burst on way to the hospital."

Katie moved to Kinsley's side and lifted her hand. "You okay?"

The girl's face was the color of the beige wall behind her, a much lighter shade than usual. Her hair was sweaty and matted. She nodded.

"Don't leave me."

"Did you call your parents?"

Tears added to the moisture in her hair. She shook her head. "They won't come."

Katie brushed the wet bangs off Kinsley's forehead.

"Stand back," the first man pushing the stretcher said.

"I want to go with her. I'm all she has."

A wave of nausea swept over Katie. The only one who had ever depended on her had been Rachel, and look how that had turned out. Katie was irresponsible and untrustworthy.

Automatic double doors from outside swished to open. Larry strode across the waiting room to where Katie and Kinsley argued with the medical personnel. He placed a hand on the first man's shoulder.

"I'm Reverend Pullman. I'm the girl's youth minister." His words brooked no argument. "Since I'm not a relative, Kinsley and I ..." he dipped his head to indicate the patient, "asked Miss Smith here to remain with her and act in Kinsley's best interest."

He glanced at Katie. His gaze held no familiarity.

"Now, please, see to Miss Martinez. Take good care of her." He focused on Kinsley. "I'm praying for you."

The nurse remained in the way. "Do you have Miss Martinez's personal information?"

"I do. Also, her father is on his way."

The nurse nodded and moved aside.

The two ambulance drivers pushed the stretcher forward, while Katie rushed to catch up. They came to several cubicles and pushed her into the third one. After lifting her onto an exam table, they took the stretcher and retreated. The nurse moved to Kinsley's side, quickly clamping on a blood pressure cuff and strapping a monitor across her belly.

After a few minutes, when all her vitals had been checked and she was attached to the screen that kept up with such info, the nurse left. Kinsley appeared to be asleep.

Katie had just sat in the only available chair, straight-back with no padding, when Kinsley's eyes flew open. Katie jumped up and grabbed her left hand.

The girl's clasp tightened, sending pain shooting up Katie's arm. She bit her lip and clamped her mouth. Kinsley needed her. She wouldn't fail her like she had Rachel.

CHAPTER

Kinsley's face scrunched into a wrinkled mask. She screamed, hiccupped, and screamed again. Katie's fingers ached from Kinsley's tight hold, but she wouldn't let go. After a few seconds, the mask relaxed.

"That was a rough one, wasn't it?" Katie said.

The teenager nodded.

"When did these pains start?"

Kinsley gnawed her lip. "About two this morning."

Katie's brow crinkled as she stared. "Why didn't you tell your parents before they left for work?"

"I . . . they . . ." The mask returned. "Yeooh!" Kinsley's screams bounced off the back wall.

Katie's stomach churned. The air was stifling, and her forehead was damp with perspiration. She'd give anything if someone would bring her a soda.

A man's head peeped around the curtain's opening. "Anything I can do?"

Larry. Katie could hug that man. "Would you mind getting me a cola?"

"Done."

He disappeared and returned soon with a cup loaded with ice and soda. Another wave of labor pains started. Katie couldn't let go.

"Set it over there."

"How's she doing?"

"Hurting, what do you think?" *Cut the sarcasm, you stupid imbecile.* She lowered her voice. "Sorry."

Larry sat in a straight-back chair at the foot of the bed. Kinsley's labor continued its torment. Sweat soaked her thick hair. She gritted her teeth and crushed Katie's hand, but she didn't scream anymore.

After a nurse came in to check Kinsley, it was the nurse that yelled. "Dr. McDonald, STAT!"

The baby girl arrived before the doctor. Kinsley never dropped Katie's hand. Larry didn't move, but his face turned scarlet. While the doctor worked on Kinsley, the baby was put in a warmer and examined.

Mr. Martinez, Kinsley's dad, joined them on the baby's first cry. With a look of worry, his gaze followed the infant.

The doctor finished with Kinsley and moved to another patient. The pediatrician wrapped up a baby burrito and handed her to the new mama. Kinsley dropped Katie's hand and clasped the baby to her chest. She unfolded the tiny fingers from a hand that broke free of the swaddling and grinned up at her father.

"Be realistic, Kinsley. We can't keep that," he said.

Her face became a prune. "She's mine. I won't give her up. Katie?" She turned to her new comrade.

A flush crept up Katie's neck. "It's not easy."

"But you did it." Kinsley's eyes were trying to close. She was exhausted.

Orderlies entered. One explained that they had a room for Kinsley. One picked up the baby.

"We'll take care of her while you get some rest."

The other two rolled her into the hall. Katie rushed to catch up.

"I'll be back in the morning. Get some rest. Your daughter is safe."

A single tear ran down the side of Kinsley's face. Her eyes widened.

"My daughter." More tears ran rivulets across her cheek. "I'm going to name her Katie Marie." Her bed rolled on toward her room.

Numbness overtook Katie's body. When she tried to move, her legs buckled. Larry's strong arms caught her.

"Come on. I'll take you home."

Mr. Martinez seemed rooted to the spot where he stood.

Katie and Larry walked side by side into the bright sunshine of late evening. His fingers looped through hers. The warmth was like a safe haven. What was she doing?

Early the next morning, Katie dressed and waited out in front of the half-way house. The second step crumbled with her weight. She cringed. Even if it took having a roommate, she would be so glad to move.

Larry looped into the driveway, jumped out of his truck, and caught her arm.

Always the gentleman. He hadn't mentioned what happened the night of the bowling party. Neither had she.

"Hey, sugar, thanks for the lift. After we see Kinsley and the baby, would you mind giving—?"

"You a ride to the police station to pick up your car?"

When he grinned, a dimple showed on his left cheek. She'd never noticed that before. It was only on one side. She dipped her head. The intensity of his expression made her uneasy.

"Yeah. I forget you policeman all share info."

"I'll be happy to. It's wonderful that they found it."

She winked, hoping to go back to a lighter mood. No way was she going to get into a conversation that included his new youth assistant, or why Katie ran out on him, and she wasn't about to ask about that "Reverend Pullman" comment at the hospital.

"Sure will be glad to get my independence back." Her head shook like a bobble doll. "Madison and I will be getting our own place next month." She clamped her mouth shut. She hadn't planned on sharing private information with a cop.

"Super news."

Was he being facetious or honest? Who could understand a cop, especially one that got all involved in religion?

They arrived at Kinsley's hospital room but couldn't see the patient for the medical personnel surrounding her. Voices, hushed. Movements, urgent. Monitors, beeping. What was going on?

"Does this hurt?" a doctor asked.

"Uh-huh," came a small reply.

A nurse spotted Katie and Larry at the door and moved their way.

"Sorry, she can't have visitors now. You might come back in about an hour."

"What's wrong?" Larry asked.

"Are you family?"

"No."

"Try coming back."

The nurse went back to the doctor's side. Katie and Larry looked at each other. Katie shrugged.

"I'm staying."

"I'm with you," he whispered. "Do you mind if we pray?"

Katie hadn't prayed since she was seventeen, didn't think it helped, but maybe it could if Larry did it.

"I guess."

He took her hands. "Lord, look down on Kinsley. You know what's happening. Heal her now, and take care of Baby Katie."

The intensity of his voice broke down her defenses.

"Amen," she said. *Baby Katie? What a beautiful sound.* Big Katie could almost believe God heard and was answering.

Medical personnel pulled away from the cluster, leaving one at a time, some pushing out machines. The only sound remaining was the *bleep bleep* of the monitor over Kinsley's bed that posted her blood pressure, pulse rate, and oxygen saturation. The doctor nodded to the pair as he left.

Katie moved toward the young mother tied to the machine. Her brown eyes lifted. She reached out a hand, and Katie took hold of it.

"You okay?"

Kinsley nodded. "Better."

She asked for a drink. Katie lifted a glass of water to the girl's lips. Color drained from her face. She tried words again.

"Will you ...?"

Her energy vanished. Katie bent closer to hear. Larry slipped to the other side of the bed.

"...keep..." A film of sweat formed over Kinsley's upper lip.

"We'll talk later. Save your strength." Katie brushed back sweaty curls and smiled.

"... Katie ..." Kinsley swallowed. "... Marie? Keep Katie Marie?"

Katie's eyes widened, not believing the words she heard. Instead, she patted the girl's hand.

"Now, now. You'll be okay. Just rest."

Kinsley was scared. Katie got that. Who wouldn't be? But giving away a daughter was a decision that just might ruin her life. *Just ask me.* Katie shivered.

Kinsley's mom and dad entered and huddled in one corner. The dad's jaw was tight. The mother sobbed, wiping her nose occasionally with a tissue. Larry stepped back and dropped his arm around Mrs. Martinez's shoulders.

"That baby almost killed our little girl." The dad's voice rose with anger.

Katie only caught a little of what Larry was saying—something about being innocent and needing love. Mr. Martinez didn't sound too loving toward Baby Katie or his daughter.

Words came from the bed like a whimpering shadow. "Her ... name ... is ... Ka ..." Kinsley was out of breath.

Katie swiped her own eyes with the back of one hand while she patted Kinsley with the other. How Katie would've loved having her mom with her when she gave birth, though having her trying to control things when Katie was hurting might not have been a blessing.

Kinsley wouldn't give up. "Keep ... Katie ... p ... please." Tears rolled down the teen's face and blended with the already wet hair. "P ... paper." The monitor showed a rise in pulse.

A nurse entered and shooed everyone out.

The four left the room and clustered in a waiting room down the hall. Larry tried to comfort the girl's parents, but the dad was full of rage.

"If she'd only tell me who the father is, I'll kill him."

"Don't talk foolishness," the mom said. "The main thing now is that Kinsley recover. Then she can give the baby up for adoption."

"She wants to keep the baby." Katie could bite her tongue for interfering.

Mr. Martinez's eyes blazed. "She'll do what I say."

A man touched Mr. Martinez shoulder. "Excuse me, are you Kinsley's parents?"

"Yes," the mom said. "How is she?"

"I'm Dr. McClure. Let's sit down so I can explain what's happening." He motioned to seats behind them.

Catching Katie's arm, Larry started to move away.

"Wait." Kinsley's mom called out. She addressed the doctor. "This is Kinsley's youth minister and his assistant." Her gaze flicked over Katie. "You may speak in front of them."

Assistant? She was no minister's assistant. She wanted to set them straight, but Larry's fingernails dug into her arm. She licked parched lips and listened.

"Kinsley's blood pressure is elevated, and the urinalysis shows high protein in her urine, causing us to believe she has postpartum pre-eclampsia."

"Is it dangerous?" the mom asked.

"It can be. I've ordered an IV of magnesium sulfate. That should reduce the chance of seizures. I'll check her again tonight."

"Thank you, Doctor. May we go back in with her?"

He nodded and left.

Larry stood. "We'll leave now, but I'll be praying for you." He caught Katie's arm. "I'll stop by again this evening."

The dad waved them off.

After the elevator door closed, Katie faced Larry.

"Assistant? Blast it all, I'm not your assistant. That would be your red-headed girlfriend, what's-her-face." Her voice escalated. This wasn't how she'd intended to broach the subject, but it was what it was. At her side, her hands balled into fists.

Larry's tone was unusually loud. "Michelle. But she's not my assistant or, I might add, my girlfriend." His knuckles popped for emphasis. His ears reddened.

The elevator opened. Three people joined them. Silence descended until the door reopened on the first floor. Katie marched ahead with Larry trailing. Nothing else was said until they arrived at the police station. He got out and circled to her side. She didn't wait but got out of the car herself and stomped toward the office. Before she reached the door, he jumped in front of her and caught her shoulders.

"I must get to work, but this isn't over."

"It is for me."

She hurried through the door. It closed with an intended bang.

CHAPTER *Twenty-Seven*

Larry's mind wouldn't stay on target. He was trying to prepare for a new series starting Sunday night. His hand banged against the side of his head.

Shame on me, thinking of an ex-con named Katie when I should be dwelling on God's Word.

The lessons about putting God first struck a chord with him. How he had failed. Bowing his head, he poured out his heart to the Lord. *I need You. Unless you anoint my words, they can't help anyone. Settle my mind. Show me Your way. Give me the fruit of the Holy Spirit called patience."*

"Hi, there." Michelle waited at his doorway. "You seem deep in thought."

He stood. "Deep in prayer."

"Oh, sorry, but Reverend Schumacher called me to come in. He just told me that the pregnant Mexican girl in your youth group has had her baby. Since you have no wife," she lingered over the term and leaned against the door, "he suggested I go visit her. Would you like to go with me?" She fluffed one side of her hair and tipped her head to the right.

He should've known better than to pray for patience. It was dangerous.

"I went this morning. Right now, I have a devotion to plan. But you go ahead. That would be nice."

She sat on the corner of his desk, crossing her long legs and letting the top one swing.

"I can wait for you or come back later."

"No, you go on."

He once again took his seat and picked up his Bible. One of her eyebrows rose.

"Are you avoiding being with me, Larry?"

She usually used Pastor when addressing him. He didn't care for the familiarity.

"Of course not."

"You do understand my being your assistant isn't a suggestion?"

His head jerked up. He narrowed his eyes. "No, I didn't."

"Reverend Schumacher said you were rushed last Friday since the kids were waiting for you. Maybe you need to talk with him again."

Larry bounded to his feet. "Yes, I guess I do. Please excuse me."

Michelle rose. She sucked on her pointer finger that had a long blue-painted nail. Her smile was strange. It sent shivers up his spine and dried up all his spit.

"Close your mouth, Reverend Pullman." The senior pastor stood in the doorway.

Larry froze. *Talk about being caught with a stupid look.* His smile went askew.

"I was just coming to see you."

"Wonderful." The pastor stopped and motioned Larry ahead of him. "You lead. I'll follow."

Larry couldn't help but see the ironic twist to that statement.

After he took a seat in the big office, Reverend Schumacher closed the door. He sat behind the enormous walnut desk and steepled his fingers.

"How might I help you?"

"Michelle says—"

"Three weeks ago, I told you that you had a month to gain the respect of the kids and parents." The pastor leaned back. His steepled hands moved to cross his abdomen. "Last week, I told you to make Michelle your assistant and lose the ex-con girlfriend."

"Katie isn't my girlfriend, and Michelle is not good at—"

"Did I ask for excuses?" The pastor's gray eyes turned to hard steel. "I've been talking to Mr. Martinez. He wanted me to check into putting Kinsley's baby up for adoption. Imagine my surprise when I learned that your brought you ex-con girlfriend to visit Kinsley."

"Kinsley called—"

Reverend Schumacher held up his arm. "No more excuses. You're fired."

Larry jumped to his feet. "Sir, I love those kids. I've tried—"

"Well, you haven't tried hard enough."

"I've developed a rapport with many of them, especially Ryan and Cody, Kimmi and Shawn, and of course, Kinsley. They'll miss me. I'm starting a new series on Sunday about putting God first and—"

"Turn in your keys, Pullman. I'll have Michelle fill in temporarily. You might give her any notes you have for the Sunday series." He stood and held out his hand.

Larry pulled keys from his pocket and handed them over.

"I'm really sorry," the pastor said.

"Me too." With bowed head, Larry left to pack up his office.

Michelle still sat on his desk, waiting. He picked up a box and began to throw things into it—pictures, books, and notes. She leaned into him, pressing her cheek to his back. He pulled away.

"Sorry, I've been distracted, so I don't have any notes for Sunday's class. You'll have to wing it." His tone was dismissive.

"Oh, Larry." She moved to face him. "You didn't quit, did you? I never meant to cause that." Her expression showed sincere shock. Did she not see it coming?

"I didn't quit. I was fired." He went back to packing.

"Why?"

"I don't have Reverend Schumacher's trust. He thinks the young people will be better served with someone else. You're my temporary replacement."

"I wanted to help you, not do your job. I'll talk with him. You're good with those kids."

Maybe he had her all wrong.

"No, I need to leave. He and I never saw eye to eye. This is best."

"Where will you go?"

He sniffed. "Back to looking for a job in the ministry. Meanwhile, I still have my part-time job in Wharton Rock."

"I forgot that's where you live."

"Yeah, I'm a small-town kind of guy. Still live with my mom." With the addition of the Bible he'd been using on his desk, he lifted the box.

"Your mom? How old are you anyway?" She giggled.

He went back for a notepad and put it in his box and walked to the hall.

"Will you call me?" she asked.

"Why?"

"Because I care. May I call you?"

He shrugged. "If you like."

He walked out.

Things moved fast for Katie. Only two weeks after picking up her car, she walked into the apartment that Madison had rented for the both of them.

"It's bigger than I expected." She strolled through the first bedroom. "Which is your room?"

"Since I was only able to get a two bedroom, I figured you should have the biggest one since your daughter will be here some of the time." Madison went over to the closet. "See, it's extra big, so you'll have room for some of Rachel's things as well as your own."

"Thanks." It was exciting, but it also made her sad. Katie wanted to do this on her own. She was still dependent on someone, but living with her family was harder, and she didn't like the halfway house. "I'll pay a hundred dollars more than my half every month until I pay you back on the deposit and first month's rent."

Madison waved her hand. "I'm not worried. I'm just glad to have a roommate." She twirled. "Our own place. Isn't it wonderful?"

Her friend expected more enthusiasm from Katie. She really tried.

"Yes. It's great." Her words were monotone, despite her effort. "Shall I move everything in today? I need to be at work at four thirty."

"Today or tomorrow."

"If it's paid for, I'll move in now. The sooner I'm out of that halfway house, the better."

Madison's grin widened. Katie had said the right thing.

"I moved some stuff in yesterday while you were working. I plan on sleeping here tonight. Can't wait to see Wanda's face when we tell her."

"Well, let's head over there now."

Madison drove her car with Katie following. Back at the halfway house, Madison took a load out while Katie began to pack. Not that there was much to that. Most stuff was still in her cardboard box from when she'd previously been thrown out.

"So, you're moving?"

Wanda was behind her. After a muscle jerk, Katie swiveled with jutted chin and firm reply.

"Yes, I am."

Madison swept back in. "Yep, we're out of here this evening. You can give our room to two other women."

Wanda crossed her arms. "Glad to hear it." She glared at Katie. "I won't have to deal with any more drug problems."

Katie's face flamed despite her efforts at bravado.

"Speaking of." Wanda shifted positions, continuing to stare at Katie. "The police called asking if I'd seen any more drugs around you. It seems your brother-in-law that's a police chief turned in drugs he claims to have found here at the halfway house." Tapping a finger to her temple, she shifted again.

Katie had more reason to be uncomfortable than the house manager.

"What's up with that?" Wanda's expression showed more interest than her manner downplayed.

Katie shrugged. "I have no idea. Where did he find it?"

"I don't know. Sergeant Morris said the police chief told him he visited you one day and found it in plain sight."

"Then it must've been in the living room."

"I would assume so. Or in the yard, while you were hugging."

"Hugging?"

Wanda covered her mouth. "Oops. I wasn't supposed to see that. Sorry."

"Whatever you think you saw, you didn't see. Got it?" Katie almost shouted. *How stupid! Her and Toby? No way.* She would be so glad to get out of Wanda's domain.

Madison moved between them. "This is all fascinating, but Katie and I have work to do."

"Don't let me stop you. I might throw a party when you're gone." Wanda walked out of the room.

Katie was still shaking. She hated Wanda's constant insinuations. For some reason, the woman had never liked her. What a shock it was that Toby didn't tell them where he found the drugs exactly. She hated being obliged to her brother-in-law, but though he drove her crazy, he might've saved her neck.

"You about ready?"

Madison loaded up two boxes of stuff.

"Yep."

Katie followed with her cardboard box, a toaster, and the metal money box—the sum total of her existence, except her car—but she was off to a new place, a new life, a new beginning.

She just hoped it proved to be better than her past.

CHAPTER *Twenty-Eight*

Three days later around noon, Kinsley and the baby arrived on Katie's doorstep.

"I need help," the girl said. Her face was as white as her shirt.

Katie widened the door. "What's going on?"

Kinsley looked right and left at the empty apartment.

"We kinda don't have money for furniture. There's two chairs and an old table in the kitchen." Katie motioned.

Kinsley took a step and swayed. Catching the girl's shoulders, Katie eased her to the floor and reached for the baby.

"Are you okay?"

"Not really."

With legs stretched in front of her, Kinsley rested her head against the wall. She reached out her hand. Her fingers clutched a folded piece of paper.

Katie took it. "What's this?"

"Read it."

Katie read the paper. "Being of sound mind on this day, I request that Katie Smith be allowed to rear my child, Katie Marie Martinez. Upon my death, I give her full custody." Katie's fingers shook. Her mouth went dry. "Surely, you don't mean this. You're young. You'll outlive me."

Kinsley stared across the room. Her breathing labored. Her head twitched. "No. Got to." She gasped.

Rubbing the girl's back, Katie cooed like she might with Baby Katie. "Relax. It will be okay."

"Need . . . hospital." Kinsley's words were jerky, with a gasp after each one.

Katie punched in 911 and ran for a wet rag to bathe Kinsley's brow.

A tick caused the girl's right cheek to sink in. The shaking of her head worsened. Though scared, Katie tried to be calm. She continued to pat Kinsley's hand while they waited for the ambulance. The girl gagged. Katie reached for a trash can, and just as Kinsley vomited, a siren sounded and someone pounded on the door.

"Coming."

When Katie opened the door, two emergency workers dropped a stretcher and squatted on either side of Kinsley. The baby let out a wail. Pacing back and forth with Baby Katie on her shoulder, Katie patted the babe's back.

"I didn't know what to do."

The man on the team lifted Kinsley to the stretcher. The woman took vitals and spoke in low tones.

"When did she begin seizing?" the man asked.

"She arrived here with the baby about thirty minutes ago, breathless and pale. She began to twitch and said she needed to go to the hospital. That's when I called. Then she vomited and . . ." Katie halted. "What's happening?"

"Looks like she's having a seizure," the man said. "So the baby is hers?"

Katie nodded.

"How old?"

"Three weeks, maybe?" Katie counted back in her mind.

Kinsley's whole body was trembling. One of the workers handed the trash can to Katie, who ran to dump it in the bathroom. When she returned, the medical team and the stretcher were disappearing across the yard. She stepped to the porch.

"You taking her to Apache Falls Memorial?"

"Yes, ma'am."

She went back inside. In the kitchen, she sat in one of the two chairs, the ones they'd never made it to when Kinsley arrived. Two brown eyes in a tiny face stared at Katie, as if she had all the answers. That was when she realized she had a baby without a diaper or a bottle. Behind the front door was a pink and white polka-dot bag. *Thank God.* Fumbling with one hand into the bag, she pulled out a blanket and laid Baby Katie across it until she found a bottle.

"You hungry, sugar?" The infant latched onto the nipple. "Yeah, you were hungry, weren't you?" Memories flooded Katie's mind of when Rachel was born. "What am I going to do with you, sugar? I need to go see your mama."

Larry. He would want to know about Kinsley. Would he keep the child?

About that time, Madison tore through the front door. Her eyes widened.

"What in the world is that? I thought your daughter was eight."

"She is." Katie handed the baby and the bottle to Madison. "Keep her a little while. I need to go to the hospital."

Madison stood like a statue. "When will you be back?"

"I don't know."

Grabbing her car keys, Katie dashed away before Madison could ask more questions. She gunned off in the direction taken by the ambulance. Her sweaty palms slipped on the wheel. A red light stopped her. She should tell Larry.

He might know.

He might not.

While she waited for the light to change, she scanned through her phone until she came to Larry's number and hit dial.

"Pullman." The rich baritone blanketed her shoulders with a comforting warmth.

"This is Katie. I wanted to let you know about Kinsley."

"What about her?"

A curtness tinged his tone that hadn't been there before they'd left the hospital after the baby was born. What did he have to be mad about? Katie had been the one angry over his assistant remark. And she still hadn't forgiven him for the night she overheard his conversation at the church. She pushed that aside. Kinsley came first.

"She's been rushed to the hospital."

"How do you know?" His voice seemed a bit critical.

"I called 911."

Silence.

"Larry?"

"Did you go to her home?"

Yeah, definitely critical.

"Look, I did nothing wrong. I thought you might want to . . . ah . . . Oh, forget about it." She disconnected.

Her phone played its merry tune when she was two blocks from the hospital. She pulled in the lot. The song played on. She'd let him know. She owed him nothing else. The automatic doors opened.

"Kinsley Martinez," she called before she reached the counter.

The woman with creases across her brow, purple polka-dot scrubs, and an ingrained scowl ran her gaze up and down Katie.

"Family?"

"All I know is her parents. Have they been called?"

The woman's scowl deepened. "Are you in the Martinez family or not?"

"No. I'm the one who called 911."

The woman went back to her monitor. Katie's back stiffened.

"Listen, Kinsley left her baby with me when she got sick. I followed the ambulance. I need to know how long I'll be keeping her child." She put out a hand to still further comment. "Not that I mind. Little Katie is adorable but—"

"Take this lady to room C." The woman directed a young man, then turned back to Katie. "Wait in there. I'll send her parents in when they arrive."

"Okay."

Katie sat in the five-by-five room that held eight chairs, one table, and one lamp. One wall featured a blissful ocean scene titled "Let the waves roar." She ripped off a thread from her jeans and tugged on the top that suddenly appeared shorter than usual. Fluffing her curls, she tucked her legs under her, then decided that was uncomfortable in the small, hard chairs, so she dropped her feet to the floor, eyeing it as possibly being more comfortable than the chair.

The door opened. The same young man motioned in Mr. and Mrs. Martinez. Kinsley's dad glared.

"What are you doing here?"

"I called 911."

"Where were you?"

Katie felt the blood drain from her head. Kinsley wouldn't want them to know she'd come to Katie's house.

"Thank you for calling them," the mom said, saving Katie from answering.

"You're welcome. I think she was having a seizure. Sure scared me."

The door opened again. A tall, thin man with prominent cheek bones and a wide forehead stepped inside and took a seat across from the Martinezes. Katie was the outsider on the end. The man swept one glance her way and focused on the girl's parents. His brows knit together.

"I'm Dr. Alvarez, the doctor on call. I'm so sorry. We did everything we could, but Kinsley had a strong seizure. Her heart just stopped. We got it beating again twice, but we couldn't sustain the rhythm." He bowed his head. "We lost her. Again, I'm so sorry."

Kinsley's mom squealed and sobbed.

"I want to see her." Her dad stood.

"Very well."

The doctor nodded to the young man who stood behind him. Mr. Martinez followed him out. With heaving shoulders, Mrs. Martinez trailed behind him. Dr. Alvarez's gaze swept over Katie.

"I understand that you were the one with her when the seizure began."

"Yes, sir."

"I'm sorry we couldn't revive your friend. It wasn't your fault. Even with the swift action, there was nothing that could be done. I saw in her records that she had a seizure after her delivery. Posteclampsia is rare, but in her case, there must've been an undetected before now heart problem. We just didn't realize in time." He stood, bowed, and left.

The room closed in on Katie. The oxygen supply diminished. Numbness swept her muscles. She fought it, rising, holding onto the table beside her. After her legs gained strength, she took a step, finally let go, and treaded forward, not realizing she was outside until the hot sun struck her face. The reality of Kinsley giving up her baby to Katie socked her in the gut. She had lost a sweet friend and had a month-old child to look after. What was she going to do?

Before Katie reached her apartment, she stopped at a superstore and bought more formula and a package of diapers. That took all the money she had. The infant's crying met her when she opened the door.

"What's wrong?" she called out and rushed toward the sound.

In the middle of Katie's bed lay the squirming child, red and wrinkled from crying. Katie picked her up and cradled her next to her heart, mingling her tears with that of the orphan babe's. Long minutes passed. The quiet of the apartment awoke Katie's reverie. Where was Madison? Katie looked through each inch of the small place, not believing her friend would leave a baby alone.

The front door opened. Madison halted when she saw Katie's glare.

"I ran to get some diapers. The bag didn't have any more, and we had a bit of an explosion."

For the first time, the stench reached Katie's nostrils. She'd been so steeped in grief she hadn't noticed.

"Okay, but you shouldn't leave her alone."

Madison handed over some wipes and a small packet of diapers to Katie. "Sorry."

"I bought some too."

"Then we should have plenty for a while."

"Yeah."

"How long are you keeping her?"

"I think forever."

"The state will never let an ex-con have custody."

"I know, especially not me."

"I'm going to work. We both work tomorrow night, so you'll have to figure it out by then."

"I know."

Katie sat on her bed with tears again flowing. Would they ever stop?

CHAPTER *Twenty-Nine*

"Kinsley Martinez."

Larry gave the name the second time to the clerk in the emergency wing. He was out of breath after jumping into his car, driving like a speed demon from Wharton Rock, and racing from his outlying parking place. He cared for Kinsley, for all the young people he'd ministered to for such a short while.

"I understand you were fired, Reverend Pullman. You have your nerve coming here." The voice came like a low growl from his right. "If Kinsley had gotten rid of that baby, she wouldn't be dead now."

A chill crept down Larry's spine. He twisted.

"Dead? No."

Nose to nose, Mr. Martinez spit venomous words out at him. "Kinsley's dead because of your assistant's stories about keeping her baby." He glowered.

Larry felt the blood drain from his face. He took a step back, but the chill swept over his entire body.

"I'm so sorry. What can I do?"

"Get out of here. That's what. You're fired. We don't want you here."

Behind them, Mrs. Martinez's sobs grew louder. The man needed to tend to his wife, but he had gone directly to the angry stage of grief.

"Yes, I was fired, but I still care. Got it?" His tone could've been nicer. *A soft answer turns away wrath.* He should've remembered before he spoke.

Mr. Martinez grabbed his wife's arm and stormed from the hospital.

Larry turned back to the clerk. "There was a woman with Kinsley Martinez. She had called 911 and, I'm sure, followed the ambulance."

"If she's still here, she'd be in Room C."

She nodded to a young man in scrubs, who showed Larry to the room. The door was open. The room was empty. Katie was gone. Larry tried to call, but it went to voice mail. After walking back to his truck, he drove to the halfway house and knocked on the door.

Wanda opened it. "Yes, may I help you?"

"I'm a friend of Katie Smith's. Is she home?"

The woman's eyes narrowed. She studied him. "I remember you bringing her in one night and picking her up another." She straightened. "She moved."

"Moved?" What a day for surprises. "When?"

"A few days ago."

"Where to?"

The woman shrugged. "She and Madison Hogue got an apartment together. Don't know where."

"Thanks."

He shuffled down the steps. The door closed behind him. He might try the restaurant or call Toby. He should know where she was living. She would've had to notify her parole officer, but he didn't want to go that route and take a chance of getting Katie in further trouble if she hadn't. He tried Toby.

"Wheeler."

"Do you know where Katie moved?"

"Katie moved? No, I didn't know. Where to?"

"That's what I was hoping you might tell me. A mutual friend passed away. Katie shouldn't be alone." *But does she need me?*

"Let me know if you find out."

"Will do."

Larry's next stop was the restaurant. When he asked Paul, he motioned to the server near the window.

"That's Madison. I think they're rooming together."

After thanking the restaurant manager, Larry stopped the server and asked. The look the girl gave him resembled that of Mr. Martinez, though he couldn't imagine what he'd ever done to her. He didn't even know her.

"Who wants to know?"

"I'm a friend of Katie's. We had a mutual friend die."

"You could call her."

"She's not answering my calls." He kept his gaze steady and severe.

She huffed. "Maybe that's your answer."

"Please."

The plea in his eyes must have looked sincere because she wrote on her menu pad, tore out the sheet, and handed it to him. "Here."

"Thank you."

He drove to the address. It had been over an hour since Katie had called him. How was she taking this? Was she home? Why did he care?

When he spotted the red Honda, his neck muscles relaxed, his breath released. Her apartment door was ajar. Holding an infant, Katie paced and cooed. She looked up before he could knock, and she stopped in the middle of the almost empty living room. A red puffiness turned her eyes into mere slits.

"She's gone and left me her baby. She wanted *me* to keep Baby Katie, but a teenage girl isn't supposed to die. What am I going to do?"

He entered, closed the door behind him, and embraced both Katie and the crying baby. Katie's skin was icy. He stood firmly, allowing her to borrow his warmth while she spilled out her grief.

When she pulled away, she turned her diva-gorgeous blue eyes to him in silent supplication. How he wished he could give her answers, but he was fresh out.

"I doubt you'll be allowed to keep the baby, even if you're willing. Kinsley's parents, or Child Protective Services, will take her.

"No." Katie clutched the child to her breast. "She's mine. Kinsley wanted me to have her."

"Be realistic, Katie."

"You be realistic and face facts, you and your policeman friends. She's mine."

Her face screwed up like the raisins in his morning cereal. He blew out a breath. What obligation did he have in this?

"Katie, I—"

"You should probably leave. Thanks for checking on me."

His phone rang. The call originated from Wharton Rock Community Church, his home church.

"Pullman."

"Hello, this is Pastor Lloyd. Any chance you could come today and talk with me."

Larry glanced at Katie. She had retreated to her bedroom. The baby squirmed beside her on the bed.

"Yeah, I could be there in about half an hour."

Katie knew when Larry left. Her body warmth vanished. Her soul comfort faded. She sagged to the bed, the babe across her heaving chest.

Moments later, a knock sounded. He'd returned. She eased out from under Baby Katie. One glance out the front door's peephole told a different story. She opened up.

"What are you doing here?"

All she needed was a drug dealer when it appeared she might be in the clear herself. Collin threw up open palms.

"I'm clean. I promise."

"I've heard that before."

Baby Katie awoke and cried. Katie turned to her bedroom. Collin followed her and closed the apartment door.

"Love the furniture." He chuckled.

"It's called no money."

Katie changed a diaper and picked up the baby, wrapping her into a tight pouch like she'd seen the hospital do. She walked back across the living room and sat in one of the two dining chairs in the kitchen. Collin sat in the other.

"Where did that come from?"

"You mean my new daughter?"

He frowned and sighed. Katie straightened.

"A young friend asked me to keep the baby if anything happened to her." Dropping her head, she gnawed her lip. "She died earlier today."

"Come live with me, Katie." He squatted at her feet.

A jolt of electricity zipped straight through her heart. The day she'd met Collin, he'd done the same thing. She'd been so full of hope. He was spontaneous, fun, and wanted her. She gnawed her lip again.

"I can't."

She also remembered the abuse, the drugs, and the betrayals.

"Live with me. I'm sorry I treated you wrong. I was strung out on coke. I'm going to NA three times a week. I need you to keep me straight." He shielded himself with waving hands. "No strings."

"And just why would I do that when I've finally got a place of my own?"

"Your own? Or Madison's?"

"She paid the deposit, but I'll pay her back." Katie shook her head. "Anyway, it's none of your business."

"Madison isn't your friend."

"A lot more friend than you."

Saliva collected in her mouth with the sting of sucking lemons. Baby Katie burped.

"She framed you."

"And you would know this how?"

"Drug dealers have their sources. You know that."

Katie shifted the baby and wiped the milk off the rosebud lips.

"Nicole framed me."

"Nicole wasn't there the last time."

Tension stiffened Katie's back. "How did you know?"

"I told you—"

In unison, they said, "drug dealers have their sources."

"Nicole was a customer. I passed her on to a dealer friend of mine." Collin paced. "Look, I'm sorry. I treated you bad, but Madison isn't your friend, and I need you." He squatted again and fingered the baby's blanket sprawled across Katie's lap. "You bring out the good in me, Katie. I don't understand it, but you do."

She giggled. "Me, the ex-con?"

"Wayne got you all mixed up. You needed money. I understand that."

"Yeah, I guess you do."

Madison bounded through the front door. Her eyes locked onto Collin, a laser of ire with flashes of rage. Her chest rose and fell. Her fists balled.

"What are you doing here?"

Katie snickered. "I said the same thing."

"I came to check up on you, Miss Madison." His glare looked more like a threat, less like a welcome. He glanced over at Katie. "Think about it." With one more eye dart directed toward her roommate, he marched out the door.

Madison's heaving slowed. Her expression softened. Without a word, she went to her room and closed the door.

Friend or foe? Katie was never so confused in all her life.

CHAPTER  Thirty

"We sure will miss you around here." Toby leaned back in his chair. "You're a real asset, but I understand the call to ministry that burns in you, and I'm grateful for it."

With legs balanced, Larry stood ramrod straight, hands to his sides.

"I'll miss being a policeman. I love it. But I won't be gone for a month yet. Got to work here until my full pay kicks in." He gave a wry smile.

"Going to seem strange going from being your boss to having you be my pastor."

"Nothing will change. We'll still be friends."

"Yep, that we will." Toby rose, walked around his desk, and stretched forth his hand. "Congratulations, Reverend Pullman."

Larry shook the hand and rocked back on his left leg. He nodded.

"What's the order for today?"

"We've got a report of a body found near Buffalo Lake. Come with me to check it out."

"Yes, sir." He gave a quick bow. His mama taught him to show respect and be a gentleman, and by Jove, he'd do his best.

"I'll be there in a minute. Have a call to return first."

Larry's cell sent out a bugle call about the time he reached his desk. "Pullman."

"Hi, Larry." The feminine voice was soft and seductive, and he was at a loss.

"Hello, may I help you?"

"This is Michelle. Don't you remember me?" The voice lost all sexual innuendo.

A vision flashed through his mind of a beautiful redhead sitting on his youth minister's desk, ready to share stories when he had needed studying time. Right before he was fired. His replacement.

"How's it going with the youth group?" he asked.

"Oh, Larry, it's a lot harder than I imagined. Last night, I started my devotion three times. The noise level drowned out my words until I threw up my hands and walked out." She lowered her voice a notch. "Not my finest moment."

"I'm sorry. Teens can be a handful." Had he misjudged Michelle? She seemed vulnerable, scared, real. God would want him to help her. "Guess you heard about Kinsley?"

"Oh, yes, so sad. The punishment for sin, I guess."

"God doesn't punish us that way, Michelle. It was just in His plan after the sin. That's all."

"I have so much to learn. Could we meet?"

Toby strode out of his office.

"Dinner would be nice." He meant it. "I'm at work, so I must go. I'll call you tonight. Okay?"

"Yes, that would be lovely."

Now why did I do that? Larry left for his current date with a murder victim.

"Ty Holden." Toby swatted his leg with his Stetson. "By George, life ain't fair. This man was really trying to go straight."

"Looks like his past caught up with him anyway." Larry examined the specks on Ty's chest. "Gravel?" He lifted some to his nose. "Yeah. I don't think this is the crime scene. Nothing here but sand."

"There's a gravel pit around the left back from the lake. I'll show you." Toby headed off.

In about ten minutes, they came to a spot up from the lake and a hundred yards above it. They used their fingers like rakes but found nothing.

"Might have to get old restaurant Willie's hound dog out here," Toby said.

They returned to the body about the time the county medical examiner arrived with his team. Toby picked up the dead man's hand to read letters on the open palm.

"Slau."

His gaze rose to meet Larry's. Larry shrugged.

"What was that guy's name you arrested back right before I left for seminary, the one who broke into Dairyland?"

"Slaughter. Good thinking, Pullman. Check that out. By George, I'm going to miss you."

Larry was comfortable with police work. It suited him and was one reason he chose to give a month's notice. He needed transition. Guilt didn't keep him from being a good cop, but being a shepherd to the people he loved, that scared him to death.

God gave Larry a second chance. He longed to tell others about God's love. But minister? *Why, Lord?*

"You coming, Pullman, or did you decide to lie down and play dead yourself."

Toby's voice came from behind Larry. His ears flamed. He twisted around to see Toby climbing into the driver's side of the squad car. Larry ran to catch up. Toby gunned it.

"You seem distracted. Short timer's attitude already?"

Raking fingers through his hair, Larry recalled his fingers last going through the gravel at the possible murder scene. He dropped his hands. One rubbed his aching leg. Seemed it never became totally pain free since the shooting. Was God telling him that was why he should give up police work?

"Toby to Larry. Over." Toby's grin covered the right side of his face, a bit mocking.

"Sorry. Got a lot on my mind."

"Want to talk about it. I've been told I'm a good listener."

"Who by? Lacey?" Larry sniffed but let his warm smile cover his unease.

Toby ducked his head to the right to check for traffic and then turned onto the highway. Larry faced forward, his body tense, while he argued with himself over his suitability for this new ministry.

"You went to seminary to become a pastor. That's what you said. Now you've got a church. Have you decided that's not what you want?"

Boy, did that hit a nerve. "God called me to win the lost for Christ."

Larry's jaw tightened. Tendons strained as he pushed against the dash. "Okay. So . . ."

"But I shouldn't be a pastor. I'm not fit." If Reverend Lloyd knew Larry's past, he wouldn't have asked him to take over the church. Should Larry tell him?

"You finished seminary with high grades." Toby sounded and looked perplexed.

"Yeah."

"Is my hard drive out of whack? What am I missing?"

"I'm not worthy to preach Christ."

"Not worthy? Or not willing?"

Larry's heart skipped a beat. He rubbed the leg harder. The car's oxygen level seemed to drop. Toby turned on a cross road.

"I'm thinking you're identifying with Jonah."

"I'm not running from God. You forget that I've already served as a youth minister." He stiffened his back against the seat.

Toby took a softened tone. "But that was temporary, and it was teens. And you were fired."

Pow! Larry slammed the glove compartment. Blood seeped from two tiny cuts across his knuckles. What a childish gesture. He slumped into the seat, as if he could, if he tried, disappear.

"First aid cream in the glove compartment."

"Thanks."

Larry opened it and dressed the cuts. Silence settled like poison gas. Oil derricks pumped on the right. The Wharton Rock loomed behind them. An occasional farm house stood in the midst of a cove of trees on the vast North Texas plains.

After entering the town named for the rock, Toby pulled the police car into a parking space beside the station. Larry opened his door.

"Wait." Toby used his boss tone.

Larry did as asked.

"When I hired you as a patrolman, I checked your background and your credit. I found nothing to prevent you from serving. I know you were raised in Apache Falls and moved here with your mother shortly after your high school graduation. If you're keeping anything back from the church that would hinder your ministry, you need to let us know. That's all I'm going to say. If you want to talk, you know where to find me." He got out and strode into the office.

Self-incrimination sent tingles down Larry's spine. Toby was right. Larry was being dishonest, not a good recommendation for the shepherd of a church. If Reverend Lloyd and the church board were willing to take on the handicap of a pastor without a wife, he at least owed it to them to confess his wayward youth and maybe actively seek a Christian life partner. Someone besides Katie, who wanted no part of him or his God.

He dialed the Wharton Rock Community Church and was soon connected to Reverend Lloyd.

When his shift at the police department ended, Larry's appointment with the church board began. His only time for prayer was during the five minute drive, but God's peace followed him into the church office.

Six board members clustered in various chairs around the pastor's study. Serving still as pastor, Reverend Lloyd was behind the desk. Larry slipped into the chair saved for him. His leg bobbed up and down against the floor, making a racket until he steadied it. *Pop!* He sat on his hands to fend off more knuckle crunching. Seven pairs of eyes zeroed in on his antics, obviously waiting for him to begin. He stood again and cleared his throat.

"Two days before my fourteenth birthday, my dad died." His voice broke. His eyes stung. "I was so angry at God for taking him. I dropped out of church, joined a gang in our neighborhood, and caused my mother enormous grief."

The memory choked him. He coughed, sputtered, and swallowed several times. Pacing the small space in the room left for him, he closed his eyes against visions that tormented him to this day. A syndicate boss that convinced him of friendship. His childhood friend, Dennis, bleeding out in his arms. Larry's mother crying when he was arrested for car theft. He halted, cracked a knuckle, and smoothed his neatly-trimmed mustache.

"Ricky became like a dad to me. We played ball. We sat around a fire and talked. When he showed me how to hot-wire a car and drive off, he made it sound like fun, but the first time I did it, I was so scared."

Several coughs peppered the ensuing quiet. Again, he paced and talked.

"Ricky ran contests. The boy who stole the most cars won great prizes. One week, I was the top guy and won a TV. So proud of my accomplishment, I took it home to my mother." He snickered. "She threw her iron at it, crashing the screen."

The noisy air conditioning shut off. Larry stiffened. One finger tapped his jaw. His injured leg throbbed.

"It was all meant to be fun. Just boys being crazy. No one would get hurt."

Reverend Lloyd's quiet voice interrupted Larry's monologue. "But they did."

Larry's head jerked up. "Yes. The police raided our clubhouse. They shot my friend. I was arrested."

With his elbow propped on top of his knees, one of the deacons, Ted Ferguson, held his chin in his hand.

"I don't understand. If you had a criminal record, how could you be a police officer?"

"Several of the guys did get a record. I was only seventeen. Praise God, my record was sealed. Had it not been, I couldn't have been a policeman or gone to seminary." With his leg hurting more and more, Larry retook his seat. "When I got out of jail, I ran to the church, fell at the altar, and pleaded for God's forgiveness. He gave me a second chance."

Several had other questions. Larry was unable to read the mood.

"When did God call you to the ministry?" Reverend Lloyd asked.

"When I was thirteen."

"So, before all the car thefts."

"Yes, sir. When I came back to God, He renewed His call. For years, I ran from it. You see, I'm not good enough to preach Jesus. I want to tell others they can have a second chance like I did. But minister? I'm just not worthy. I owe it to you to explain. I'm only whole through God's grace."

Several shook their head. Reverend Lloyd stood.

"Seems to me that's the reason we're all here. Without God's grace, none would be worthy to serve."

One man said, "Amen."

"If you don't mind, will you wait in the outer office while we discuss what you've told us?" Reverend Lloyd said.

"Yes, sir."

Larry stepped out and paced a rut in the old carpet while he waited. Despite the air conditioning blast, sweat dampened his underarms. Flies leapfrogged about his stomach, leaving him almost sick before the inner door opened. Reverend Lloyd was still standing but offered Larry time to sit.

"With today's vote, we still would like to invite you to be our pastor. What's good enough for God is good enough for us." The old pastor beamed.

With one long sigh, a load dropped from Larry. God forgave him. So had this church's leadership. He couldn't stop the moisture forming in his eyes. He blinked.

"Thank you so much."

"Thank you, young man. That took courage. I'm more convinced than ever that you're the man for the job."

"Thank you, Pastor."

"You mentioned seeking a wife to help you." The man's eyes danced with mirth.

"Yes, sir, a lady I worked with at the Apache Falls church."

Pounding Larry's back, the pastor smiled brighter. "Good luck. Any girl would be blessed to have you as a husband."

"Thanks."

After everyone dispersed, Larry walked to his car and dialed. He had promised and somehow felt excited about it.

"You did call."

Michelle was back to her soft tone. He could almost see her sexy smile. She was a good woman. They had gotten off on the wrong foot since he'd had eyes for the impossible.

"You free for dinner tomorrow night?"

The restaurant's atmosphere was conducive to romance. Larry and Michelle sat in the corner—the lighting low, the music soft, the Italian dishes delicious.

What did it remind Larry of? Katie talking about the lack of any privacy in prison. *Shame on me.* He shifted positions and concentrated on Michelle's telling about when she and Reverend Schumacher visited Kinsley's parents.

"They're, of course, so distraught. It's so sad. It shouldn't have happened. Sin caused Kinsley's death. I know you thought she should be allowed to have the baby, and I don't believe in abortion either, but it's just so stinking sad." Michelle's lower lip covered her upper one.

"I agree, but abortion wasn't the answer. It just happened."

"God's will?" Her gaze lifted to him.

The Scripture from Esther came to his mind. *For such a time as this.* He placed a hand across Michelle's long, slender fingers with soft-pink nails.

"The Christian life isn't a democracy, Michelle. God reigns sovereign. He decides who lives and dies and when that happens. He's the only just judge."

Her eyes glistened with unshed tears. "I don't understand."

"I don't either."

Her hand pulled away as she reached for a tissue.

"So, tell me about Wednesday night."

"It was awful. How did you do it?"

"Seeking help."

Her eyes widened after she dried them. "You didn't have an assistant at first."

"I didn't have an assistant at all."

"Then how?"

"Ryan is a real leader. Cody guides them into worship if you allow him to play his guitar."

She dropped her hands to her lap. "I never thought of that. I made everyone sit, and I tried to teach."

"No music?"

"Well, I don't sing." Her tone was soft. She picked lint off her linen jacket. "So, I should ask Cody to get them singing first. Good idea."

By the time the two left the restaurant, he'd shared lots of ideas. Michelle seemed receptive. A peace settled over him. He felt like God had used him.

He pulled into Michelle's apartment building lot and parked near her spot. He circled the car and held open her door.

"You're such a gentleman, Larry. I'm so proud of you for taking over as pastor of your local church. What an exciting opportunity."

When she stood, her face came within inches of his chest. She lifted her head and licked her lips. A jittery feeling turned his stomach. His leg jerked. With it hard to breathe, he shifted away from her and offered an I'm-not-ready smile. She dropped her head and moved around him.

"Call me."

"I will. Honest. I will."

Her smile broadened. "You really will?"

He stood ramrod straight. The jerking eased. He nodded, then ushered her up the sidewalk. When she opened her door, he gave a brief wave and walked back to his car.

Michelle would make a wonderful pastor's wife. She loved God. She was willing to work in church, and she cared for him. He was sure of that. Then why did he keep comparing her with Katie, who didn't love God and didn't care?

CHAPTER *Thirty-One*

Katie's cell played a tune. Her head ached. She opened one eye to look at the screen. Seven in the morning. The baby had fallen asleep at five. It was Lacey.

"Hello."

"Did I wake you?"

No, sis. I never sleep more than two hours. "Mmmm."

"Sorry." Lacey sounded way too bright for this early.

Katie rose on one elbow. Baby Katie slept on.

"What's the problem?"

Lacey's voice softened. "How did you know anything was wrong?"

"No way you'd call me to catch up, sugar." The sound of sobbing reached out and brought Katie fully awake. "Is Rachel okay?"

"Yeah, she's fine. It's me."

"Look, sis, I haven't had much sleep. I worked yesterday, and the baby cried all night. I'm exhausted. I don't feel up to chitchat. I need sleep. If you have a problem, spill it." Katie's tone was sharp and cranky, but it's how she felt.

"Just forget it." Lacey hung up.

Katie dialed back.

"Look, do you need something or not?"

"Toby is short-handed and can't get away. Mom has a stomach virus. Rachel is out of school. I'm so weak and sick. Look, I've called everyone I know, and no one can take Rachel today. I thought maybe . . ." She paused and then struck. "Well, you are the girl's biological mother."

Katie guffawed. "I love it. You need me."

"Don't enjoy it so much."

"I can't believe it. My always-competent big sister needs her screw up little ex-con sister." This was priceless. "What's wrong with you anyway?"

"Cancer. Shingles."

Katie sobered. "I'll shower, dress, and grab the baby. We'll be there in forty minutes."

"Thanks."

"Sure. Why didn't you tell me?"

"It hasn't come up."

"Yeah. Guess we haven't talked since I left. Did you know then?"

"Suspected. What baby are you keeping?"

"Mine."

Silence. Then, "I'm not touching that. See you when you get here. Thank you."

"Yep."

Hot water blasted Katie's shoulders and back, easing the tiredness, waking her up. She dressed. It was now twenty after seven. She'd wait until later to call Paul, and she'd leave a note for Madison. No use waking up everyone this early.

The drawer of an old chest made into a bassinet remained quiet. Now the baby slept instead of earlier in the night.

Tiptoeing to the kitchen, Katie searched for a sack to serve as her suit-case. Whispering behind Madison's closed door carried through the quiet house. Katie couldn't help but listen. A male voice came across louder, especially his laugh.

"Like you care. You planning on leaving drugs on her bed again?"

"Shh."

Madison?

Splat!

"What you hitting me for?" The male voice again.

"She might hear you." Madison, only louder.

Frozen in place, Katie waited. Collin had been right. Madison wasn't her friend.

The male voice was familiar. He was up, roaming around Madison's room. *Going to the bathroom? Coming to the kitchen?*

Katie rushed back to her room, her heart galloping like a horse racing across the open plains. She swallowed and willed her pulse to slow. She threw underwear, jeans, tops, and driver's license along with diapers and wipes into one of the empty moving boxes. Perching the box against one hip, she swaddled the infant to her chest with the other arm and slipped through her bedroom door, letting the note drop to a living room chair where Madison would find it.

The sounds from the other bedroom were more raucous than teasing. Katie ran for the front door. She was down the steps before a man came to the balcony, yelling.

"Hey, Madison wants to know where you're going."

"Got a call from my sister. She needs help. I left Madison a note. I didn't want to wake her."

He blinked. Under an overhead light, his face reddened.

"Oh, okay, I'll tell her." He turned and went back inside.

Katie knew why the voice was familiar. That was the man who had stolen her car at Collin's apartment. How did Madison end up with the thief? Did she arrange it? Was Collin in on it?

Thunder crashed overhead. In front of her, lightning streaked across the sky. Her questions brought turmoil. Rage coursed through her mind. Buckling a seatbelt across the baby and starting the car with her trembling fingers was no small task. She sped off, fighting to keep the Honda in one lane.

Baby Katie awoke. The same squeals Katie had fought all night began anew. Was she hungry or wet or just scared, like her guardian?

Rain lashed the windshield. The clashes of thunder drowned out the backseat screams. Katie battled the car onto the main highway. Her headlights pierced the darkness of the storm. The center line was her guide on a morning where daylight was diminished.

An emptiness settled on Katie. She had no one. Madison had been her only friend. Katie had to be the worst judge of character ever. That made her wonder about Larry. She'd judged him harshly. He'd been the best thing that had ever happened to her, but she tossed him aside like drug's temptation.

Alone. Unwanted. Unloved.

The usual twenty minute drive took thirty-three. Finally, she parked in front of her old home, now Lacey and Toby's abode. When she got out, the rain plastered her curls to her head. When, at last, she undid the belt around Katie's blanket, she clutched the shaking child to her breast, holding the saturated blanket to block some of the rain, and ran for the covered porch. The next paycheck had to go for a car seat. Her brother-in-law might give her a ticket.

She lifted off the wet blanket. Baby Katie's cries increased. She shook from head to toe. So did big Katie. She knocked. The door was answered by Rachel. Her eyes widened.

"A baby? Where did you get a baby? Can we keep it?"

Katie slid through the door, running first to the sofa to strip the chilled baby girl.

"Can you get Mama a dry blanket out of that bag?" She pointed to where she'd dropped the polka-dot diaper bag in a rush to find warmth.

By the time Rachel handed her the extra threadbare blanket, Katie had the baby stripped except for her diaper, so she wrapped her into a baby burrito. She rocked and swayed until the cries slowed. Turning to Rachel, she said, "Show me where your Aunt Lacey is."

Rachel skipped away, almost tripping Mom hobbling from the kitchen. Katie reached out a hand to stabilize her.

"Mom, you okay?"

"Yeah. Got a stomach bug." Her face screwed into a mass of wrinkles. "I called for Rachel to get me some crackers, but she ran to open the door instead." Her milky blue eyes glared at Katie, as if all the misery was her baby daughter's fault.

All I did was knock.

Mom gripped three crackers.

"I see you got them," Katie said. "I'll get you a glass of water as soon as I go check on Lacey."

"What's that?" Mom's focus moved to the squirming bundle in Katie's arms.

She jutted her chin. "My new daughter."

"Humph." Mom shuffled on to her room.

"Is she really ours?" Rachel opened the blanket a little to peek in. "She's not very big, is she?"

"No, she's not. That's why we have to take care of her."

"I'll be real gentle if you let me hold her."

"Maybe later."

Rachel had wound through the kitchen and dining room and entered Lacey's bedroom.

"Mama . . . ah . . . I mean . . . ah . . ." Rachel giggled. "Mama, my mama is here."

"Thanks, sweetie. Show her in." Lacey's voice was either breathless or hoarse, or just weak.

Katie moved into the room. Her mouth opened, but no words came. Lacey's long, dark hair had always been so thick and full. Now it was scraggly and thin. Big red blisters covered her right shoulder. The light in her brown eyes was gone. Katie inched toward her sister. Her hand reached out to touch her shoulder. Lacey winced. Katie jumped back.

"I'm sorry. Did I hurt you?"

Rachel lugged a dining chair close to the bed and a child's chair next to it. She sat there.

"We can't sit on the bed. It hurts my mama." Her eyes turned serious. She was so grown up for only eight.

"That's right." Lacey cupped the girls head, with long brown hair like her aunt's. "Thank you for helping. What would I do without my big girl?"

Rachel smiled and spread out her skirt, as if visiting a queen.

Katie sat in the big chair her daughter had brought for her. Thankful that Baby Katie had dosed off again, she looked up at her sister.

"I'm not much of a nursemaid, so tell me what I should do."

Tears welled in Lacey's eyes.

"Thank you for coming. I didn't know what to do. These shingles are giving me excruciating pain. I can't do anything."

"Your hair." Katie brushed through the top of her sister's hair.

"Chemo."

"Where's the cancer?"

"My breast."

"When did you find out?"

"Actually, the day you went back to Apache Falls."

A flush heated Katie's cheeks. "I'm so sorry."

Lacey touched Katie's knee and then reached so her fingertips caressed the baby's hand.

"She's beautiful. You'll have to tell me the story sometime when I feel better. As for what to do, whatever you see. Play with Rachel. In a while, get lunch for Rachel and Mom, and yourself, of course. Just let me rest."

Katie jumped to her feet. "I will. We'll be fine. Call if you need us."

She ushered Rachel from the room.

"Let me check on Grandma, and then we'll play a game of Go Fish. How's that?"

Rachel clapped her hands and bobbed her head.

Katie shifted the baby to get ice water for Mom and then peeked into her room.

"Here's your drink. Anything else I can do?"

Mom had several tasks. Rachel wanted to keep playing. Baby Katie slept on her blanket in the corner. Katie forgot to call her boss until two hours before she was due to be at work. He was mad.

CHAPTER *Thirty-Two*

A piece of peanut butter fudge sounded so good right now. Like that would solve everything. *No!* God won a great victory in Lacey's life three years ago. She wouldn't undo it because of a few trials. If she could get through her adopted daughter's kidnapping, she could get through cancer. And shingles. Though the shingles had been her biggest challenge yet. The pain never stopped.

Toby strolled into the bedroom. "Want me to rub that cream the doctor gave you over the blisters?"

"Yeah."

She eased over on her stomach. A painful rash lined her spine, went over her right shoulder, and covered her right ear. Toby's rough fingers smeared the prescription cream down her back. Her breath caught. She moaned. Never had she experienced such a throbbing ache. His hand pulled back. Her rough cop husband sniffed and swiped.

"I'm so sorry."

"It's okay. Everything hurts."

"I can't touch it any more gently."

"I know." It became easier for her to breathe. "Toby?"

"Yeah." He lay across the bed, facing her.

"Are you sure you don't love Katie?"

He'd sworn that what Wanda saw was a sisterly thank you for helping her escape a frame up, but with Lacey so weak and ugly, the worry still nagged.

"Of course not, silly. I won over the best sister. I'd be a fool to look further." He tweaked her nose. "Now, you quit worrying about me and just work at getting well."

She aimed for a gleaming smile, but it was weak, like the rest of her.

"I'm thankful to Katie for coming."

"Oh, I am too." He lifted the sweaty wisps off his wife's brow. "I am worried over the situation with the baby. I've made inquiries, but so far, it does seem that the baby's relatives don't intend to search for her."

"That's sad. Katie does seem to love that baby."

"Humph," Toby mumbled.

"Toby?"

"Yeah?" Mischief danced in his eyes.

"We knocked Katie out of her job."

"Shall we pay her a salary?"

With some measure of relief, her lids were heavy.

"She needs a car seat for Baby Katie."

"I'll bring one home. Now sleep."

"Mmmm."

She drifted off in slumber, dreaming about a time when she and Katie were children, and she had taken Katie's hand and helped her cross the street. She had been such a pretty little girl with those blonde curls and eyes almost as dark a blue as Toby's.

"Katie." Mom's voice boomed, sure to wake up her younger daughter.

Katie scanned her environment, trying to remember where she was. Red, green, and brown recliners lined up in a row across from a forty inch TV. To the side of the room, a sofa with mounded blankets and pillows served as her bed. On the floor beside her, a baby blanket covered the infant, who, thankfully, kept sleeping. Three days of waking in this spot had still not prepared her for the morning sight. She ran to help her mother before she woke up the baby.

"What?"

"I can't find my crutch. I know I put it to the side of the night stand."

The covers wound around Mom like the burrito Katie turned the baby into. Katie spotted the crutch and picked it up.

"It slipped under your bed. Here."

"Thank you, sweetheart. I'm so glad you decided to come home."

Like I had a choice. Well, maybe she did, but she wasn't heartless. She loved her family, despite their constant interference and attempts at control.

"Oh, it's time to get Rachel up for school." Katie dashed out of the room, wondering if she'd ever get used to this hectic lifestyle. "Wake up, Rachel." Katie shook the child and started toward the kitchen. "I'll get you a bowl of cereal."

"Don't want cereal. Want eggs."

Katie cringed. "Sure, sweetie."

She ran to the kitchen, broke an egg into a bowl, picked out the shell, and scrambled it in a pan. On second thought, she broke two more. Sure enough, Mom came to the kitchen door.

"Make me two eggs too."

"Waah!"

Baby Katie was awake and needed changing and feeding. Well, she'd have to wait a moment. No sound came from Rachel's room. Sure enough, the girl was back asleep when Katie shook again.

"Get up." Her voice was sharper than she intended.

The girl sobbed. "I'm sleepy."

Katie went to the closet. "Would you like to wear your purple shirt today?"

"No. Jeremy made fun of me. I never want to wear it again." Rachel sat on the side of the bed. "Want the red flag shirt."

Katie thumbed through the choices. "I don't see one."

Mom poised behind Katie. "Needs washing."

Laundry. This was crazy. "How about you wear the blue one with the panda bear today. I'll wash the red one, and you can wear it tomorrow."

Rachel began crying.

"Look," Katie held up the blue shirt. "This shows off your beautiful brown hair."

Damp eyes glistened, but Rachel nodded.

Katie ran for the baby, jostling her with coos. A terrible scent accosted her nose. She ran for the kitchen. The eggs were burned. She poured water into the skillet and found another. Needing both hands, she laid the baby on the floor and cracked three more eggs. Baby Katie squealed as soon as she touched the cold floor. Pajama-clad Toby shuffled in about the time Katie found another pan.

"What's burning?"

Lacey eased in behind him. Seeing the mess, she yelled, "What in the world happened?"

Tears ran down Katie's cheeks. The sobs grew heavier. She hid her face in the baby's blanket and sprawled on the floor herself. Toby yanked out a dining chair.

"Have a seat up here. I'll get the eggs."

Katie remained where she was and let the tears roll. Seven a.m., and she was already done for.

Sunday morning marked nine days in Wharton Rock for Katie. The last Sunday no one had gone to church. Not up to facing the whole town yet, she hoped that didn't change today.

"I wish I could go welcome the new pastor." Lacey nibbled on toast.

"I'm thankful your pain is less," Katie said.

"Me too. Tell him I'll come when I can."

"He'll understand."

Toby poured himself and Katie some coffee.

"I'll stay with you," Katie said.

"Nonsense. You go with the family."

Lacey bustled in the kitchen, obviously much improved.

"I have nothing to wear to church." That wasn't a lie.

Mom took her baby daughter's arm. "Folks nowadays wear jeans on Sunday morning. You'll be fine."

"That's settled," Lacey said. "I'll get a nap while you're gone, so I'll feel like enjoying my family this afternoon."

It always happened. When she was with Mom and Lacey, Katie was pushed into doing things she didn't want to do. She stiffened.

"I'll—"

Toby swallowed his last bite of breakfast. "Larry will be glad to see you, Katie. He's been worried."

Her shoulders slumped. She sucked in defeat like a familiar companion. *Church, here I come.*

While she dressed, a tingle of excitement sparked her mind. She chided herself for believing Larry might want to see her, but she couldn't calm her jumping pulse. Along with her nicest jeans, she chose her only top with sleeves and a higher neckline. How fun to find that Lacey had picked out a dress for Rachel the same color as Katie's top. Katie had brought nothing for the baby but pajamas, but Lacey insisted, if she took her to the nursery, no one but the workers would see her anyway.

Lacey slipped the dress over Rachel's head. "Do you have more clothes for Baby Katie at your apartment?"

"Nope."

"Do you have anything else for her?"

"Nope. I left a few diapers I couldn't stuff in that bag. That's it."

"Toby brought home one of the department car seats. Just until you can buy one."

A wave of discomfort hit Katie's tummy, leaving it turning and tumbling.

"Yeah. I was going to buy one with my paycheck. I have three days coming, but then I'm not working now."

Her tone trailed off. What was she going to do? It was one thing to help out family, but she needed a job.

"I'm a lot better. I should be able to get to usual activities soon."

"Really?"

Katie's mind whirled with possibilities. Maybe this was merely temporary, and Katie could go back to her life. Her life where? *With Madison? No way. Collin?* She might have to take him up on his offer, but could she trust him?

"I'm ready to go, Mom, Katie, Rachel," Toby called from the front door.

Chattering all at once, the family marched to the car. Toby had the car seat fastened in and ready. Katie buckled in the baby, while Toby hooked Rachel's seatbelt.

"Thank you, Detective Dad."

Rachel bounced on the seat. Toby reddened.

What was that all about?

In big old Wharton Rock, it took all of five minutes to reach Community Church, where they then unbuckled and got out of the car. Toby led the way.

Katie shook from her nose to her toes. The last time she'd set foot in that church was when she and Rachel were visiting for a while with Lacey and Mom—before prison, before the kidnapping, before she'd given away her daughter. Everyone would know. Katie couldn't inhale.

When she tripped going across the lobby, she almost dropped the sleeping baby. Toby caught her arm. Her face flamed. Everyone stared.

They walked down the hall. Rachel ran into her classroom, shouting friends' names. Toby led Katie to the nursery, gave the baby's name, and ushered Katie into the sanctuary beside Mom.

The dreaded middle. No escape. She crossed her right leg then shifted and kicked out her left leg. The music began. Katie faced forward.

Why was Larry sitting on the platform?

Something was dreadfully wrong. Katie's mouth was as dry as the baby's bottle that morning, which sent Toby after formula before church. She put both feet on the floor. She swallowed what little saliva she could collect. Her whole insides were on fire. A wave of nausea struck. A familiar-looking man stood.

"Most of you all know that Reverend Lloyd took retirement this past Monday. Our new pastor is no stranger to you, so without further ado, I wish to introduce Reverend Pullman."

Larry stood and strode to the pulpit.

The blood drained from Katie's face. The nausea worsened. She slipped past Toby's protruding knees and ran from the church.

CHAPTER *Thirty-Three*

The morning breeze was already stifling. Still, Katie's nausea subsided in the fresh air. The anxiety did not. On the side of the church building, she paced from the front to the back. By the time her pulse slowed, so did her steps. At the back, she turned once more and collided with Larry. His hands clasped her arms.

"What are you doing here? Shouldn't you be preaching, Reverend Pullman?"

"Everyone is singing. I only have a moment."

"Blast it all, isn't that just terrible." She broke away from his hold. "Wasn't it bad enough that you're a cop who works in your church? Did you have to be a real preacher? God deliver me."

The pacing started again, and her pulse skipped ahead of her. He raced around in front of her.

"I'm sorry. I thought you knew. I was over the youth in Apache Falls."

"But that was temporary volunteer work." She hesitated. "But it wasn't, was it?" Her hands covered her face. "What a fool I've been?"

"I never meant to deceive you. Look, I have to get back inside, but we need to talk."

With her hands still hiding her face, she shook it with a downward look.

"What about?" She turned laser eyes on him. "I'm not fit to be a preacher's girl."

She walked away. The wonderful aroma of roses on the side of the building mocked the morning's hope of seeing him. How foolish her dreams were.

His footsteps retreated. She waited. The next one to come out was Toby.

"Come back in and listen to Larry's first sermon in this church. He's been there for you. You owe it to him."

The nausea returned. Her cheeks were hot. She fanned herself with a church bulletin.

"Okay."

Toby led off. She trailed behind until she reached the back row. There, she slipped into a corner by herself.

Reverend Pullman read from Psalm 103: 8-12. "The LORD is merciful and gracious, slow to anger, and abounding in mercy. He will not always strive with us, nor will he keep his anger forever. He has not dealt with us according to our sins, nor punished us according to our iniquities. For as the heavens are high above the earth, so great is His mercy toward those who fear him; as far as the east is from the west, so far has He removed our transgressions from us."

Katie's mind focused on one sentence: "He has not dealt with us according to our sins." What did that mean?

Her first thought was to ask Larry. *Foolish.* She should stay clear of him. She'd told him once. She'd tell him again. Forget her. She was no good.

Was prison her only punishment, or did God reserve future punishment for her? No, what Larry read included something about God being slow to anger. *Slow, but sure?*

She squirmed and wiped her sweaty palms on her jeans. Lacey might explain it to her. She'd drawn closer to God when she had lost weight. Katie scooted back in the pew and lifted her head. That was a good plan.

The music director replaced Larry, leading them in song. Everyone was standing but Katie. After jumping to her feet, she walked out to search for her daughters.

Toby remained quiet on the trip home. Mom, of course, did not.

"Where in the world did you think you were going, Katie?" Mom's breathing was loud and noisy. Her knuckles were white as she braced against the dash. "I was never so embarrassed in all my life. I didn't raise you to be disrespectful in church." Her voice truly squeaked.

"I'm sorry, Mom. I was shocked."

"About what? Did you forget in three years what church was like?"

Mom would never understand. Katie's tone softened.

"I didn't know Larry was a preacher."

"So, big deal."

Mom heaved another loud intake of air. Katie clamped her mouth shut.

"Lacey was putting on a roast this morning."

Toby drove in their driveway. Katie chuckled at his changing the subject. *Wise man.* When the car stopped, she reached over to pop the buckle for Rachel and then opened the car door. The girl crawled over Katie and dashed off. Katie circled to extract the baby from the car seat while Toby assisted Mom, still huffing and moaning so they all knew she was unhappy.

Katie got the message.

By the time the group had changed clothes and sat at the table to enjoy Sunday dinner, the doorbell rang. Toby blotted his lips.

"I'll get it."

"I can't believe a salesman would call on Sunday. Ridiculous." Mom grunted.

"Is Katie Smith here?"

The voice sent jitters to Katie's insides. She had never expected Collin to follow her to Wharton Rock. She scooted out of her chair.

"Excuse me."

She went to the door. With hand raised, as if to block Collin's entrance, Toby glanced her way.

"It's okay." She eased out to the porch and turned her wrath on her old boyfriend. "What do you want?"

"I told you I wanted you to stay with me." He glanced at his feet. "Did you find out what I said about Madison was true?"

"Yes."

"I thought so. Jordan told me he thought you overheard him and Madison."

"I did."

"Last chance, sweet stuff. You have a home with me. No drugs. No pressure. I promise."

She believed him for now, but how long would it last? Lacey was there when Katie was dumped by her husband in Colorado. She was there to take Katie in when Collin was abusing her. Lacey was there to pick up Katie at the prison after she had put Lacey through torment with Rachel's kidnapping. Now, for the first time ever, Lacey needed Katie. She liked being needed. It made her feel better about herself.

"Sorry, Collin. Thanks, but the timing stinks."

"What are you going to do? Madison is looking to you for half the rent."

"Oh, boo-hoo for her."

Collin cracked a grin. "Yeah. Will you live here?" His head bobbed toward the house.

"Yeah, for now. My sister has cancer."

He scraped muddy athletic shoes against the bottom step. "I'm sorry."

"Me too."

He trudged on toward his car. "See you around."

"Yeah."

"Oh, Katie, what did you do with the kid?"

"Rachel or Katie?"

"That baby."

"Taking care of her."

"Madison said the grandmother came looking for you last week."

A numbing agent soaked through Katie's veins. It's what she'd feared but prayed wouldn't happen. With the loss of a daughter, did the couple decide a granddaughter might be a compromise? Katie had Kinsley's note, but the seizure had hit before she signed it.

"You can't win that fight." Collin laughed and left.

Larry could answer that question, as well as the one from his sermon. Maybe seeing him just once more would be okay.

CHAPTER *Thirty-Four*

The Sunday afternoon picnic and walk with Michelle had been just what Larry needed, relaxing and mind clearing. His nerves were stretched like a too-full-of-air balloon. Minister by day. Cop by night. This month of double duty was taking its toll.

Then there was Katie. Several times he had picked up his phone with the idea of calling her for a we-need-to-clear-the-air talk. He hadn't been fair. He knew she thought of him only as a policeman who was helping in church, and he'd allowed her to keep thinking that. After all, being a cop was one black mark in her book. Being a minister was a long, dark smudge.

He'd been so foolish, letting a pair of iridescent-blue eyes charm him into denying the call of God on his life. *Never again.* Michelle was pastor's wife material.

Then why, God? Why couldn't he get the blue-eyed ex-con out of his mind?

Sitting in his chair behind Amber, the receptionist at the police station, his mouth dropped in disbelief, and he leapt to his feet. Katie Smith had entered and was walking toward Amber.

"Is Larry Pullman . . . ?" Her gaze drifted backward. "Oh, hi." She sent him a half wave.

Leaning against his desk, he straightened and nodded.

"Katie, what might I do for you?"

The receptionist returned to her keyboard. Katie moved to face him.

"Can we talk?" Her voice was low.

He motioned to the chair.

With a brief scan, Katie took in the office, glancing toward the back room where Toby usually sat. Her cheeks were scarlet. Her eyes were hypnotizing. *Drat it!* Larry almost missed his seat when he lowered his body. Privacy was best for this kind of talk.

"I need to go out to Buffalo Lake to check out a few things," he said. "You got time to drive out there with me?"

She nodded. He ushered her out the door.

When they were seated in his truck, Katie unfolded a slip of paper for him to view.

"This is all I have. Could I win if Baby Katie's grandparents try to take her?"

The hand scrawled note read: *Being of sound mind on this day, I request that Katie Smith be allowed to rear my child, Katie Marie Martinez. Upon my death, I give her full custody. K . . .*

"I take it Kinsley wrote this."

Katie's cheeks lost some of their red tinge, but she'd crossed and recrossed her legs numerous times. Her chin lifted. Her lips narrowed. She nodded.

"Right before her last seizure. She brought the baby to my house, laid her on the floor, and had this note in her hand. I guess she got too sick to finish signing her name. When I couldn't help, I called 911." She lowered her head. "As you know, she didn't recover."

"Kinsley's parents didn't want the baby?"

"No. And Kinsley didn't want them to have her."

"Child Protective Services will pick up her up and put her in foster care."

"They can do that?"

Larry nodded. "If the family doesn't want her."

"They might now."

"How do you know?"

"Collin said they stopped by the apartment last week and asked where I was."

His body tensed. "Oh, yes . . ." His words trailed off. "Collin." He cleared his throat and drummed up some cop steel. "You living with him again?" How could she after the way he'd treated her last time? If she was around drugs, she'd be back behind bars in no time. Then where would the baby be?

A spark lit her eyes. "No." Her tone was defensive. "Besides, where I live is no business of yours, preacher man." She faced the window.

He cringed and turned the ignition. He wound through the city streets to the freeway before he continued the conversation.

"I apologize. You were right. I didn't make it clear that the youth group was my job. I didn't tell you that I was in the hospital with a gunshot to my leg your first two weeks in prison. I didn't tell you that when I got through rehab I registered for seminary in Fort Worth and have been searching for months for a job in ministry. Guess I didn't tell you a lot, and I'm sorry."

Wind whipped trash left by the side of the road onto the windshield. A soft voice from the radio advertised the Apache Falls tire place on Southwest Boulevard. Katie's fingers drummed on the arm rest. He couldn't take it anymore.

"Katie?"

"What?"

"I said I'm sorry."

"What am I supposed to say? You're forgiven?" Tears pooled in the corners of her eyes. "Well, it hurt to see you up there and know you'd lied to me." Her brows lifted. "Were you shot during Rachel's rescue from the kidnappers?"

"Yes."

That helpless feeling rushed in on him again, that moment he realized he would be a cripple for life. He swallowed the lump forming in his throat. A quivery sensation tickled the back of his neck.

"I'm sorry." Her head dropped to her chest. "Is that why you decided to change careers?"

His hands gripped the wheel tighter.

"No. Back in my rebellious youth, God gave me a second chance, and He called me into the ministry. For years, I lived in denial. Laid up in the hospital and at home, I had way too much time to think. I decided to quit running from God."

She snickered. "Yeah, I'll bet you were a real bad kid. What did you do? Stick gum underneath your desk at school?"

His jaw tightened. The lump in his throat enlarged. "Stole cars."

"You what?"

"Stole—"

"Cars. Yes, I heard you. Then how could you be a policeman or even a preacher if you have a record?"

"I never got charged with anything worse than a misdemeanor. It started when my dad died. I was fourteen. It stopped when I turned seventeen." He glanced her way. His neck was hot and itchy. "I'm not proud of it, Katie. I'm just thankful to be forgiven."

She gnawed the nail on her pointer finger. "That's something else I wanted to ask. You gave a Bible verse last Sunday that I didn't understand, something about God not dealing with us according to our sin. You mean God doesn't care if we sin? That can't be right."

Larry went back to the Scripture and gave a condensed version of his message.

"God forgives our sin and puts it out of His mind forever."

"Ah, but can God forgive every sin?" She glared at her nail and sat on her hand.

"Every sin."

"Even drugs?"

"Even drugs."

Her voice softened. "Even having your daughter kidnapped?"

He reached across the console and tugged her hand out from under her legs.

"Even that. All you have to do is ask God to forgive you. He will, and it will be just as if you had never sinned as far as God is concerned."

His heart raced. This was the part of ministry he loved, drawing sinners to Christ. He would love to see Katie get a second chance.

Her hand lay warm in his. He longed to keep holding it, but he was at the crime scene. He took back his hand and stopped the truck. Her red cheeks now held a rosy glow. The moisture made her eyes sparkle. It was the first time he'd seen any trust in her expression. He hated to shut it down.

"Just sit here. I've got to walk over that area between here and the lake. Be back in a few minutes."

Her nail biting began again. By the time he reached the spot where the body had been found, she was out of the truck and following.

"What are you looking for?"

He explained about the body. "Toby found a tie into the drug traffic around here. He wanted me to scan the area again, looking for anything we might've missed."

She brightened. "I'll help."

He made eye contact and gave her a teasing smile.

"You know, you just might turn that inside knowledge into helping the police."

The red returned to her face, but her grin was bright.

"Never thought my bad days could turn into something good."

His eyes probed her blue ones, more beautiful than the vast sky above. He loved having her beside him. He couldn't resist catching her hand again.

"God is in the business of turning the bad into good, the harmful into helpful, the scars into stars."

Her expression showed a lack of turmoil for the first time since he'd seen her at the Apache Falls restaurant, where he'd fallen hard and long despite her anger—maybe because she was so broken and fragile. *Dangerous territory!*

He straightened, dropped her hand, and got to work.

When Katie returned from her morning with Larry, she had time to think, to process what she'd learned about Larry, about herself. The house was quiet. After two weeks off work, Lacey had returned to work. Rachel was at school. Toby was working, as usual, and Mom was asleep.

Katie had put Little Katie down for a nap before she'd left to see Larry. For once, Mom agreed to watch the baby, probably because she thought Katie went back to working at Willie's. Katie hadn't lied, but she hadn't told the truth either. She had stopped by Willie's and offered to work. He had told her to come in Saturday, so then she had gone to see Larry.

Larry. Memories of the time with him felt warm and fuzzy, a new sensation for Katie. In her experience, men were either aloof and critical or exciting and risky. Katie nestled the baby in her arms while she fed her.

The front bedroom used to be Lacey's, before she married. When Rachel moved there at four years old, she had slept beside her aunt, a twin bed pushed next to a double. Before Katie moved in, Rachel had the room to herself. Now she shared it with her mom.

Rocking in a squeaky chair created a soothing melody for Katie's somersaulting thoughts. With the two beds, the small rocker was the only chair that would fit between the chest and the beds. Katie was just glad to not be sleeping on the sofa anymore.

Afternoon light spilled from the west window. In early July, that window should be basking her in heat, but the memories of Rachel being kidnapped, bouncing a ball against that house while Lacey hurried to get outside, brought a chill and goosebumps to Katie's arms.

"God can forgive you, even of kidnapping Rachel," Larry had said. He should know. He was a preacher, and he said all she had to do was ask. Could forgiveness be that easy? Surely not. Katie couldn't forgive her ex-husband for coming up with the kidnapping scheme and hiring those two guys that hurt her daughter. What about forgiving Lacey? She couldn't. She just couldn't. Her sister was hateful. Her words always sent Katie to the depths.

Her breathing labored. She'd stopped rocking. The infant stirred. Katie rocked again. *Squeak. Squeak.* After switching the babe to her shoulder, she patted her back. Katie's tension evaporated. Her breathing eased.

Lacey had done a kind thing, buying Rachel a birthday gift and saying it was from her mother. Katie rocked faster.

Wayne lost his life trying to save Rachel from the clutches of mean men. *Squeak. Squeak.*

Burp. It was amazing how such a small baby could create such a loud noise. Katie giggled and rocked.

Why not try Larry's solution? It couldn't hurt.

Little Katie drifted off to sleep. Big Katie got up and laid her in the middle of the double bed before she returned to the rocker.

Last week, Lacey had handed Katie a white Bible.

"When we built on the back addition and I moved my stuff, I found this."

It was the Bible Katie had carried as a teenager. She hadn't seen it since she was seventeen. Not since the attack. The chill returned. Could she forgive that? The tension returned. Her legs pumped.

"Oh, God," she cried out. "Help me. I can't do this."

Let him who is without sin cast the first stone.

How could she not forgive? Her life was steeped in fornication, adultery, drug addiction, and kidnapping. Who was she to cast stones at even her rapist?

Her body shook. Her heart drummed so loudly, the pulse pounded in her eardrums. While a child, she'd memorized the Lord's Prayer. She remembered the words.

Forgive us our trespasses, as we forgive those who trespass against us.

She whispered words that only she and the Lord could hear.

"Lord, forgive me. Come into my heart again, like You did when I was seven. Lord, I want to forgive those who've hurt me. Help me do so. I'm willing, and You're able. Amen."

Moisture clouded her vision. Words filled her mind, words to an old hymn that women prisoners sang in the Christian dorm at Seagoville Prison.

"Amazing grace, how sweet the sound that saved a wretch like me," she sang out loud.

A childish voice blended with hers. When Katie looked up, Rachel stood at the door, home from school and singing in the most beautiful voice Katie had ever heard.

"I never knew you could sing."

The child's cheeks were rosy, her eyes gleaming.

"I sang a solo in our Christmas program last year."

"You did?" Sadness pressed down on Katie. "And I didn't get to hear it. Maybe this year."

Rachel skipped to the bed and stared at her adopted sister.

"Come sit in my lap." Katie held out her arms.

After twisting around, Rachel took two skips to the chair, climbed up, and laid against Katie's breast, like the baby did. The warmth from the young body brought a peace Katie had not experienced in a long time, maybe ever.

"I love you, Rachel Marie Smith."

She giggled. "I love you, too, Mama Katie. What's the rest of your name, Mama?"

"Katie Marie Smith. I gave you my middle name."

"And the man who helped me when those mean men had me was my dad, Mr. Smith. Right, Mama?"

"Yes, Wayne Smith."

Rachel hung her head. "He went to heaven."

"Yes, he died. We hope he went to heaven."

"My teacher said we'll go to heaven if we ask Jesus into our hearts." The child's smile was as wide as the North Texas plains, where you could see no end.

"That's true. Have you done that?"

The girl nodded. "So I'll go to heaven when I die."

"Right."

"Mama?" Rachel's lips puffed out. Wrinkles lined her small brow. "Have you asked Jesus into your heart?"

"May I tell you a secret?"

Rachel nodded with vigor.

"Just before you got home, I asked Jesus into my heart."

The girl clapped her hands and bounced on Katie's lap. "Yay! I'm glad you'll go to heaven too."

"So am I."

After Katie finished the dinner dishes, she took the baby out on the porch. The summer sun inched down in the west, sparking shoots of bright purples, pinks, and oranges high into the sky—a true masterpiece of God. A sweet aroma wafted from the rose bushes on either side of the steps. She inhaled and smiled, feeling cleaner than she had since her early teens.

Lacey opened the door. "Mind if I join you?"

"Sure, come on."

Imitating the rocking chair, Katie leaned up and back. The baby's eyes drooped. Soon she was asleep.

Lacey eased into the other lawn chair. An "oh" escaped her lips when she made contact with the web-laced seat. She still had some pain.

"Don't be mad at Rachel, but I have to ask something."

"I could never be mad at Rachel."

"She told me that you gave your heart to Jesus this afternoon. Is that true?"

Katie flinched. She'd really tried to forgive Lacey's unkind words, but she wasn't sure if she was ready to talk about it. She remained quiet. Lacey stood.

"Forgive me for prying." Her tone held a note of hurt. "It's none of my business."

Katie heaved a sigh. It had to stop. Could she be the one to begin? *Amazing Grace. He gave me amazing grace.*

"Don't go. Really."

Lacey eased back into the chair. She cleared her throat and sat straight. "Listen, Katie—"

"No, you listen." Katie's body and spirit stilled. "You've always been there for me when I got in a mess." Raising her right hand, she chewed the nail on her middle finger. "But you always took every opportunity to condemn me and make me feel like poop." Her heart jumped ahead of her.

"I know." Lacey faced her sister. They locked eyes. "I'm so sorry. I was wrong to do that. I couldn't understand how you could keep taking drugs when you saw what it did to you. Then God showed me it was no different than when I kept overeating, knowing it was killing me, mentally and physically. I'm still struggling with why you continue to choose the wrong kind of men, but . . ." She choked. Tears filled her eyes. "I've never walked in your shoes."

"I was raped behind the school when I was sixteen. Wayne found me. He cleaned me up, took me to Apache Falls, and married me." She bit her lip. "He was kind and tender." The memories lingered. *Even if his scheme sent me to jail.*

Lacey reached for Katie's spare hand. "Oh, my, I never knew that, sis. Why didn't you tell us?"

Katie's bottom teeth bit into her upper lip. "I couldn't, don't you see? I wasn't living for Christ." Her voice lowered. "And it seemed God failed me by not protecting me. I still struggle with that, but I know bad things happen to everyone."

"It's up to us how we handle them."

"Yes. I didn't do well at that. I compounded the failure again and again."

"I almost committed suicide," Lacey admitted.

Katie's eyes widened. "Why? When?"

"Shortly after you left Rachel with me. I thought Toby was going to marry Sandra, and they could adopt Rachel. I was an awful mother. I thought everyone would be better off if I wasn't in the picture," Lacey almost whispered. Her pain was evident.

"We both failed."

"Yes, but we both did right in the end."

Katie's gaze searched her sister for answers. She sniffed.

"Maybe you did. You stopped overeating and decided to live. I, on the other hand, never quit choosing bad men and taking drugs until I ended up in prison for kidnapping."

While halfway turning in her seat, Lacey placed a hand on either side of her waist.

"That's not true. Did you give your heart to Christ today or not?"

Rachel stuck out her head. "Mama, can I have some ice cream?"

"May I," said Lacey.

"Well, may I?"

With her critical expression, Rachel favored Lacey. Katie had always thought she looked more like her sister than herself.

"You may," Lacey said. "I'll be there in a minute."

"Detective Dad will get it for me."

Lacey snickered. "Yeah, he probably wants some for himself."

"I want some too." Mom's voice could be heard from farther back in the living room.

Katie and Lacey laughed.

"Okay then," Lacey said.

Silence descended for a while.

Baby Katie became heavy. "I think I'll go put her in her drawer bed for the night."

"Will you come back out?"

"I will," Katie said.

And she did.

Lacey caught hold of Katie's hand and swung it between the chairs like she used to do when she walked with her little sis across the street.

"I'm so sorry for what happened to you. If I'd known, I think I would've been more understanding. Maybe not. I was pretty selfish back then."

"I did give my heart to Christ this afternoon." Katie's words were softly spoken, but retained emphasis.

"Then don't you see? You didn't give up. It may have taken you longer than me, but you turned to God. That's not failure. It's success."

Lacey's eyes twinkled with moisture, her smile beaming with love. That love melted Katie's heart like ice on the July sidewalk.

"I forgive you." She said it. She meant it. *One step at a time.* "NA teaches us to make amends."

"You demonstrated amends to me because you came when I needed help."

"And you forgave me when you bought Rachel a present she'd love and said it was from me."

The sisters laughed together.

"Would you like some ice cream?" Lacey asked.

"I think so. Yes."

Toby met them at the door. "I just had a call. Katie, I need to talk with you. It's about the baby."

CHAPTER *Thirty-Five*

The circle of family looked peaceful and calm. Mom sat at the head of the table, her bowl of ice cream finished. To her right, Toby sat before his empty bowl. Beside him, Rachel took small spoonfuls while making yummy sounds. On the left, Lacey and Katie dawdled over their treats.

To Katie, it tasted bitter, like secrets. Even her sense of smell failed her. The smell of the cut up strawberries was foul, unappealing. Her head throbbed—stress-related, she was sure. With Rachel and Mom there, Katie acted as if everything was wonderful, and that was harder than asking forgiveness. What news did Toby have about the baby? The spoon shook in Katie's hand so badly she feared the cold treat would dump into her lap.

By the time her anxiety almost blinded her, Mom stood and announced, "Think I'll go climb in bed and watch the dancing show from there."

After all said their goodbyes and Rachel gave her a good-night kiss, Mom hobbled to her bedroom and closed the door.

"*May* I have more ice cream?" Rachel said with emphasis.

"No, you may not, young lady." Lacey stood. "We must get you in for a bath."

"Are you sure you can handle getting down to bathe her?" Toby asked.

Resembling Katie for a moment, Rachel jutted her chin. "I can bathe myself. I'm not a baby, you know." She sounded more like Lacey.

They retreated to the back bathroom. Katie glared at her brother-in-law. "What's the bad news?"

It was bad. She knew it with every fiber of her body, every beat of her heart, every throb of her headache. She willed her hands to quit shaking, but she finally laid down the spoon.

One of Toby's fingers twirled his bowl.

"As police chief, some of my jobs are distasteful. This is one such task."

He stared at the empty bowl, as if it gave him courage.

Katie pounded the table. "Blast it all, spill it. Are you going to try to take Baby Katie from me?"

"I have no choice." His tone was husky, hoarse, scratchy. He leaned his elbows across his knees, resting his chin in his hands. "When you first came, we applied to be foster parents. Lacey and I signed the papers to have temporary custody of Baby Katie, and it was granted since the family didn't want her."

Katie glowered. "Why? Y'all never told me that." She whammed the table. It bounced and made a terrible racket. "You deceived me into thinking poor old Katie was doing something good while it was old goody two shoes Lacey that was making it happen."

Lacey stuck in her head. "Are you okay?"

Silence followed. Lacey left again. Toby reached for Katie's hand.

"Think about it. CPS wasn't going to allow you custody of a child. It seemed to be the perfect solution as long as you and the baby were living with us anyway. What else could we do? You love that baby."

"You can leave me alone. Kinsley's parents don't want that baby. Kinsley brought her to me when she feared she was dying."

He held up hands, palm outward. "I know, I know. It's not fair, but it's the law."

"Blast the law."

She stood and paced from the stove back to the table.

"Do you have any documentation that the mother named you as guardian to her daughter? I need proof."

"I'll be right back."

Katie marched to her room and pulled the wrinkled piece of paper from her purse, the one she'd showed to Larry. She hastened back to the kitchen, laid the paper in front of Toby, and pressed out the wrinkles with her hands.

"There."

She went back to her pacing.

"K could be anyone. Why didn't she give a full signature?"

Katie's voice softened. A lump lodged and swelled.

"She went into that last seizure that took her life. She tried, but she lost all control, but she came to my apartment specifically to ask me to take the child. I know it. I must care for her, for Kinsley's sake." She squared her tiny shoulders. "That's what I've done. It's the right thing to do." Her resolve crumbled. Her vision blurred. "What am I going to do?"

Toby came around the table and took Katie in his arms.

"Baby Katie's grandparents have lost their daughter. They want a second chance with their granddaughter. Theirs is the legal right. A woman from CPS will be here tonight, or they'll allow us to return the child to the grandparents. I suggest that Lacey and I go with you to return the baby."

"Return her?" Katie jerked away, her voice escalating.

"From what I hear, they have softened a lot through their grief. Maybe they feel guilty about the way they acted. We might suggest to them offering you visitation, a way to stay in her life and tell them about her mother's love." Keeping his voice low, he stepped back. "What do you say?"

"You don't think I should even fight for her?"

"You could try, but really I think you'd spend a lot of time and money, the lawyers would get rich, and you'd still lose. I could be wrong." He shrugged.

She sniffed and sobbed. "I just can't give her up. She's mine. Right from the beginning, we bonded."

"That's why I suggest working it out privately with her grandparents."

"They hate me."

"You don't know that."

"I most certainly do. They made it pretty plain, especially Kinsley's dad."

Toby smirked. "Kinsley's dad isn't rich, but he's not poor, and Kinsley was their only child. You don't think you should even fight for Little Katie's inheritance?"

She gave him a touché smile. "I'll fight for that."

"Okay then. I understand the grandparents are out of town for this Fourth of July weekend. CPS will give us until Monday. I'll see if I can set it up and arrange for Lacey's friend to keep Rachel so Lacey can go with us. I think she could help soften the grandparents' hearts."

Katie grimaced. The blinding headache was making her sick. She went to the living room to cry and pray. Prayer was a new thing for Katie. Strange as it seemed, prayer seemed to help her make up her mind on certain things, like needing to call Larry. She punched in his number.

"Pullman . . . ah . . . Reverend Pullman, how may I help you?"

Katie guffawed. "You really stink at this preacher stuff. You've been a cop too long."

She heard him exhale. "You're right. I must work on my greeting."

The rich baritone timbre of his voice sent her heart to racing. He sounded delicious, making her mouth water for his kiss. With that thought, she felt the need to bend over for a spanking. It felt naughty but nice. Kissing a preacher that was a cop? Lacey used to worry she was going crazy. Instead, it was Katie.

"I could use some counseling, preacher man."

"I'm all yours."

No, he wasn't, and Katie knew that was for the best. Despite her coming back to Christ, she still had all the ex-con, ex-druggie, ex-sinner baggage. A pastor shouldn't have to cope with that. He needed someone with a heart to win others for Christ, someone like Michelle. Katie closed her eyes. Dealing with that picture made her jumpy as a grasshopper. Katie went back to pacing.

"When?"

"How about I pick you up and we go for an ice cream at Dairyland?"

His voice could soothe a rattlesnake. She plopped on her bed to dream. "Sounds wonderful."

The headache diminished. Her anxiety took on a new form.

By the time Larry appeared at the door, Katie skittered out like she had no worries, feeling ever so like a teenager in love. Lacey had told her to leave the baby asleep. They would watch her. Katie hadn't been picked up at the door since the sophomore dance at Wharton Rock High School.

The chatter between she and Larry was lighthearted, as if neither of them wanted to dip into the weightier issues. Finally, Larry's expression turned somber. His long tongue took a swipe at his chocolate ice cream cone.

"So, what is it you need counseling about?"

If only she were someone else. If only she were sixteen and could begin anew. *If only* didn't count. She faced heartbreak, and Larry deserved better. She explained the situation with the baby and told him Toby's suggestion. Larry stroked his mustache, as if that helped him think.

"And you want to fight?"

She raised her brows. "You bet I do."

"What would happen if you tried it Toby's way first?"

The air went out of her anger. Her shoulders slumped.

"I guess I wouldn't be any worse off." She tensed. "Yes, I would. They'd have my adopted daughter, and they'd keep her. I'd lose her without a fight."

His voice was soft but pierced her square in the heart.

"I believe you'll lose her while you fight. Child Protective Services will pick her up so fast it will blow your mind."

She teased her lips with her teeth. Some friend he turned out to be. He and Toby were on the same side, opposite of her.

"Not if me and the baby run away. I won't let her out of my sight."

"What kind of life is that for a child, running from the law before she has her first birthday? And what will happen to you? You'll be back in prison, and Baby Katie will go to her grandparents anyway."

"It's none of your business, preacher man. Take me home. Now."

His hand crushed his cone. "You know what? You're a spoiled brat, always thinking about how hard it is for you. Why don't you think of others for a change? Like Baby Katie, and the grandparents who are grieving. Like Toby, who could jeopardize his career if he doesn't apply the law?"

"Save your advice for your congregation of Wharton Rock country hicks. Don't try it on a city girl like me." She crossed her arms and pouted.

"You're not a city girl. You were born and raised here."

"Yeah, and I got away as soon as I could."

She dumped the rest of her cone in the trash and remained standing until he got up and led the way to his truck.

When they reached Lacey's house, he walked her to the door. She started in. He caught her hand.

"Don't be mad."

She offered an aloof smile and tilted her head downward with a seductive eye flutter.

"Why, Reverend Pullman, I'm not mad. We just verified that a relationship between you and me is ridiculous. Go be a pastor, and I'll go be a parent. I have two daughters, and I plan to get a place and have them both come live with me." She hesitated and dropped her head. "Good night."

She shut the door in his face and remembered she hadn't told him about her salvation. He would've wanted to know. She shrugged. It didn't matter. Not really. She had decisions to make, and they didn't include Larry Pullman.

CHAPTER

With her pulse still thumping, Katie leaned against the closed door and aimed for nonchalance.

"I've got a great idea," Lacey said.

It took a while before Katie realized Lacey was talking to her.

"Yeah, what's that?" Katie's tone hadn't shed all the irritation. She tried again. "I'm all ears." *That was better.*

"Toby works Sunday. After church, let's have a ladies' day at the lake. We'll take the girls. I'll call Joanne and see if she can bring her girls. Why, even Mom might go with us. We'll take a picnic. How does that sound?"

Slow and unexciting. "Do you feel up to all that?"

"If you prepare the picnic, drive, and help with Rachel swimming and fishing."

Lacey had a winsome look, a sort of please-please-please expression.

"Now we get to the truth."

Katie sat in the recliner near Mom and faced Lacey on the sofa. Pajama-clad, big ears Rachel skipped across the living room.

"Please, Mama." No subtlety with a child.

"Fine."

Except for church and facing Larry at the pulpit again. If she stayed in Wharton Rock long, maybe she should change churches. There was no Bible verse that said "thou shalt go to thy sister's church."

Rachel bounced, clapping her hands. Baby screaming came from the front bedroom.

"You woke the baby." Katie bit her lip at her critical tone. Wasn't that what Katie had always hated in Lacey? Katie patted the child's head. "I'm sorry. She is probably hungry."

"Can I feed her?"

Katie glanced at Lacey. "Is it okay? It's late."

"Tomorrow is Saturday, so she can stay up later."

She smiled at the girl. Rachel went back to her celebrating, while Katie picked up Little Katie and warmed her bottle.

The talk was all about Sunday. Even Mom chimed in. Katie sat quietly, chewing on a hangnail and dreading the long work day Saturday at Willie's Restaurant. She was grateful that Lacey and Mom would watch the baby. And at least it put money into the metal box.

Sunday began gray and drizzly, not a good picnic day. Toby left early for the station. The proposed trip to Kinsley's parents' house was not mentioned. The rest of the group headed to church. Katie still preferred the back row. Mom obliged, so Lacey didn't argue.

Larry's gaze locked Katie's. She picked an imaginary string from her jeans. Squirming, her hips settled tightly against the pew's back. A few moments later, she slouched into a semi-reclining position. Massive long hair on the lady in front of her hid Katie. *Perfect.*

The sermon began with Psalm 139:14 about being "fearfully and wonderfully made," focusing on God's love for His special creation—man.

All those years, Katie had sought love in all the wrong places. Could it be that God's love had been available to her all the time? That thought dropped warmth around her shoulders like the baby's blanket. Her jitters calmed. For once, her you're-no-good video quit playing in her mind. Lost in the touch of Christ, Katie kept her seat. The closing prayer ended. Lacey went after the girls. Mom folded her arms over an ample bosom.

"You staying here all day?"

Katie jumped. "What?"

"Hi, Katie."

That all-male voice sounded secretive while raising her blood pressure. She turned away from Mom and took an appreciative view of a guy too luscious to be a cop, much less a preacher.

"Reverend Pullman." She offered a quick nod.

"Good to see you."

His gaze could melt ice. She bit her lip.

"I liked the sermon about love. It meant a lot." She never expected to hear that come out of her mouth.

"That's good, Katie. I appreciate that."

His glance drifted from her eyes to her neck, only to jerk back to her eyes. She giggled. Her low-cut blouse made him nervous. *Interesting.*

"Anything change?" he asked

"No."

"So you still have the baby?"

Lacey saved her from answering when she placed Baby Katie in her sister's arms.

"Are we going to the lake, or are we standing here gabbing all day?" Mom asked.

"The lake?" Larry asked.

"There you are, Reverend Pullman. We're ready to leave for lunch." Sandra was the old pastor's daughter. She and her youth minister hubby waited at the back.

"Excuse me." Larry moved away. "Have a good day. It's a good one for the lake. Sun's out now."

"That's what we thought," Lacey said. "Let's go."

She led her family out the door, to the car, and back home to change and pick up the prepared lunch.

Rachel splashed in shallow water. Katie straddled a nearby rock. The babe slept under an umbrella on the quilt spread over the only grassy area they could find. Mom and Lacey lounged in chairs under oak trees, overseeing the scene. The picnic of bologna sandwiches, carrot sticks, and apples was devoured. Only cheese, crackers, and more Diet Cokes were left in the basket.

Lacey's pain was all but gone. Tuesday, she was scheduled for a partial mastectomy, which was why Toby insisted they visit the baby's grandparents on Monday.

"I've got to hand over that infant, and who knows when you might go with us if we don't do it Monday," he had told her.

She didn't disagree. She just dreaded telling Katie. It was probably best that Joanne and her girls couldn't come to the lake. If only Lacey could work up the courage to spill the news. Was this carefree outing a way of softening her sister? Absolutely. *Lord, give me the right words. Take care of the baby, and allow Katie to stay in her life.*

How many times had Lacey prayed that lately? When her sister was softening and had even turned to God, Lacey feared this could thrust Katie back into drugs. Mom might not be able to take the disappointment. Neither could Lacey. She had begun to hope again.

Rachel bounded up to her aunt. "Do we have any more cookies?"

Lacey brushed the child's head. "No, missy, you ate them all."

The warmth of the July day put Mom to sleep. A bead of perspiration trickled down her face while she snored.

Frowning, Rachel laid her head in Lacey's lap.

"I have some snack crackers. Want some?"

Rachel nodded her head. Her chin poked Lacey's leg. Lacey opened the cracker box and handed over two.

The baby awoke. Katie opened the diaper bag and grabbed a bottle. The open bag smelled of baby powder, while Rachel and Katie smelled of fish and algae. The two fragrances vied for prominence.

"Can I go back in the water?" Rachel asked.

"You can stick in your feet, but don't get in until your mom finishes feeding the baby," Lacey told her.

The girl scampered away. Obviously, stomping through the water wasn't getting in. Lacey sighed. The area was silent except for Rachel's sloshing, Little Katie's slurping, and an occasional squeal from a boat on the lake.

Spill it now. Lacey scooted closer to her sister.

"You know I've got the surgery Tuesday?"

"I remember. Don't worry about a thing. I explained to Willie. We have it covered. The girls and I will be fine." Katie winked at Rachel.

"There's one thing we should do before Tuesday."

"What?" Katie put the little one on her right shoulder.

"We should take Baby Katie to her grandparents' house."

"Am I going too?" Rachel was quick.

"No, sweetie," Lacey said, her gaze still fixed on her sister.

Katie stiffened. She nibbled the nails on the hand looped around the infant.

"Baby Katie isn't going either." The words were pushed through tight lips.

"It's the law, Katie. If you don't at least try, you'll give up any chance to stay in the baby's life. Besides, Toby and I must take the baby, whether you go or not."

Katie sagged. She looked like she might cry. "Don't you think I can beat them either?"

"No, I don't." Lacey softened her tone. Fear mounted like the granite of Wharton Rock. *Please, Lord.*

CHAPTER *Thirty-Seven*

An acrid smell brought a twitch to Lacey's nose. The clock at the side of her bed read two thirty. Surely everyone in the house was asleep, so where could the smell be coming from? Probably her vivid imagination. She turned to the other side, plumped her pillow, and tried to go back to sleep. The chemo had left her energy depleted. By taking a nap after work, she couldn't sleep well at night.

Dreamland had started over when a shrill blast woke her for real.

Toby jumped from the bed. Lacey sat up.

"What is that noise?"

"Smoke alarm. I'll check." He dashed out the bedroom door but returned moments later. "Get up. The house is on fire. Our way through the kitchen is blocked." He jarred open a window. "Hurry."

An orange glow cast evil-looking shadows on the wall. Snatching her robe, along with their wedding picture and Rachel's four-year-old picture from the nightstand, she rushed to the open window. She threw her legs over the sill and eased to the ground, with Toby holding her hand until she got her balance. Behind her, a red tongue of fire curved around the wall, moving toward their bed. Toby jumped to the ground.

"I'll get your mother. You get Katie and the girls."

Toby was already slipping through Mom's always unlocked window. Lacey had warned her to lock it so many times, now she was thankful she didn't. Lacey strained against the window in the other bedroom but couldn't loosen it. She ran to the front door. The lock held. Frantic, she raced back around the side.

Toby climbed back out with Mom right behind him.

"I can't get this one open, Toby, and the front door is locked. Can we cross from Mom's room to theirs?" Even she could hear the panic in her voice.

After Mom was over the sill, he reached back for her crutch.

"Call 911. I'll get them."

Rachel's basketball rested in the bushes. He bounced it against the front bedroom window, then climbed back into Mom's room and out with a vase. Lacey kept bouncing the ball against the window. How could her sister keep sleeping? Surely, the baby was crying by now.

Toby hurled the vase at the window, shattering both. Smoke released. Katie's bloody head poked through the shards.

"What in the world?" A spasm of coughing almost choked off the words.

The baby began to cry. Katie turned.

"Get out," Lacey yelled. "Fire in the kitchen."

The smoke alarm should've been loud enough to wake the block.

Toby used the ball to clear glass and climbed in. He laid the bedspread over the ragged edge and handed first Rachel and then Baby Katie to Lacey. By the time he got her sister out, a fire truck pulled up in front, and the chief took charge.

Toby gathered his family near the curb and ran to the porch to grab lawn chairs for Mom and Lacey.

Dressed in his robe, the next-door neighbor Mr. Barnett watched from his porch. The dad of a big family across the street walked across.

"Anything we can do?"

The man's wife passed out water bottles.

"Thanks," Toby said, taking a long gulp. "Right now, I just don't know." He shook his head.

Baby Katie wouldn't stop crying, no matter how hard Katie rocked her. Watching the dark clouds of smoke billowing against an almost full moon made Lacey want to cry too. So much damage. Who knew if anything could be saved?

Rachel's cough worried Lacey. She hugged the girl to her. Toby's warm arms covered Lacey's shoulders. The rein on her emotions dissolved. She buried her head in his chest so her tears wouldn't scare the kids.

The baby stopped crying, but her gasps were wheezy. With unsteady legs, Katie edged over to the fire chief.

"My baby seems to be having trouble breathing. Have you seen that before with the smoke and all?" She had to shout over the noise of the fire and the firemen.

"How old is the baby?"

"About two and a half months."

He yelled at one of his men, rubbed his forehead, and focused on Katie.

"Yes, ma'am, but the ambulance should—"

As if on cue, a siren blasted the air. One of Wharton Rock's ambulances pulled behind the fire truck. Billy Reynolds and another EMT rushed over to the fire chief. He pointed to Katie and the baby.

"Age?" Billy asked as he shone his flashlight on Baby Katie's face.

The baby screamed, gasped, and coughed.

"Two and a half months," Katie said.

"Poor little thing," Billy cooed.

He reached for the baby. Katie let go. Holding the baby carefully, Billy ran to the ambulance and went inside. Katie's pulse thundered in her ears. She rushed after the EMT and climbed in behind him.

"Wait for me."

Billy hauled a portable oxygen tank from the side. The mask swallowed the tiny face.

"Does she have a history of asthma?"

"No," Katie said.

"What are you doing to my baby sister?"

Peeking into the back doors, Rachel poised her arms on her small hips. She coughed again. Toby tugged Rachel to his side.

"Sweetie, this man is trying to help Baby Katie breathe better." He smiled. "How are you doing, Billy?"

Billy straightened. "I'm fine, Chief Wheeler. With so young an infant, we need to get her to the hospital right away."

"Do something here. It's a long ways to Apache Falls." Katie's voice escalated over all the noise.

Busy taking the baby's vitals, Billy didn't answer Katie. He worked in silence. Toby placed a hand on Katie's shoulder.

"Don't forget, Wharton Rock has a nice hospital of its own now."

"Oh, yeah." Katie's fingers brushed the sweaty forehead of her tiny baby daughter. "So are you taking her to the Wharton Rock Hospital?"

"Yes, ma'am," Billy said. He turned to Toby. "Let me check your daughter there, Chief Wheeler. She has a terrible cough."

After Billy checked Rachel, he determined she seemed fine.

"We'll get the baby off to the hospital. If Rachel's cough doesn't improve, take her to her doctor tomorrow."

"I sure will, Billy. Thanks."

Toby stepped back. He motioned for Lacey, and she came running.

"I'll watch after Rachel and your mother. Go with your sister. She needs your support."

Lacey looked as if she were near tears. "That's a good idea." She glanced up. "Move over, Katie."

Rachel clung to Toby's leg. He lifted the big girl into his arms.

The ambulance took off. Through the windows, Katie saw little but darkness until they reached the highway. A siren coming from their vehicle caused Katie to cover her ears. The few cars on the road at this time of night moved to the side. The ambulance took the last Wharton Rock exit, where a large building with flashing lights on top directed low-flying planes away. Katie's pulse seemed to race ahead of the ambulance. The salty taste of tears gathered in her throat.

Billy kept the oxygen over the infant and conversed with medical personnel at the hospital.

With a screech, they stopped. Doors slid open. Bright lights and signs directed them down the hall. The EMT rolled in a stretcher carrying the tiny baby. Katie and Lacey rushed to keep up. A lone woman sat behind a counter. A man with a little boy sat on one side of the waiting area.

The woman looked up at the newcomers, took one look at Baby Katie, and pointed to the right. A nurse seemed to magically appear beside them and led the way to an exam room. The EMT and the nurse gently moved the babe.

"You're in good hands now," the EMT said. He removed the oxygen mask and left.

Baby Katie was still and quiet.

"Ah, sweet little one." The nurse clamped a monitor around the baby's tummy. She glanced at Lacey. "So the baby was in a fire. Tell me about it." She looked down at a folder.

"Our house burned. I think the smoke—"

"How old is she?" the nurse asked Lacey.

"I'm the momma here." Katie scowled and paced.

"How near was she to the fire?"

Katie stopped. "Blast it all, just do something. She's not breathing right."

"I take it she was close."

The nurses' tone was critical, but she bent over and listened to the baby's breathing. Then she left.

By now, Katie was bawling. Lacey patted the babe with one hand while she rubbed her sister's back with the other.

The nurse returned carrying an oxygen tank. This mask wasn't as enormous as Billy's had been. She slipped the loops around the babe's ears, and soon her skin color grew pinker and even reddened.

Before the nurse disappeared through the door, she turned. "The physician's assistant will be in to check on her in a few minutes."

Lacey stiffened. Her fists closed into tight balls beside her hips.

"Well, hurry please. This is an infant. She won't make it if you delay treatment. You have medicine that can help, but she needs it now."

The nurse smiled and walked out.

Long minutes ticked by. Baby Katie gasped, seeming to choke with the mask over her face. Katie's breathing was almost as labored as her namesake. An ache settled at the nape of her neck. Though she held onto the mask to keep it from slipping off the baby's face, Katie could do nothing more. When she glanced up at her big sis, she breathed easier. The tension in her neck eased.

"Thanks for coming with me, sis."

"You're welcome." Lacey massaged Katie's back. "I just wish they'd hurry."

A man with shaggy hair and a stethoscope dangling from his neck entered.

"I'm Gregory Martin, PA." He reached out a hand, but when neither woman took it, he sputtered and sighed. "Well, let me see."

Lacey and Katie stepped away from the exam table. Gregory Martin probed the infant, listened to her heart and lungs, and then reopened the door and called out. He asked the usual of Katie.

"How old is she?"

"Two and a half months."

The nurse came back in with a breathing machine.

"We'll give her ten minutes on it before we test her lungs further."

Hours later, and lots of coffee for Katie and Diet Cola for Lacey, they left the hospital. The baby was now sleeping evenly. Lacey weaved in front of Katie, whose legs could barely hold her up. They climbed into the cab that would take them to their temporary home.

Lacey turned to her sister after they got on the road.

"This may create a new problem. Baby Katie's grandparents might no longer want the child if there is permanent damage to her lungs. A child with asthma requires more medical attention and special care."

"But I can't keep her."

"No," Lacey said.

As they bounced along the highway, Katie's thoughts returned to worrying about whether she had turned off the stove when she finished in the kitchen the night before. She couldn't remember. That must have been what started the fire.

It's my fault the fire started, my fault she probably has asthma now. Katie slumped in her seat, all fight gone. *I knew it all along. I'm not worth forgiving.*

When Katie entered the motel where Toby had secured rooms for temporary lodging, the noontime sun burnt the top of her head. Inside, heavy drapes and the blasting air conditioner cooled and darkened the room. Mom snored from the closest bed. Clasping the infant to her breast, Katie felt her way around in the dark, yanked off her clothes, and slipped under the covers on the other bed.

As her eyes adjusted to the darkness, she noticed what appeared to be a huge basket near the window. She stood again and circled the bed. Her fingers brushed over a satiny texture. It was a bassinette, smelling of baby powder. She didn't know how it got there, but it sure was thoughtful. She laid Baby Katie on the tiny pad. She never woke, but her breathing sounded regular.

When Katie lay back in her bed, her body melted into the soft mattress, relaxing one muscle at a time. The thick comforter brought solace in the cold room. If only her mind would calm as easily. Snippets of conversation kept her awake, replaying.

"Her lungs are not yet fully developed."

"The smoke overwhelmed one so young. She can't process out poisons yet."

"She'll probably live with asthma all her life."

If only I'd stayed up and done the dishes last night as Lacey had asked, maybe I'd have seen the fire in time. Did I do something to cause the fire? I must have.

Katie must've been crazy to think she could be a responsible parent. Why was she clinging so tightly to this baby that everyone said she couldn't keep? She loved the child, and Kinsley had wanted her to live with Katie. That was why.

Are you sure you're not trying to replace Rachel?

A chill swept Katie. Could she be that callous?

What would Kinsley's parents say when they learned Katie caused a fire that hurt their grandchild? They already believed she was evil.

Maybe I am.

Did God really save her, or was she living in an impossible dream? Her actions couldn't be forgiven. With everything she'd done wrong, she must have committed an unpardonable sin.

What was she going to do? Baby Katie was lost to her. And no matter that her relationship with Rachel had improved, Lacey was now her mother. Rachel would never live with Katie in their own place. What was she thinking? Wayne was dead. Larry was better off with Michelle.

Collin still wants me.

Could she trust Collin, or would he pull her back into the drug scene? A dose of cocaine would put such worries out of her mind. It was tempting.

One thing she knew. If she was to stay clean, she needed to get back to her meetings. Living in Wharton Rock had derailed her regular attendance. Without help, she would seek comfort in the wrong places. Just like she'd done all her life.

The next week brought a whirlwind of activity. The tiny two-bedroom apartment they had found frustrated each of the family members so that yelling had become commonplace. Lacey's surgery had been postponed. They were back to where they started with her surgery scheduled for Tuesday and Toby insisting they take the baby to her grandparents on Monday.

Fatigue weighed heavier on Lacey than the hundred pounds she had lost. She rubbed her temples. A headache throbbed. Two friends in construction were working on the old home in their spare time to give her and Toby a break on cost. The insurance wouldn't begin to replace what they'd lost, which was nearly everything.

Lacey's stomach churned. Perhaps it was connected to the headache. She couldn't be sick or the surgery would need to be postponed again, a fate that her cancer doctor said shouldn't happen if she was to defeat the disease. She lay back on the leather sofa and wished she had her comfy flowered sofa back, but it, like most things, had been burned.

The walls closed in on her. Toby was at the station. Mom turned her dancing show up loud, which didn't help Lacey's pain level. Rachel played with the baby. She was going to miss her temporary sister. Lacey settled on the floor beside the two girls.

"I need to talk with you, sweetie."

Rachel swung the baby's hands. Call it gas pains or whatever, but that baby laughed out loud, bringing a chuckle to Lacey.

"You know that Baby Katie is not your real sister, don't you?"

"Yep, but she's my mama's daughter. Right?"

"Not really."

Eyes wiser than an eight-year-old should have lifted in understanding. "I know. Her real mommy died, but she gave her to my mama, so now she's hers." Rachel's matter-of-fact tone seemed to settle the issue.

"It's more complicated than that."

Lacey explained about Baby Katie not being kin and the baby's grandparents wanting her back.

"But that's not what Baby Katie's mommy wanted."

"But we can't prove that."

"If my detective daddy told them, that would prove it, wouldn't it? Policemen don't lie."

A smile came all the way from Lacey's insides to her mouth. She hugged her girl so tightly, and she remembered years ago the child complaining about shutting off her air after Rachel was rescued from the kidnappers.

"No, your daddy doesn't lie, but it has to be something more than him saying it. He wasn't there when it happened."

"Does Mama lie?"

Rachel's eyes flashed confusion. The baby began to whimper.

"No, sweetie, but Mama still has to have proof, and she doesn't, so tomorrow, we'll take Little Katie to her grandparents."

"But you'll bring her back."

"We'll ask if she can visit us sometimes, but Little Katie will stay and live with her grandparents."

"That's not fair." Tears sprang to Rachel's eye.

She's had so much sadness in her young life. It broke Lacey's heart. She wished Katie had never brought the baby here.

Katie. Was she going to survive this? Would Lacey lose her sister again when she only just found her?

Lord, help us.

CHAPTER *Thirty-Eight*

Sitting at his desk on the Monday afternoon of his final week with the Wharton Rock Police Department, Larry scanned the room. He would miss this place—the camaraderie of the officers, the feeling that he was protecting his town from criminals. God had called him to be a fisher of men, not a symbol of law and order.

"Wake up, Pullman." Willie Brandt, Toby's top detective, tossed the latest crime report on Larry's desk. "You're not off duty yet."

Larry liked Willie. Toby was still trying to win him for Christ, but Willie was a good guy. Larry spread out the paper.

"What's up?"

Willie's grin was a big splash of white in a black face.

"Get out on patrol, officer."

"I haven't had a piece of my goodbye cake yet." Larry offered a pathetic-plea expression. "Ruby made it special. She'll miss me."

"Earn it first."

Willie's eyes narrowed. His mean look never did quite work, but Larry saluted and headed toward one of two squad cars on the side of the station.

He drove east to west, from one end of town to the other, then rounded north to south. He pulled to the side of the Valero on the freeway and jotted down notes for Wednesday night's prayer meeting. His text would be Romans 8:28, "And we know that all things work together for good to them who are the called according to His purpose."

That verse got him through his teens while he tried to live up to his second chance. He'd clung to it when the tug of the ministry had weighed on him and again when no one would allow him to preach. God had led him full circle from Wharton Rock to Apache Falls and back to Wharton Rock. He met his every need and guided him into the hometown pastorate.

A short, curvaceous, ex-con blonde tested his resolve on so many levels. Though she revved up his pulse, God continued to drum into him that she wasn't the one chosen for him. Why did God allow his awareness of Katie as a woman if she wasn't right? *All things work together for good.*

He noted "blind faith."

With static, his radio awoke with an urgent call. "Officer needs assistance at Rocking Saddles Bar."

Larry hit his siren and lights and zoomed to the edge of town. The setting sun nearly blinded him. After parking at the far side of the parking lot, he used his hand for a visor. Two men and one woman surrounded Willie Brandt. The biggest of the men held a pistol, and the policeman's hands were in the air. The small guy headed toward Larry.

After sliding across the seat, he eased open the door on the opposite side and pulled out his service pistol. He dashed to the cover of trees edging the lot.

A semiautomatic gun shook in the small guy's hand. He circled the squad car.

Larry called for backup while he peeked through the branches of a mesquite. The spindly tree couldn't hide much. Would stepping out from cover help or hurt Willie? Number one rule of police work: any delay in crime was helpful. Dry twigs snapped. He crouched lower.

"I see you in those trees. Won't help you to hide. I can shoot the bark off that there tree."

Not with his hand shaking, he couldn't, but the voice was dangerous and near.

The cock of the pistol pointed at Willie fifty feet away was loud in the quiet lot. The only thing louder was Larry's breathing. If there was anyone left in the bar, they weren't budging.

A police siren blasted.

An anxious voice shouted, "Take care of business, Brandon, and let's get out of here."

A gunshot exploded.

Willie? With a sudden plunge, Larry thrust the mesquite aside and shot at the man. And missed.

The center of Larry's chest stung. Pain soaked his whole front and seeped through to his back. A pungent taste saturated his mouth. Light dimmed until blackness overtook him. He'd failed to protect his friend. *Help us both, Lord.*

CHAPTER *Thirty-Nine*

Toby drove a police car to Apache Falls. It was official business, returning a child to her family.

I'm her family, not them. In the back, Katie sulked and sobbed. This last week, she'd cried enough tears to fill up Buffalo Lake.

Lacey twisted in the front seat. "You okay?"

"Mm huh." Katie sniffed.

"I'm sorry," Lacey said.

She was sorry. So what? That didn't help Katie. That didn't keep Little Katie from the clutches of those mean grandparents who never wanted her.

"Don't let it throw you, Katie." Lacey's tone was desperate. "You've come so far."

Katie stiffened. Just a little more money and she could get a place of her own, but she wouldn't have a daughter living with her, Rachel or the baby.

The truck pulled to a stop in front of a low-slung red brick home. The hedge was nearly dead, but the Bermuda grass was mowed, and a big crepe myrtle added a burst of fuchsia. A white cross poked up in front of the dead shrubs.

Though Toby and Lacey jumped right out, Katie took her time. If she could only think of a way out of this, but she couldn't, not short of going back to prison. She bit her lip. Prison might be easier, at that. Lacey put a hand on her sister's shoulder.

"I sat Rachel down last night and explained."

Low blow! Tears welled in Katie's eyes again. With the sleeping babe on her shoulder, Katie shuffled behind her kin. The door flew open before they reached the porch.

"It's about time. I expected you two hours ago." Mrs. Martinez glared through piercing brown eyes and crossed her arms over her obese torso. Her red-and-green flowered top billowed over black pants. Her expression turned kinder, and she held out her arms toward the baby. "Give me my granddaughter." Kindness didn't seep into the tone she used.

Katie froze, clutching the child tighter.

Toby reached for Baby Katie and, with the gesture, ripped out Katie's heart.

Lacey stepped back, her hands resting on her sister's shoulders. *Why Lord?* Life wasn't fair. It was so hard to understand how God allowed Katie to fall in love with this child, only to snatch her away. She massaged her sister's tense shoulders.

"May we come in?" Toby asked.

The baby let out an ear-exploding cry. Mrs. Martinez rocked her back and forth.

"I don't see why you should."

Toby twirled the Stetson in his hands.

"Please, ma'am, there's extenuating circumstances you need to hear about."

While still bouncing the baby on her shoulder, the woman shrugged and pivoted toward her door.

"There, there," she cooed.

Inside, Mrs. Martinez sat in a rocking chair. Toby, Lacey, and Katie stood until their hostess finally motioned them to sit. The only place was a well-worn sofa.

Toby launched into a lengthy explanation how Kinsley found where Katie was living and brought the baby to her when she believed herself out of options. He handed over the handwritten note to Kinsley's mother. She stood again, trying to quiet the baby.

Katie exhaled, jumped to her feet, and tugged the child away from the grandma.

"Oh, blast it all." She walked off with a swinging motion until the babe quit crying.

The grandma tore up the note. Silence descended.

"That was a copy," Toby whispered.

"What do you want from us? We aren't pressing charges, but we could." Those brown eyes sparked fire.

Toby straightened, his voice becoming more authoritative. "Ma'am, we only desire what your daughter preferred, for Katie to remain in the baby's life, to be able to see her and keep her for a few days at a time, but then always bring her *home*." He stressed that word. "Seems a reasonable compromise for y'all and for my sister-in-law, as well as your granddaughter."

A male voice sounded from the back door. "Give my wife the baby and get out of my house."

"Sir," Toby swiveled toward Mr. Martinez, "your wife will explain how your daughter's wish for Katie to raise the baby could be satisfied, while you enjoy a relationship with your granddaughter. We only want—"

The man eased forward, pushing his face a nose away from Toby's.

"I don't care what you want, officer, or what that . . . that . . ." he pointed to Katie, "*convict* wants. Now get out. Now!"

Toby nodded to Katie. The sweet baby was almost asleep. Katie kissed the top of the tiny head, handed her to Mrs. Martinez, and ran to the car.

Lacey cringed and yelled, "You are mean people, just like my sister said."

Tears welled in her eyes. She dashed after Katie.

Before she got out the door, her husband's stern voice could be heard saying, "You've not heard the end of this."

The ride home was as gloomy as the days while little Rachel was kidnapped, but without the extreme fear. Since they were so late, they drove straight to school to pick up the only daughter Katie had left.

At the school, Katie jumped from the truck. Her arms opened and embraced Rachel. Minutes ticked by. Rachel squirmed. Only then did Katie let go.

Lacey kept her mouth shut. On the drive home, Rachel bubbled about her new friend and learning about division from Miss Young. The normalcy brought a measure of comfort.

The afternoon and dinnertime went by with Rachel and Mom carrying the conversation. Toby only grunted, and Katie said nothing. Shivers snaked down Lacey's spine. She hadn't felt so hopeless since she was a hundred pounds overweight and considering suicide.

They were still at the dinner table when Toby's phone rang.

"Oh, my God, how bad is it?"

His anxious words were like a blast of doom.

CHAPTER

By the time Toby asked the question on the phone, "How bad is Larry?" Katie was on her feet. When she heard Toby's words, "...room three twenty-two at Apache Falls Memorial?" she was out the door.

After aiming her Honda in the direction from where she'd come earlier in the day, her heart raced faster than her car. Larry had to be okay. She didn't take time to wonder why that mattered.

The drive took forever. She stilled the pace of her pulse with a new-found skill called prayer.

Lord, heal Larry. Don't let him die. Take away his pain. Even though I'm not good enough for him, he's a good man and loves You. Please, Lord, heal.

Strange as it seemed, Katie felt better. The hospital had been far too frequent a stop for her lately: when Little Katie was born, when Kinsley died, and now for Larry. She slid in another plea to the Lord.

The old elevator creaked and squeaked but opened on the second floor. The sign across the hall sent her right to the ICU, not a good sign. A large waiting room teemed with people. She spotted Reverend Lloyd, the minister whose place Larry took at the church. With her head down, she dashed past him, not wanting to see anyone except Larry.

She stopped at a nurse's station.

"Are you family?" a clerk asked.

Flipping a nail against her teeth, Katie lifted her eyes. "No, just a friend."

"He already has two guests. That's the limit. Sorry."

The woman turned back to her paperwork.

Katie gnawed her lip. Of course, his family would be here. She should've guessed, but she had to know he was okay, to let him know she cared, to tell him she was sorry, that he was right. It wasn't all about her.

A nurse buzzed the door open for another guest. When the nurse turned away, Katie slipped in before the door closed. One cubicle after another lined both sides of the hall. Room three twenty-two was in the corner. An older woman stepped out, heading back the way Katie had come. She resembled Larry. *His mother?* Katie paused and waited for her to disappear. Then she pushed past the curtain.

The face of the man on the bed was pale, lifeless. He seemed asleep. Tubes erupted from his left arm and out the foot of the bed. A blood pressure cuff tensed and relaxed. Readings appeared on a monitor above the bed.

A woman with long red hair bent over him. His hand was limp in hers. She looked up.

"What are you doing here?" the woman asked.

The blood drained from Katie's face, leaving her chilled. *Michelle.* She bit her lip.

"Hello. I'm just a friend."

"Since when?" The redhead's right eyebrow quirked. "I would've thought, after that little disappearing act you pulled, you'd never show your face around Larry again."

Katie jutted her chin and hiked her shoulders. "Larry understood."

"Oh, did he now?"

"Yes. Besides, he's now my pastor, as well as my friend, so I have every right to be here."

The older woman reentered the cubicle.

"I talked with the doctor. If Larry can make it through the night—" She stopped, smiled at Katie, and stretched out her hand. "I'm sorry. I don't believe I know you. I'm Larry's mother."

Katie glanced at Michelle while shaking hands with Mrs. Pullman. "Nice to meet you. I'm Katie Smith."

The woman's eyes widened. "Aren't you Betty Chandler's girl?"

Great. My past precedes me. Katie wished for a vanishing act.

"Yes, ma'am. Your son is a good friend." She chewed more on her lip.

"Oh." The lady nodded, as if she understood. "I know so few of Larry's friends anymore, but I know he would appreciate your concern." Tears pooled in the corners of her eyes as she looked at her son. "He's in critical condition." She sniffed.

Michelle touched the woman's hand. "But we're trusting God to heal him."

"Yes, yes, we are." Mrs. Pullman smiled up at Michelle. "I never thanked you for coming. It would mean a lot to him."

Of course, his mother knows Michelle. Guess she is a special friend. The chills were gone. Katie's blood fired up. She nudged Michelle to one side and retrieved Larry's hand when Michelle let go.

Katie rubbed the hairs on top of his hand and, with the other hand, brushed back a dark curl from his forehead. She spoke to the unmoving man, but her words were meant for his mother.

"Tell him I'm praying, and I'll return another time."

She gently laid his hand on the bed and turned. Mrs. Pullman pulled her into an embrace.

"Thanks again for coming, and thanks for your prayers. He needs us all." The smile was genuine and kind.

Katie gulped. Shouldn't she be comforting the older woman? She tried, but her throat closed so that returning the hug was the best she could manage. Maybe tomorrow Katie would catch Larry awake without Michelle. If God would spare his life.

The lunch shift at Willie's the next day was abuzz with talk of the shooting. Toby wouldn't give Katie any details, but town gossip filled in the gaps.

After Katie served Marian Ferguson, the woman jerked her into the booth beside her.

"I heard you went to see our two cops in the hospital."

"Yes, ma'am."

"Reverend Lloyd said you sneaked into ICU, so I know it was Reverend Pullman you went to see because Willie is in a regular room."

She dipped her head down to the left, as if waiting for confirmation. Katie stood. Her boss wouldn't appreciate her sitting on the job.

"Larry. . . ah . . . Reverend Pullman," *that title was a mouthful,* "has been a good friend since I returned."

She matched Mrs. Ferguson in a demure head dip.

"Oh, I know all about that. When you left prison, you stayed in a half-way house. What's that like anyway?"

"Different." Katie stiffened. "Excuse me, I need to get other orders out."

She pasted on a smile. Gossip was one thing Katie couldn't stand. Probably because she'd been the brunt of it far too often.

"Wait a minute," Mrs. Ferguson called. "You might want to know that Reverend Pullman is out of his coma."

"That's wonderful. Thank you."

Katie escaped. Joanne, Lacey's best friend, who was also a server, winked as Katie went by with a tray full of burgers.

"She does that to everyone."

Katie bobbed a nod. The cook sat out two more chicken-fried dinners. Katie swished them off the counter and onto a tray. The next two hours flew. Willie's was the place to eat for lunch in Wharton Rock. By three, Katie was tired and hungry. She flopped into a chair and nibbled her own burger and rings, remembering that was also Larry's favorite meal.

So, he was out of a coma. Would Michelle be there again today? The next day? Friday? Maybe Katie should wait until he left ICU, but what if he didn't?

When Katie pulled into a space beside their corner apartment, Rachel was playing dolls on the stoop. Unwanted memories flooded Katie's mind. Tremors teased her nerve endings. Four years ago, Wayne had spotted the girl outside alone, pulled to the curb, and confessed to being her dad. That had been the beginning of a nightmare few days for Lacey and Mom.

How could Katie have been a party to that? She loved her little girl and would never want to see her hurt. Her downfall came with a price. Surely, she had mistaken the good feeling for God's forgiveness. She was damaged goods.

After she perched beside her daughter, the front door opened and Lacey stepped out.

"Oh, hi, Katie. I was hurrying to change clothes and get out here with Rachel. I don't like leaving her alone for long."

Shutting off bad memories, Katie mashed down Rachel's cowlick and ran her fingers through the child's long hair.

"Believe me, I understand your angst, and I appreciate your care."

"I'll bet you do." Frowning, Lacey sat beside them. "Sorry. That wasn't nice. You're welcome. I love Rachel too, you know."

"I'll watch Rachel if you need to start dinner," Katie said.

Pink tinged Lacey's already rosy cheeks. "I'm good."

You still don't trust me alone with her? Katie gnawed her pointer fingernail.

"Are you okay?"

Lacey didn't make eye contact. Since they gave away Baby Katie, the household tension affected them all. Katie shrugged and continued working on her nail.

"Toby consulted a lawyer on your behalf in regards to the baby."

"Why? He said I couldn't win."

"He's taking a second look. Mr. Martinez's attitude changed his viewpoint a mite."

"Poor little old Toby."

Katie couldn't keep the sarcasm from her tone. She didn't even try. The situation made her feel like meat on a portable grill, pressed hard on both sides. Lacey stood, her arms crossed, her jaw tightened.

"It's not our fault."

Katie dropped both hands to her sides. "Oh, really? Then whose is it? I distinctly remember your insisting on giving Baby Katie to those people."

The next sound was the door's slam. Lacey was gone. Rachel snatched her doll and threw it down the stairs.

"I don't want to play anymore."

Following the doll, she raced down the stairs and away with Katie running after her but unable to keep up.

When Katie neared the apartment office, the back door to her right closed. She opened the door then went into the nearby ladies room. The sound of sobbing could be heard in the quiet. Beside the sink, Rachel clutched her knees to her chest and faced the wall. Katie slipped her arms around the girl's shivering shoulders.

"Mama's sorry. Forgive me." *What a stupid thing to say.*

Forgiveness. Why did it always come down to forgiveness?

Katie brushed back Rachel's wisps of thick, black hair, so much like Lacey's and not at all like Katie's blonde curls. Rachel had always been more Lacey's daughter, though Katie distinctly remembered giving birth in a dirty duplex in La Junta, Colorado, where Wayne drove off and left her. If it hadn't been for the crusty old woman in the front of the house, Katie would have bled to death, and Rachel would've died too.

Two days after the birth, it was Lacey who drove six hundred miles one way to pick up her sister and new niece. Her tender care had taken Katie back to their childhood when Lacey doted on her baby sis, not unlike Rachel had loved Baby Katie.

Ah, memories. Some good. Some bad. Just once, Katie wished she could live up to her sister's expectations.

Katie smothered Rachel with kisses and tears. Their hearts beat in rhythm, like when they were one person. She rocked the child and crooned a lullaby. Rachel relaxed and quit crying.

"You hungry?" Katie asked.

The girl nodded.

Katie helped her up. They walked out arm in arm.

Lacey waited on the stairs to their apartment. Her eyes were moist. Rachel ran to her. Over the girl's shoulder, Lacey mouthed one word. "Thanks."

"I should thank you. You've done so much." Katie dipped her head to hide her smile. "What can I do to help you with dinner?"

"I ordered pizza."

Rachel jumped up and down.

"Sounds good."

The tension was relieved at last. Would it stay gone?

CHAPTER *Forty-One*

The alarm was set for four, but Lacey awoke an hour earlier. Who could sleep when, in a few short hours, doctors would be cutting on her, stripping away part of what made her a woman?

A full moon cast evil-looking shadows on the ceiling, adding to her unease. Toby snored in peace. Easy for him. Her surgeon said she should be out of the hospital within forty-eight hours or less so, since he was short-handed, he hoped to be back at work full time by the weekend.

Willie was out of the hospital but still unable to work, and of course, the police department would no longer have Larry, even if he survived. God would heal him. The church needed their pastor. Toby needed his friend, and Katie needed ... Lacey didn't understand that relationship. Toby said Larry was dating a woman from Apache Falls and seemed to be headed toward marriage, but he was important to Katie, somehow.

Please, Lord, heal Larry. Lacey should think of others, not herself.

When the alarm sounded, Toby sprang from the bed and dove into the shower. She crawled to her feet and found her baggiest, most comfortable shorts.

Shorts were exchanged for a paper gown when she arrived. Vitals taken, blood drawn, Lacey waited in a cubicle. Toby held her hand. Katie would see to Rachel and Mom. Right now, Katie's help was a blessing, even with her sullen attitude, but she seemed to relish the idea of being in charge. Lacey worried about her having to give up the baby. As much as Lacey tried, she still couldn't quite trust her sister.

After they wheeled Lacey into surgery and asked her to lie on her side and count to ten, she remembered nothing until she awoke with only one breast and cried.

❧

Two days after Lacey's surgery, she came home. The next day, Katie was off work. Three days of getting gossipy updates on Larry made her anxious, angry, and apprehensive.

"He's in God's hands," Reverend Lloyd told her one day.

"They don't give him much hope," Marion Ferguson had said last night.

Enough. Today, Toby would be with Lacey, and Katie would go see for herself.

By the time she dressed and started toward the door, Mom stopped her.

"Since you're off today, would you mind taking me to the retirement center to see my friend Pearl?"

Katie let out a long breath. "I want to visit Larry today."

"Pshaw." Mom waved her hand. "You can still drive to Apache Falls afterward. You're off all day, aren't you?"

"Yes, but ... how long do you plan on staying?"

"I called Pearl. She said I could have lunch with her. She arranged for it, so you could drop me off and pick me up when you return."

"I can do that." Katie took in Mom's tattered robe and fuzzy house shoes. "How soon can you be ready?"

"Not long."

"Well, snap, snap, get to it then."

"I can't hurry. You know that."

Why should she be irritated? She's the one that waited until the last minute to ask.

A tension headache pounded Katie's right temple. She rubbed it, marched to the rocker, and pumped with her legs. Would Larry be awake? Would he be glad she'd come? Would she have to face Michelle?

One hour later, when the rug should be threadbare from Katie's rocking and silently cursing her mother, Mom hobbled into the bedroom.

"I'm all ready."

Katie willed her jitters to calm while looping Mom's free arm to help her to the car.

The Golden Oaks Nursing Facility sat spread-eagled, with parking in between the two wings. Katie pulled into the drive-through and jumped out to help her mother. Poised in her seat, Mom scanned the entrance.

"I'm thinking about moving in here. Maybe I could get an apartment right close to Pearl. That would be nice."

Katie shrugged. Mom drove her crazy, but Katie would be out of that house when Lacey recovered.

"Let me help you."

Mom shook her off. "I've been doing things on my own since before you were born. I may be slow, but I'm not addled."

Katie stiffened. Then why did she insist that Lacey help? Mom needed Lacey, but not Katie.

"I'll leave then. Enjoy your visit."

"Mmmm." Mom hobbled away.

When Katie reached the car door, Mom swiveled and called out Katie's name. She paused.

"Come back after your hospital visit."

Katie's mouth went suddenly dry. "I said I would."

"I just don't want you to stay in Apache Falls."

A lump grew in Katie's throat. "I wouldn't do that."

"Mmmm, yeah, it's happened before." Mom shuffled on down the hall, leaving Katie with another claim to guilt.

The sunshine hid behind a cloud. Katie's fingers shook against the steering wheel. She swallowed her lump, stopped for a soda to help with her dry mouth, and found the Christian music station on her car radio.

By the time she reached the Apache Falls hospital, not having any idea what she faced, she had added some steel to her backbone. She didn't care what anybody said to her, even that blasted redhead.

The elevator was empty. Few people waited for ICU. A clerk opened the door, and Katie went to where she'd last found Larry. This time, he was alone. He still looked fragile, pale, and asleep. She took his hand.

"Listen here, Larry, this has to stop. You've got to get well, you hear me?"

The monitor kept up a steady beat.

She closed her eyes. "Lord, please heal Larry. He's a good man. I deserve stuff like this, but he doesn't. He tries to serve You. This man even preaches for You. Please, God." Tears ran.

"Katie." A weak, breathless voice came from the still figure.

Her eyes sprang open. "Larry?"

"I'm so glad you came."

The dry mouth was back. Her neck heated. She cleared her throat.

"I came before." She heaved a long sigh. "I'm so glad you're better." *Lame.*

"God loves you, Katie." His eyes closed. His hand went limp within hers. "And so do I." The volume trailed off.

Had she heard him correctly, or was she dreaming? Did he really say "So do I"? Her pulse swooshed in her ears. She didn't have enough saliva to swallow.

"Hi, nice to see you again. How's our guy?" Mrs. Pullman returned.

At least it wasn't Michelle.

"He spoke to me." Katie rubbed Larry's hand.

The mother nodded. "Good to know. He came around this morning for the first time. I feel like that's encouraging."

"Yes, yes, it is." Katie's pulse was still pounding. She needed to get out of there. The oxygen was not sufficient. "I must leave."

She tripped as she raced out of the room, wanting to think about what Larry said, or what she thought he said.

Lord, please heal Larry.

Later that day, Toby eased into a chair beside Katie.

"I wanted to talk to you. First of all, the guys are making great improvement on the house. It wasn't as bad as we thought at first. We plan on moving back in this weekend."

"Super-dooper. I can help on Sunday."

"That would be nice. There's something else."

"Have at it."

Katie knew her tone was unkind, but Toby had been a bear ever since the trip to drop off Baby Katie. As if he had a reason to be mad. She was the one who'd been wronged. He rested his elbows on his knees.

"I went to see a lawyer. I took the original of Kinsley's note."

"I know. Lacey told me."

"He said the handwriting could be analyzed and proven to be Kinsley's with a ninety-five per cent assurance."

Katie straightened. Her brows went up. "He did?" She stood, went down the two steps, and paced the yard, her hands on her shaking head. "I told you we should fight. I told you."

Bending lower, he clasped his hands in front of his legs. He spoke through gritted teeth.

"But he worried that there was no date."

She halted. "So proof that it's her handwriting isn't enough?"

His head remained tucked. Unusual for her brother-in-law to not make eye contact. Almost like he was talking to her and avoiding her all the same. Katie cringed. A prickly sensation peppered her neck. She clasped her arms in front of her and waited. There was more. She could feel it.

"That was last week." Soft words with the power to crash all hope. He faced her, walked her way, and dropped his arm around her trembling shoulders. "This week he learned about why you spent time in prison."

Despite the July heat, a chill swept over Katie. Again, it was her actions that defeated her. They should've locked her in prison and never let her out. Life would be much simpler. No Larry to worry about, no babies to lose, no money problems, no life, just existence, but easier, way easier. She felt like she was going to be sick.

"Thanks for trying."

She ran for inside and escaped to the bathroom, but the red letters that seemed to be stamped on her heart couldn't be erased.

Unforgiven.

CHAPTER Forty-Two

Through the next three weeks, Katie's savings mounted with extra hours and good tips at Willie's. When Rachel was out of school, she and Katie played Go Fish and dominoes. Katie couldn't believe it, but she was actually enjoying a life in Wharton Rock. She must be losing her mind. If only . . . *Quit it. I need to face facts.*

Number one, Rachel would never live with her again.

Number two, Baby Katie was gone forever.

And number three, Larry was too good for her, even on the slim chance that he cared.

The God forgiving her thing still bounced around in her head like a bunny on weed. When she read her Bible and prayed, God gave her hope, but when she remembered her past, reason told her it wasn't possible. How could she believe in God's forgiveness when she couldn't forgive herself?

During the next month, she would find a place to live. Mom talked more and more about moving to Golden Oaks. Lacey improved daily. Rachel was content, Toby was back at work, and Lacey would return to normal soon. They no longer needed an extra mouth to feed, nor an extra pair of hands to work.

Katie drove to Narcotics Anonymous meetings in Apache Falls so she wouldn't have to try another meeting. Without the group, she'd fall on her face, but they couldn't work miracles.

Word around town told her Larry was better and out of ICU. It was time for her to visit again. Time to know for sure if he meant what he said. With a morning shift off, she slipped quietly out of the house before Mom came out of her room. There had been a time when Katie didn't do hospitals. Now she was a regular. Once she arrived, she asked the room number and headed that way.

To the side of the cracked-open door, a note read Larry Ray Pullman. She was at the right room. Would she find him all smiles and encouragement or glum and despairing? Would his mother be there or Michelle? Katie's heart rose to her throat. The hallway was hot, making her short of breath. Before she entered, she heard voices and stopped.

"I feel so much better." *Larry's voice.*

"I'm so thankful. I was so worried." *Michelle.*

A long pause.

"Larry?"

"Yes."

"Before you were shot, I told you that you needed to make a decision. I know you haven't been well, but I just wondered, have you given *us* any thought?"

"Yes, I have." His voice was deep and clear. "I want to marry you. You'd make a great pastor's wife. You're what I need."

Michelle had her answer, and so did Katie. No need to visit. God healed Larry, and he had chosen a wife. End of story.

She lifted her head, squared her shoulders, and marched from the hospital.

With two hours until her dinner shift, Katie drove around Apache Falls, ending up at Kinsley's old church. The 1930s architecture with a white steeple and four pillars was beautiful. Stained-glass windows lined the sides. It was Katie's idea of a typical-looking church, but she knew its walls hid hatred and anger.

The memories weren't all bad. There, Larry believed in her enough to ask for her help with teens. There, Kinsley's brown eyes had lifted in trust, not to just an ex-con, but to one who had lived the trauma and survived. There, Ryan, Cody, and others had searched for her.

She dug out a tissue and dried her eyes. There, the senior pastor had judged her for being a drug addict and ex-con. She was marked.

Damaged. Without hope. Unforgiven.

Her shoulders shuddered. Unable to drive, she parked in the lot. Her hands trembled. Nausea gnawed at her gut like internal poison. Sobs wracked her body as memories flooded her mind—of the bush where she'd hidden for hours, of Larry's decision for a more suitable wife, of her heart-to-heart talk with her sister. Of her prayer for salvation.

Larry didn't love her romantically, but he'd never promised that. Larry was a friend, a pastor, a good Christian desiring to lead her to Christ.

There is now no condemnation in Christ.

That Scripture entered her mind and spread out like the azure sky above.

She glanced at the clock. Time to go to work. She knew what she had to do. She'd set the plan in motion as soon as she got off work that night.

Willie's was busy with customers all evening.

"You okay?" Joanne asked.

Katie was lost in her thoughts. "Huh?"

"You look like you lost your best friend. Your face is pale, and you have this woe-is-me expression."

"Thanks for the kind words."

Joanne laid a hand on Katie's shoulder. "I didn't mean to be mean." She sighed. "Is it Larry? Is he okay?"

"I have no idea."

Katie swayed her way to where her next order was up, but she could feel Joanne's stare hot on her back. She only had three more hours before she could ditch Wharton Rock for good.

When the dinner trade slowed, she made her way over to her boss.

"I'd like to talk with you."

"Shoot."

"I'm moving back to Apache Falls. I'll drive back and help out for two more weeks if that's okay. It will give me time to find another job, and you time to find another server."

Willie's squatty frame eased onto a bar stool. Wrinkles bunched around his sagging jaws.

"You sure this time? We went through this once before. In no time, you moved back wanting a job. If I hire someone, I can't take you back."

Katie dipped her chin. "I understand."

"Katie, are you okay? You've seemed down today. Is there anything I can do?"

"I'm fine. Lacey is better now. They don't need me anymore, and my home is the city."

He nodded. His fingers raked the scruffy whiskers on his chin.

"Wharton Rock has apartments and houses to rent, and you could stay on here."

"Thanks, Willie. There's not many nice people in this town, but you're one of them."

His hairy arms embraced her in a hug. "There's lots of nice people here if you give them a chance."

"I've given them most of my life." She marched to the back and grabbed her purse. When she went back past Willie, she paused. "Anyway, thanks. I'll see you Saturday."

He blocked her way. "I'll start trying to find a new server. I hope you find peace. You're a good employee. I hate to lose you."

"Thanks."

Time to get out of there before she started bawling.

It was nearly nine o'clock when she returned to Lacey's partially renovated house. That's what it would always be. First it was Mom's, then Lacey's. Never Katie's. One more reason to move.

The TV blared. Mom's head bobbed in her recliner. Lacey and Rachel came out of the bathroom. In her Bugs Bunny pajamas, Katie's daughter bounced across the room like the emblem on her attire.

"Guess what?" She didn't allow Katie time to respond. "My friend Brianna has a birthday party tomorrow, and I'm going. We're going bowling. I've never been bowling in my whole life."

Rachel smelled of baby powder and no-tears shampoo. Katie's eyes stung. How she'd enjoyed this time of playing mother to her daughter when Lacey was unable to do the simple things like drive her to birthday parties and give her baths.

"That's exciting. You'll have to call me and tell me how it went."

"I won't have to call you, silly. I'll tell you when I get home. Mother and I bought Brianna's gift this afternoon. Guess what we got her?"

"I have no idea."

"A Princess Fashion doll. She's going to love it."

"I'm sure she will, but we need to talk." Katie looked to Lacey for help.

"Baby, have a seat. I think your mother has something she wants to say." Lacey sat beside the girl and waited.

Katie's stomach churned. She picked up the girl's hand, so tiny, even in Katie's small ones.

"I'll be moving tomorrow."

A gasp came from Lacey. Rachel appeared confused.

"Where will you go? Don't you want to live with us anymore?"

Katie's tummy was turning cartwheels, and her mouth had a sour taste.

"I love living with you and Aunt Lacey ..."

"And Grandma and Detective Daddy too. Don't forget them." A sorrowful expression crossed Rachel's face. "I wish our baby still lived here. Are you going to live with Baby Katie?"

"No. Mama will get a place of her own. Maybe you can visit some time. Would you like that?"

The girl nodded.

Katie let out a pent-up breath. Would Lacey allow it? Katie glanced up. Lacey's eyes were damp, but her smile reminded Katie of the day Lacey had bought a candy bar with her own money and given it to Katie. She'd been six and thought her big sister was the best in the world.

"You're welcome to stay here as long as you want, you know. You've been a big help. Thanks for dropping everything and coming when I needed you. I'll never forget that, sis."

"No problem." It'd been a long time since Katie felt proud of anything. "I hope to have a place secured before tomorrow night." If what Collin told her could be believed.

"Where will you go?"

"I'll let you know."

Lacey cuddled Rachel to her. "Let's get you in bed, missy." She reached out for her sister and hugged her in with them. "Be careful in your new home and find a church to attend there."

Katie chuckled. "That's just what I intend to do."

Lacey's eyes widened. "Oh, wow, you have changed."

Had she? Katie hoped so. If only she could be a good influence on Collin and not the other way around.

CHAPTER *Forty-Three*

The nurse gave Larry his discharge orders and two prescriptions.

"Glad to see you getting out of here, officer. We almost lost you."

"God wasn't going to allow that. He's got plans for my boy," Mrs. Pullman said.

She looked ten years younger since Larry had been pronounced officially out of danger.

"Thanks for all you did." Larry shook the nurse's hand. He was a lucky man, but he frowned as they brought in a wheelchair to take him out. "I can walk. Thank you."

The wrinkled nurse frowned. "Hospital orders."

"Yes, ma'am." He saluted.

Michelle balanced an ivy in a fishbowl-looking vase and a bunch of roses in a clear glass tube.

"I'll bring these."

She'd been a permanent fixture while he was hospitalized. He couldn't ask for more in a life partner.

When they reached the house, Mom hastened to unlock the back door. He eased from her Toyota to diminish the pain. He felt like he'd been kicked in the sternum, and his right calf stung as if cut open, which, of course, it had been.

After parking behind them, Michelle rushed past with the two vases.

"I'll put these inside and come back to help."

"I'm a grown man. I can make it inside by myself." But maybe not without an "ouch" or two.

He stumbled along. When she returned, he offered her a tired smile and took her arm. His brown leather recliner looked like heaven on earth. Bracing himself with the armrests, he sprawled across the chair, allowing his body to give into the softness. Mom handed him a cup of coffee.

"That was fast," he said.

Her face beamed. "You griped about the hospital coffee. Thought it was time you had some real brew. I'm going to cook us a bite to eat."

"Now, Mrs. Pullman," Michelle reached to pat her arm, "sit here with your son. I'll go pick up some lunch."

Michelle was gorgeous, but her smile appeared a bit condescending. Mom slumped onto the sofa.

"But I love to cook. Really, it's not a bother."

Michelle perched beside her future mother-in-law.

"How sweet. Larry is so lucky to have a mother like you, but now is time for you to rest. I'm younger. Let me do this."

"Okay." Mom's lips thinned.

With her purse on her arm, Michelle scooped up the tube vase of roses. She focused on Larry.

"I thought perhaps we'd leave the ivy here for your home, but, with your permission, I'll take these roses to the church. They'd be lovely on the communion table in front of the pulpit."

"Wait." Larry voice lacked force. "There's someone at the church who handles the weekly floral arrangement. I can't remember . . ." He glanced at Mom.

"I think it's Reverend Lloyd's daughter, Sandra."

Larry snapped his fingers. "Yes, that's it." With his gaze lifted to his fiancé, he said, "Best not to interfere with her plans."

Michelle bent to kiss his cheek. She waved her hand in dismissal.

"No problem. Leave it to me. I'll work it out. You just rest."

She dashed out, and silence descended. He and Mom locked stares. His muscles tensed. How was a wife going to change their lives? Mom gave him a we'll-get-through-this smile.

"Glad I made a chocolate pie before I went to the hospital. At least I have a dessert."

She scurried to the kitchen to set the table, cut the pie, or whatever else Moms might do.

Larry squirmed. "Is it time for a pain pill?"

Mom brought him a pill and a glass of water. "Here you go. Try to sleep while Michelle is gone."

He chuckled and pushed the chair to the reclining position. Had he been too hasty in his decision to marry the gorgeous redhead? She was insistent, and he didn't want to string her along. His wayward heart burned for a certain petite blonde, but her life was a mess, and she didn't seem to want him to be anything more than a sounding board and whipping stick. His eyes stung. This injury had made him dependent on others, and he hated it.

Shut in with the Lord on Saturday evening, Larry prepared his first sermon in almost five weeks. He was eager to get on with his life. The weeks of recovery had weakened him. He had no resolve, no confidence, no joy.

"Lord," he prayed out loud, "guide me. You protected me and healed me for a reason. Now anoint my message, and renew my vision."

For two blessed hours, no females—not Mom, nor Michelle—interfered. No one forced a pill on him or coddled him with tender loving care. God's word spoke. His prayers brought peace. He was his own man again, a minister for the Lord Jesus Christ, but no longer a cop. He hadn't quite recovered from the disappointment of that.

A doorbell rang, and a delicate knock sounded on the room he'd turned into a study.

"Yes, come in."

"I'm sorry to disturb you, son, but Reverend Lloyd and one of the deacons are here."

Larry stood. "Show them in."

He pointed to the two extra chairs as they entered and then sat. Reverend Lloyd studied Larry.

"I know you're still weak. We don't want to push. Are you sure you're up to preaching in the morning?"

They're worried I'll mess it up. Collapse on the platform. "How thoughtful, but yes, I'm fine and looking forward to getting back to work."

Ted Ferguson, the deacon, cleared his throat. "Your fiancé tells us you're very weak. She's concerned you're beginning too quickly."

Heat zipped up Larry's neck, leaving his ears aflame. His jaw tightened.

"I do plan on making Michelle my wife, but she doesn't speak for me." His words were clipped, brusque.

"Okay." Ferguson gave a brief nod and smiled. "I know not being married is a handicap in the ministry. Michelle will make a wonderful pastor's wife."

"Thank you."

Larry's tone hadn't changed. She would make an excellent pastor's wife, but would she be a good choice for him? If she was God's will, why did he feel chained to a decision that brought anguish, not joy? He had prayed about it but received no peace about marrying, or breaking up, so he stalled and prayed—a lot.

Reverend Lloyd scanned the room, and his tone softened.

"Katie Smith had eyes for you, but honestly, it's just as well she is moving back to Apache Falls."

Larry's jaw ached. His right pointer finger smoothed his mustache. He shifted positions.

"She's moving, then?"

Ferguson coughed. "Already moved, from what Toby told me. She has a boyfriend there, I think." His voice grew tough. "A drug dealer." He stood. "I feel for her mother and sister. They don't deserve the turmoil Katie has dished out through the years."

Katie. Oh, Katie, what have you done? Larry's stomach churned. A headache began.

Reverend Lloyd reached for Larry's arm.

"Are you okay? Your face is so pale."

"I don't feel well. Please excuse me." He needed some air.

Reverend Lloyd walked behind him before he spoke. "Our offer is still available. I can prepare to preach another Sunday."

Larry halted, his back stiff as a rifle.

"I will preach in the morning, but thanks for your offer."

He rushed through the back door, closed it, and looked up at the darkening sky.

"Where are you, Lord? I need Your strength and Your wisdom. You called me to preach. I thought You wanted me to choose a wife to compliment that ministry. Why am I so tired and full of despair?"

He dropped to the outdoor rocking chair, sensing God had things to teach him.

"Police Chief Wheeler is here to see you, Pastor."

Larry rubbed his eyes and leaned back. The last two weeks had been tiring, but exciting.

"Show him in."

The receptionist left, and Toby strode across the room. Larry stood and shook his outstretched hand.

"Good to see you, Toby."

"How you feeling by now?" Toby twirled his white Stetson.

"Much better. I'm growing stronger each day. I was fortunate."

"Yes, you were." Toby watched his twirling hat. "I have a proposition for you."

"Shoot."

"We're still short-handed. God called you to the ministry, and I would never get in the way of that call." Toby scrunched his lips. "I have a couple of possible recruits, but I thought you might want to keep your finger in the business, so to speak." He cleared his throat and straightened. "Would you consider working on the force from, say, three in the afternoon Friday to three in the morning Saturday?"

Larry's pulse charged forward. His mouth went dry. He had so missed being a cop.

"On one condition."

"Name it."

Larry felt lighter than he had in weeks.

"Tell Willie Brandt you couldn't do without me."

His mouth turned up in mirth.

Toby held his Stetson brim to brim, stood, and shook hands with Larry again.

"That's just what I'll tell him."

The door opened and Michelle entered.

"I told the workers I wanted the kitchen light grey, not tan, but they ignored me. I need you to come and tell them." She sat on the edge of Larry's desk. "Obviously, they don't listen to me."

Toby put his hat on his head.

"Hello, Michelle. Good to see you."

"Oh, yes, hi, Captain."

"Chief," Toby said.

She waved her hand. "Chief. Sorry, I never can keep that stuff straight."

"So, Pastor, I'll see you next Friday, or is that too soon?" Toby backed away.

"Friday's fine."

Toby nodded and left.

With crossed arms, Larry turned to his fiancé.

"What in the world are you talking about?"

"Now that Reverend Lloyd has moved out, I'm getting the house ready for us to move in after the wedding. I'm having trouble with the workers."

His jaw tightened. So did his fists.

"Nobody told me the house was available. And what makes you think you can make changes without my input?"

Michelle jumped off her perch and sidled up to Larry, using all the seductive moves she knew so well.

"Oh, sweetie, I'm so sorry. I thought I'd told you. As far as the house, I assumed you would leave that to me. You're so busy." She used her coaxing tone.

Larry went to his door and spoke with his receptionist.

"I don't wish to be disturbed."

"Certainly, sir."

He closed the door.

"We need to talk."

CHAPTER *Forty-Four*

Mrs. Martinez watched Katie, who jutted her chin and marched to the fifth row. The hymnal shook in her hands. This was Katie's third Sunday at the Apache Falls Covenant Life Church. Each time, Kinsley's parents scrutinized her every move. Was Katie crazy for choosing this church?

She swallowed a lump and croaked out a tune. Unlike her sister, Katie was no singer. When the music ended and the pastor began his sermon, her mind drifted to the preacher she longed to see—Reverend Pullman.

Was he back preaching?

Was he okay?

Was he married?

No, he wouldn't be married, yet. She would've heard. That would be the event of the year in Wharton Rock.

After the service, Katie inched down the hall, keeping Mrs. Martinez in sight on her trip to the nursery. The worker handed the older woman a baby wrapped in a pink blanket. Katie's pulse roared in her ears so loudly she didn't hear a man coming up behind her until it was too late.

"Are you stalking us, Mrs. Smith?" The menacing voice was close to her ear.

She jerked around. "No. I—"

"Stay away from us, or I'll turn you in to the police."

She longed to vanish, but her feet were rooted to the floor.

"I just wanted to see—"

The baby started crying.

Mrs. Martinez halted in front of Katie and pulled the top of the blanket from the baby's face. The woman's words were gentle, understanding.

"Would you like to see her?"

The babe's brown eyes, black hair, dark complexion, and the screwed-up face, ready to scream with even greater strength, was Kinsley in miniature. Warmth soaked Katie's pores and ran through her veins, heating the chill that had frozen her to the spot. Katie's heart did a somersault, but with an intake of breath, it calmed. She reached an unsteady hand to her lips for a kiss and touched the infant pucker.

"Thanks," she spoke to Mrs. Martinez, who nodded to her husband and walked out of the church.

On Katie's trip home, a well of gratitude overflowed. Her whole afternoon had brightened.

After making a sandwich, Katie sat cross-legged on the bare floor. The apartment was small, but it was hers. She liked that, but it was also lonely. Oh, she had Collin. Wow, did she have Collin. She appreciated the fact that he'd helped her find this place, the cheapest in town that wasn't a dump. Having him near was a safeguard, but it came with a price. He kept pushing for becoming a couple, but though she talked to him about God, he didn't share her faith and didn't seem to want to.

Everyone else whom she cared for lived in Wharton Rock. The more she prayed, the more God spoke to her about that. Funny, after all the years of running away from that place, she continued to visit several times a week. She had even worked for Willie one afternoon when he was in a lurch.

A knock sounded.

She got to her feet, looked through her peephole, and opened the door. "Hey, Collin. You eat lunch?"

He shook a white sack in front of her. "I come bearing tacos." In his other arm, he held two folded lawn chairs. He strode to the center of the living area and opened the chairs. "Now you have furniture, sweet stuff."

She chuckled. "They blend perfectly with my décor."

Her savings had gone for deposit and rent, with nothing left over for furniture. The floor worked for chairs, and a sleeping bag from the Goodwill served as her bed. Not fancy, but hers. She took the white sack from Collin.

"Thanks. I just finished a peanut butter and banana sandwich. This will be dinner."

"Then hand a couple my way. It's my lunch."

His dimple sunk into his right cheek in a provocative way. She knew what she'd seen in him before prison. He was a hunk, sought out by every female she knew. He chomped away on his tacos while she placed hers in the refrigerator for later.

"Did you go to that church again?" he asked between bites.

"Yes."

"Did you see those people again?"

"Yes."

His brow furrowed. "Why do you punish yourself like that?"

"I promised God and my sister that I'd go to church on Sunday, and that's what I'll do."

His last bite of taco was huge. He swallowed.

"Fine, but why not go to a different church?"

"I don't know." Looking for connection? Trying to ... what? See Baby Katie or change the Martinezes' minds? "They have good music."

"Humph." Collin sprawled out on the floor. "I've got better use for my Sunday mornings. Like sleeping."

"God loves me, Collin. That's major." She understood his feelings. Hadn't she been the same way until the Lord got her attention? "He loves you too."

"A drug pusher. Sure He does."

"An ex-drug pusher. Isn't that what you said?"

His jaw tightened. "Yeah, and that's right. I'm clean. I don't do that stuff anymore."

She lay beside him. The tile floor was hard. She threw her arms over her head, stretching out all the kinks. Her voice softened.

"Of course, I'm a real prize. Addicted to drugs, I had my own daughter kidnapped. God could never forgive that. Right?"

"Sounds right to me."

"That's what I thought, but He did. God forgave me. It took me a while to believe it, to trust it, but you know what?" Her head lifted and rested on her elbow. "Trust isn't knowing where you're headed. It's trusting in the nature of God to forgive and guide. God is love. He never condemns."

Collin kept quiet.

She hoped her words struck home. God wanted her to tell others about what He'd done for her. She knew that much. He'd given her a second and third chance. How could she not tell Collin? Time to let up and go lighter.

"Do you ever see Madison?"

He let out a long sigh and scratched his head. "Two weeks ago."

"She doesn't work at Country Dinner Restaurant anymore. I thought maybe we kept missing each other, so I asked Paul."

"No." Collin drew out the one word into two.

"What are you not telling me?"

"The cops suspect her of dealing, but I think it's Jordan dealing from her apartment."

"Is that the guy who stole my car?" With a nonchalant tone, she slid out that question and watched for his reaction.

His lips narrowed. "You know about that. Huh?"

"Yep."

"I was a jerk that night, but I knew nothing about what he did until the next day." He swung to her hand. "You gotta believe me."

She did. Jordan had been a heel in a roomful of heels. She shook her head.

"I shouldn't have been there."

"But I wanted you there."

"To keep me under the influence."

He hung his head. "Yeah."

"So Madison still lives at our old place?"

"Yeah. With Jordan."

Would God want Katie to tell Madison about God's love, or would that open her up to police investigation? She would like to ask Larry, but she'd have to be content to ask Lacey. Surely Mrs. Good Christian would know how to advise her. Katie looked at her watch.

"I've got to get out of here. Almost time for my dinner shift."

"Come to my place tonight. We'll watch a movie or something."

"Sorry. By then, I'll need my sleep." *And need to keep my distance from Collin.*

෧

Katie was as nervous as a thief on the run. Rachel and Lacey were waiting on the front porch when Katie drove up. She took a moment to still her pulse. She hadn't been alone overnight with her daughter since the child was four. When Katie climbed out, Rachel jumped up and down.

"I'm bringing my Go Fish cards."

Katie smoothed back the girl's wayward hair.

"Sounds good."

Lacey stood. "She's been so excited."

"Me too." Katie gave Rachel a big hug and moved on to her sister. "It still amazes me how small you are. I was used to Fat Lacey." She slapped a hand over her mouth. "Sorry, that wasn't very nice."

Lacey waved it away. "No problem. I was Fat Lacey all my adult life until God healed me."

"And forgave me."

"Yes, he did." Lacey ushered them into the house. "Get your bag, Rachel."

The child scampered off.

"May I ask you a question about God? I'm still new at all this," Katie said.

"Of course you can."

"I would like to witness to my old roommate, Madison, but our relationship is strained." Katie explained the situation. "Do you think I should wait a while to contact her?"

Lacey puckered her lips and heaved a sigh. "I think I'd wait."

"That's kind of what I thought, but I want to be willing. I've been so mad at her, and I know God wants me to let go of that."

"Pastor Larry would tell us to keep them in our prayers."

Perspiration broke out at Katie's hairline, and it wasn't because of the temperature.

"So what's up with him?" *Did that sound pathetic?*

"Who? The pastor?"

Rachel lugged out her bag. Katie picked it up.

"Yes." The bag shook in her hands. "Is he okay? Back preaching?" *Married?*

"Oh, yes, he's been back in the pulpit for three or four weeks now. Seems to be doing well."

Katie waited, hoping, but Lacey seemed to have nothing left to add. Maybe Katie didn't want to hear. Rachel tugged on Katie's hand.

"Come on. I want to see where you live."

"Well, you better take this young lady before she yanks off your hand." Lacey snickered.

"Yes," Katie said, her voice shaky from pulling her mind away from Larry. She was forgiven, but not deserving. Her past haunted her still, like an extra scar.

Rachel waited with expectant eyes. Katie's sister was smiling and accepting. That was a blessing of forgiveness from God, and Katie needed to remember that.

"Let's go," Rachel squealed.

Mom and daughter skipped to the car. The engine roared to life, and Katie drove away.

"So, would you like to go for a burger and fries where I work?"

"Yes." Rachel bounced. "Will you work tonight?"

"Better not."

"Good. Then yes, I want to go. Can I get onion rings?"

"If that's what you want."

"Then that's what I'll have."

Katie and Rachel chatted and planned their Sunday over dinner at the Country Dinner Restaurant. Katie introduced her daughter to Paul and the other workers.

"I've never come here just to eat before," Katie confessed. "It's fun."

"I think it's fun too."

Rachel picked up a sign stuck on top of the napkin holder. Her gaze lifted.

"Yes, you can have ice cream if you eat your burger and fries."

"You mean burger and rings." Rachel giggled.

"I mean burger and rings."

They both ended up having ice cream for dessert, and Katie left feeling like a stuffed Thanksgiving turkey with a smile.

Before she opened her apartment door, she halted. A bad case of nerves struck her voice and worked its way down into her gut.

"At my place, we act like we're camping." The words came out with a quiver.

Questions crossed Rachel's eyes. One tiny thumb pointed up her cheek. Her jaw rested on her fist.

"How can we camp inside? Camping is outside."

"Not at my house."

Rachel shook her head. "I don't understand."

Katie squatted before her daughter. With all the food she'd eaten plus the worry over what she had to offer her daughter, her stomach lurched.

"It means we sleep on the floor in sleeping bags."

She had purchased one with colorful zigzags for Rachel.

The girl still showed confusion.

Katie stood. *Spit it out, woman.* "I don't have a bed."

Rachel's eyes widened. "No bed at all?"

"No. Just sleeping bags."

The questions slowly disappeared from Rachel's expression. Her mouth turned into a smiley face.

"That sounds fun."

Katie's shoulders dropped with relief. She swung open the door and allowed Rachel to examine the small apartment. When she stopped at the kitchen, she tilted her head to the left.

"Do you have food?"

"I have Twizzlers and Tootsie Pops. Does that count?"

Rachel bounced. "That's my favorites."

"Mine too."

The relief sunk into each muscle. The last roadblock to a real relationship with her daughter had been swept away with a daughter's bounce.

The night went well. In the morning, Katie sprang for donuts. Rachel devoured two of them with milk.

A soft knock came at the door.

Katie froze. Would she ever get to where change didn't bring fright?

Rachel started toward the door.

"Wait." Katie caught the girl's hand. "First, we look in the peephole." She pointed.

"But I can't reach that high."

Katie glanced around the place. There was nothing to be used for a stepstool other than unsteady lawn chairs.

"We'll buy a small stool that we'll place beside the door for you to use. Right now, I'll lift you." She picked her up by her waist.

"It's a dressed-up lady with a big package in a pink cover," Rachel said.

Katie set down the girl and looked for herself. She swung open the door.

"Hello." Her voice trembled.

Mrs. Martinez traipsed into the middle of the room. Her gaze circled her surroundings. Her fingers drew the bundle closer to her heart. She took a couple of steps and peered into the bedroom with its sleeping bags and backpacks and she grimaced.

After a deliberate move around the woman, Katie shut the bedroom door and turned to face her nemesis.

"So, I'm not wealthy, but it's mine."

The bundle began to squirm.

Tears stung Katie's eyes. "Is that . . . ?"

"Kinsley's daughter. Yes." Mrs. Martinez spread open the pink blanket. The woman bent to kiss the tiny forehead. Her face was red. Her words were husky. "It's been a long time since I had the full responsibility of an infant." She gave a weak smile. "It's exhausting, especially with all her coughing and everything."

"It's my sister." Rachel bounced again and held out her arms toward Baby Katie. "Can I hold her? I'll be really, really careful."

Katie's eyes were locked on the baby.

"Excuse me, what did you say?" she asked Mrs. Martinez.

Mrs. Martinez repeated it and thrust the baby toward Katie.

"You offered to share custody. Do you still want to?"

A vision of Kinsley's face when they met at the skating rink sprang to Katie's thoughts. How could she have known how it would affect her life? She nestled the babe in her arms like an unwrapped present.

"I would love that, but is it okay with your husband?"

"I told him I needed help, and you offered. Unless he planned on getting up at night with her every night, he couldn't argue."

She held the babe toward Katie. Katie's arms wrapped around the child. Her legs were shaky. She walked to one of Collin's lawn chairs and dropped. Her right pointer finger traced the baby's cheek and allowed the tiny hand to get a grip on it. She motioned to Mrs. Martinez to sit in the other chair. Rachel stood beside Katie, adoring, and touching.

"Do you want me to keep her now?" Katie asked Mrs. Martinez.

The redness in the woman's face had dimmed to pink.

"I would give anything for a full night's sleep." She took one more examination of the apartment. "I could bring anything you needed."

Heat now set Katie's neck on fire.

"Rachel and I will be going to my sister's house in Wharton Rock this afternoon. I can pick up what I need from there. A few diapers, wipes, and a bottle or two should suffice. I told them to sell the cradle I bought for the baby." Her voice cracked. "I don't think she has yet."

She eyed the sleeping lamb diaper bag the woman had dropped at the door. The woman nodded to it with her head.

"That bag should provide those things. Except for the cradle. I'm truly sorry for what we put you through, but you ..." She stood but paused. "What time tomorrow would I need to pick her up?"

"I go to work at four tomorrow so ..."

Both women said "three thirty" at the same time, and Katie gave a quick nod. Mrs. Martinez slid to the door.

"We'll work out the details later, depending on your work schedule. I'm more flexible."

"Sounds good." Katie stood and reached out a hand to shake. "Thank you. This has been an answer to prayer."

"I've noticed you in church the last few weeks. I'm praying for you."

Then the woman was gone. Baby Katie lay in Katie's arms, and Rachel leaned against her shoulder. It was a good day. One of those that Katie suspected would soon end.

CHAPTER *Forty-Five*

The weekend was perfect. Katie couldn't get enough of rocking the baby. The cradle sat in the corner of her bedroom, still unused. Katie couldn't lay her down. Her night with Rachel had been God-sent and blessed. Katie's peace mirrored that of the sleeping babe.

Midnight came and went. She needed sleep. Gently placing Baby Katie in the cradle she had gotten from Lacey's house, Katie stretched out in her sleeping bag. The hard floor seemed harder than usual, but it would take two more paychecks and good tips to regain enough to buy a bed.

With gratitude, she remembered the lack of privacy in prison and blessed God for this dark, quiet room that was all hers, as long as she could keep up the rent. She drifted into blissful slumber, only to be woken by the baby's coughing.

In the moonlight streaming through the bedroom window, Katie crawled from her warm cocoon and bent over the cradle. With arms and legs moving vigorously, the infant's face looked contorted and irritated. Each cough caused her breath to catch, scaring Katie.

She clutched the small frame against her breast, paced, and prayed. After the fire, the doctor had warned them that the smoke injured the tiny lungs. Mrs. Martinez had mentioned her coughing. Did they have medicine to give her? She picked up the phone to call the woman but noticed the time was one in the morning. Could it wait? All Katie needed was to get on the bad side of the Martinez the first time they allowed her to keep Kinsley's daughter. She lay the phone aside and continued to pace.

The baby relaxed. The cough halted. Her breathing evened out to regular and quiet. Still, Katie feared laying her in the cradle. She plopped to the floor, still holding the thankfully breathing child and waited.

Sometime, about dawn, she awoke, slouched to one side on the floor, with the babe across her arm, crying with all her might. How could Katie have fallen asleep? It was a dangerous position for the babe. What if she'd rolled over on her?

Thank you, Lord, for protecting her.

After feeding and changing the babe, she laid her in the cradle and sat watch until the next feeding, her faith stronger than ever.

Two weeks passed after that first night with Baby Katie, two weeks Katie had missed both Rachel and the baby, but Katie's days were full. She talked with Lacey nearly every day. Strange how their relationship had grown. At the time of her attack at sixteen, the devil had stolen Katie's childhood love for her sister. In weeks, God had restored that blessing. Even Mom was less controlling, more submissive, and accepting of her baby girl's life.

Larry had moved on. She would too. A new dream formulated in her mind of a home for wayward girls with young babies. Kinsley became Katie's driving force. She worked hard and prayed harder.

In the middle of her Saturday evening shift, her phone pinged. She gave a quick glance on the way back to the kitchen. It came from a number she didn't recognize and said, "Call ASAP."

She picked up three platters and delivered them to three men in the corner booth.

"Does that look okay?"

"Wonderful, as usual, Katie."

One man winked. She returned the favor.

After she scurried over to Paul, she held up her phone message.

"May I call back?"

"Who is it?"

"I don't know." But tremors slithered down her spine just looking at it.

"Okay, but hurry. More customers are coming in. I need you on the floor."

"Will do." She stepped to the back of the kitchen, faced the pantry, and dialed.

"Hello," a gruff male voice answered.

"This is Katie Smith. Someone texted me from this number."

Silence.

"Hello, are you still there?" The phone was hot in her hand. Her stomach churned.

The voice cracked but began. "This is Horace Martinez." A pause. "Kinsley's baby is dead."

"What?"

"It was God's judgment on my daughter's sin."

He hung up.

The phone slipped from Katie's grasp. Stacks of hamburger buns swam before her eyes.

Voices called in the background.

"Burger and fries."

"Two specials up."

The bell clanged.

So normal, yet so out of place. The world couldn't be continuing when a baby died.

"Katie. You okay? You're white as a ghost." Paul touched her arm.

Her sight glared his way, but she didn't see him. Swiveling, she stormed from the kitchen, through the dining room, and out the door. Somewhere in the background of her mind, she heard her name called, but her legs pumped harder. She couldn't breathe. Lunging into the driver's seat, she started the car, heading toward Wharton Rock, toward home.

A floodlight on the sign and the building illuminated Wharton Rock Community Church. Larry's white truck was the only vehicle in sight. Katie stopped her car beside his and marched inside, following an internal light.

Behind a desk, Larry poured over papers scattered in front of him. She eased inside and waited. Her pulse roared in her ears. He glanced up and jumped to his feet.

"Katie." His voice quivered.

During her last days in prison, she'd marked off the days, longing to break through that last door to the real world. Now she knew the real world kicked you in the teeth worse than prison.

"Baby Katie died." She maintained eye contact.

"I'm so sorry." His eyes gentled, his mouth grew tight.

Her eyes stayed dry. "Mr. Martinez said it was God's judgment for Kinsley's sin, but I don't think so. It was my sin."

"Oh, Katie, I told you. God doesn't work that way."

With a ramrod straight back, she stomped her foot.

"She had asthma. Did you know that? I gave it to her."

"You couldn't have—"

"Lacey asked me to do the dishes. I didn't. I might've noticed a fire starting if I had stayed up later. The smoke gave the baby asthma."

"No, it was faulty—"

"I killed her. I'm bad."

She crumpled, her eyes rolling back in her head.

Before she reached the floor, strong arms caught her and carried her to the Wharton Rock Urgent Care Clinic. Voices blurred. Her mouth was forced open to swallow medicine. When she shivered, a warmed-up blanket was tucked around her.

The next thing she remembered was waking up in Lacey's front bedroom with her sister rocking in a chair and humming "Amazing Grace."

CHAPTER *Forty–Six*

Mourners filled the Apache Falls Church two days later. Mr. Martinez glowered at Katie, but his wife had insisted she sit with the family. Forty people jammed in a side room until it was time to file into the service.

In the corner, Katie tried to disappear. The inquiring looks and laughing of children felt like pins poking—first an arm, then a leg—until her body seemed to be in a vise. All the attention went to Mrs. Martinez, whose loud cries could be heard over the clamor.

The door opened, and Lacey ushered Rachel into the room. She spotted her mother and ran her way. Katie lifted thankful eyes to her sister, who waved and stepped out. Rachel climbed into Katie's lap.

"Mama Lacey said I should come today because church would be an honor to my baby sister." She smoothed her new skirt. "Do you like it?"

Katie examined the material. "It's beautiful. Did you buy it for today?"

"Yes. Mama said it was important because my sister went to heaven and would never come back again. That makes me sad."

"It makes me sad too." One of many emotions—anger at the Martinezes, fear, worry, self-condemnation, confusion.

Reverend Schumacher didn't speak. It was his new assistant minister. The word pictures he painted were beautiful and gave Katie room for thought. She longed to ask Larry about it, but that wasn't wise. The organ music filled the room. Since the Martinez family had vied for only a memorial without a casket, people filed out after the service. At the end, so did the family.

When Katie and Rachel entered the lobby, Lacey and Toby slid to each side. Toby picked up Rachel. They led Katie to one corner. Her eyes widened. Probably twenty or thirty people from Wharton Rock stood with outstretched hands, ready to embrace the local girl gone bad, but none of them brought up her sins—not prison, not drugs, nor her failures with men. They offered comfort, an offer of prayers, and lots of love. For Katie.

Clinging to her sister to hold her up, the dam on her tears broke. Lacey patted her back, like she'd done when Katie had been Rachel's age.

"Well, I don't know about everyone else, but I'm ready to get out of this fancy church."

Mom thumped her cane. Several laughed, but many moved toward the door. Katie swiped at her tears and fought for control.

"Typical mom," she said to Lacey. "Guess we better move."

With a clearing of the throat and a touch on the arm, Mr. Martinez stopped Katie.

"They did an autopsy. Her lungs were okay. They're calling it SIDS." He shrugged. "My wife said you should know."

"Thank you," Katie said. "I'm sorry for both your losses. I'm glad I met Kinsley. She was a wonderful young woman, and that baby was a blessing." She sniffed twice, but those words needed to be said.

The man merely grunted, but his shoulders sagged. He looked older, less sure.

Rachel slipped one hand into each of her mother's hands.

"I'm hungry."

Katie smiled. "I must go."

She dipped her head to the man and left with a drove of family and friends.

Just ahead of Toby's truck that had transported the family to Apache Falls, Larry opened a truck door for Michelle. When he turned, his gaze locked on Katie. An electric jolt struck her heart. He stepped toward her. She tugged Rachel his way. It was like a pull toward freedom. Then he smiled and dropped his head. He circled the truck, got in, and drove off.

"You're going the wrong way, Mama," Rachel said.

"Yes, I was. Sorry."

She climbed into Toby's backseat to go home.

CHAPTER *Forty-Seven*

Yellow and blue tiles backsplashed an older-looking white stove. The refrigerator was new. The walls around the dining area sported a new coat of off-white paint. Michelle had good ideas to spruce up the old house owned by Community Church and provided rent-free as part of the pastor's salary. It wasn't her ideas that had bothered Larry, but he would not be controlled or manipulated.

How could he be so insensitive—engaged to one woman and drawn to another?

A chill swept over him. He loved the big house, but it was meant for a family. Michelle was in her element at this church. Already in love with the small congregation, she seemed to be everything to everyone, the perfect pastor's wife, but she didn't want children.

Arms propped on top of the table, his head dropped to his hands. The pain in his chest and leg had diminished, but today his forehead ached. Flashes of light danced at the edge of his vision. Stress, most likely. Ever since Katie had burst into his office to tell him about the babe's death, two voices had vied for prominence in his mind, shredding the volatile threads of his assurance for the future, ripping his life apart.

Was he a fool? Or a love-sick puppy? He stiffened. A man strong enough to stand against criminals and church deacons couldn't be described as a puppy. He sipped his coffee and opened his Bible.

Lead me, Lord.

A mockingbird sang in the pear tree outside his window. A dove cooed, coordinated like God's symphony.

He read, "Let me hear Your lovingkindness in the morning, For I trust in You, Teach me the way in which I should walk, For to You I lift up my soul."

That was Psalm 143:8. He loved the Psalms, so he continued to read as his vision cleared and his thinking meshed with His Lord. The pain relieved.

The remembrance of his second chance brought him to his knees.

Moving forward with grief was new to Katie. Anger, yes. Rejection, oh, yes. Envy too. But not grief. Numbness battled each muscle, rendering them less efficient. Her brain was in a permanent fog. Work days marched on without her remembering that she'd traveled to the restaurant or back to her apartment. Only Lacey and Rachel's visit last week had broken the cycle of sadness. She still wondered at the restoration brought by God in those relationships.

After a while, she admitted the sorrow didn't only stem from losing Baby Katie but the saying of a final farewell to her dream of romance with Larry. She'd known it with her mind. Hadn't she been the one to tell him she wasn't pastor's wife material? When she saw him with Michelle at the funeral, an arrow aimed and let go the realization straight into her heart.

Her Friday lunch shift ended. She had just stretched across her sleeping bag when her doorbell rang. Shaking off the fatigue with a sigh, she went to peep through the hole and then opened the door.

"What's up?"

Collin moved inside and turned to face her.

"I'm ready."

"Ready for what?"

His arms opened in a come-hither gesture.

"For this salvation stuff you keep telling me about."

Feeling both warmth and chill, she opened her mouth, but all that came out was, "Oh." Her mouth seemed stuffed with cotton candy. She was so out of her comfort zone.

"Mmm, let me get my Bible."

She thumbed through trying to find the Scripture Lacey told her about that time after Katie gave her heart to Christ but wanted to know if she did it right. It was something about confessing and believing. Her hands shook so she couldn't find anything. Dropping the Bible to her side, her gaze rested on her friend. Collin paced a five-foot line in front of her. She inhaled, exhaled, and took him by the arms.

"You realize that this is all new to me."

"I know, but what did you do?"

His ears were firehouse red, but his expression was one of fear.

"Do you love God?"

"I think so. The best I know how."

"Are you sorry for all the bad things you've done, and do you intend to quit doing them?"

"I've already stopped." The red of his ears darkened and spread. "Guess I need to stop lying and drinking too. Huh?" He nodded. "I'm sorry. I'll quit."

"Collin." She shook his arms. "You can't do it in your power. God helps you."

"Really?"

"Really."

A big grin split his face. "Then, piece of cake."

"I know there's a verse about confessing the bad stuff, and you did that, and believing that Jesus died on the cross for you."

"I do," he said and giggled. "Sounds like I'm getting married."

Her body relaxed. She threw her arms around Collin and whispered in his ear. "That's it. Jesus loves you and forgives you. I'm so excited for you." She kissed his cheek.

A breathless voice came from the open door. "Oh, my, I'm so sorry."

Her arms dropped from around Collin. She'd forgotten the door. Racing out and along the platform, she spotted Larry's tall figure taking the steps two at a time. Already with a catch in her breathing, she hurried down the steps, yelling for him to stop.

His white truck sped away, and her heart broke. With slumped shoulders and ducked head, she walked back to her place.

Collin stood in her doorway.

"You love him, don't you?"

Did she? Her ribs ached from the hammering of her heart. Life seemed incomplete without her preacher man.

"Go after him."

"I don't know where he's going. Besides, he might not love me."

Though warm on the outside, she felt chilled deep inside. Her mind grasped for good things. God forgave her. He loved her. She had a relationship with Rachel. Collin had come to Christ. So much good. Was it at the cost of losing Larry?

"Hey, sweet stuff, you'll never know unless you go after him." Collin's voice sounded far away. "Guess I can't call you that anymore." He sniffed.

Her eyes locked on his. The tips of her mouth turned upward as hope warmed her deepest parts. She snatched her purse and keys.

"Lock up," she yelled.

"You got it."

"And, thanks," she called from near the bottom of the stairs.

CHAPTER *Forty-Eight*

Enormous waves rolled to Buffalo Lake's shore. The wind bowed trees. Clouds scattered over the setting sun, striking the landscape with abundant color, a typical North Texas sunset. Katie's mother always told her, "You can't have pretty sunsets without clouds." Katie had lived through lots of clouds, but with God's second chance, well, maybe.

Tears blinded her. She'd checked the police station, his house, and the church without success. Then she parked down the road and hiked around the lake until she spotted him.

On the mound of the murder site he'd investigated, Larry stood tall, thin, and tough. The wind rumpled his short hair. His hands rose toward heaven.

"Why?" His words rumbled with the wind and resounded like an echo.

He hadn't heard her. His agony loomed larger than life. She swiped at her wet face, but the wind did the best job of drying it. While biting her lower lip, she climbed across boulders to the bare mound. When she neared, she stopped. In a quiet voice, she called his name.

He whirled. In the dim light, shadows crossed his cheeks, his expression a mask of horror, his taut body in a fight-or-flee mode. Upon seeing her, his features softened.

"Katie. What are you doing here?"

She didn't move. "Looking for you."

"Where's Collin?" He rubbed the back of his neck, and his voice cracked. "Look, I'm sorry I walked in on you, but the door was open."

She took one step forward. "I know. And all you walked in on was Collin being saved."

His arms dropped. He blinked.

"Saved?"

"Yeah. I've been telling him about Jesus." She took another step closer and straightened. "Aren't you proud of me?"

"You won Collin to Christ?" He grabbed his forehead and shook his head. "Oh, my . . . a second chance." His words were lost on the wind.

She halted. The wind pasted her swishy black top to her skin. Blonde curls beat against her neck.

"I love you, Preacher Man."

His head snapped to attention. "What did you say?"

"I'm not saying it again."

He closed the space between them. His arms encircled her. Her face buried in his hard chest. She had never felt more safe. He bent toward her, his lips two inches away, his breath warm on her cheeks. She pulled away.

"Listen, Buddy, no kiss unless I know how you feel."

A grin changed his whole persona. "Didn't I tell you?"

"No, you didn't. I bare my soul, and you come for a kiss. I don't think so." She bowed her head. He lifted her chin with one finger.

"I love you, my second chance Katie."

A ray of the sun set his brown eyes to glistening. Her pulse nosedived.

"We must think logically here. You're a preacher, and I'm still an ex-con."

"An ex-con with a second chance." His first kiss was soft as velvet. "An ex-con worth forgiving and worth loving. Did I tell you I love you?"

His crushing kiss shut up any retort.

The End

DISCUSSION QUESTIONS
FOR
Worth Forgiving

1. Longing for love, Katie has always used her sex appeal to attract men. What changes her mind when she first gets out of prison?

2. Katie spurns going to live with her sister, preferring to live in a halfway house with other ex-cons. In your opinion, is that a wise choice or a bad one?

3. Do you feel that Katie's sister, Lacey, really wants her sister to move in with them? Why? Why not?

4. Katie's mother wants Katie to move back home. What reason does she give? What reason do you feel is the truth?

5. Larry can't find a ministerial job because he doesn't have a wife. How does that hamper a pastor?

6. Katie often claims that prison was much easier than living on the outside. Why do you think that would be?

7. From a preacher at church, Katie experiences severe prejudice. Have you ever known someone who claimed to be a Christian that was prejudiced against a class of people?

8. Larry strayed away from God when he was a young teen and lost his father. A man took advantage of Larry's pain and led him into breaking the law. Have you or someone you know trusted the wrong person?

9. Katie, Lacey, and their mother make up a dysfunctional family. Do you think the reason is keeping secrets? Should Katie have immediately told her family about her attack as a teenager?

10. Kinsley is expecting a baby. She's only fifteen, and the dad isn't in the picture. Her parents insist she get rid of it. How do you feel about abortion in this case? In Kinsley's case, should she have vied for giving the child up for adoption rather than raising her alone?

11. Larry wants to minister and lead others to the second chance that he was given. When offered a ministerial job, why does he feel unworthy?

12. How does Katie and Larry's individual relationships with Christ affect their relationship, or does it?

13. When Larry chooses a wife in the hospital, why does Michelle seem to be the better choice as a pastor's wife?

14. Lacey is raising her niece and has often baled Katie out of trouble. What did she do that hampered the reconciliation?

15. Toby insists on taking Baby Katie to her grandparents. Kinsley wanted Katie to raise the child. Why was that a bad idea? Should Katie have taken back the baby immediately even though the grandparents said they didn't want her?

16. Katie witnesses to her old boyfriend Collin and ends up winning him to Christ. She wonders if she should witness to Madison, who betrayed her. Do you think that's wise?

17. Have you ever felt that you were not worth forgiving?

Acknowledgements

Thank you, Duke and Kimberly Pennell of Pen-L Publishing, for pushing me to write a sequel to *Worth Her Weight*. After they started my motor running, I discovered Katie wished to tell her unique story of forgiveness and redemption.

Without my young friend, Stephanie Bailey, I would never have been able to grasp the prejudice and difficulty of a woman coming out of prison and wishing to make a new life for herself and her daughter. Thanks loads for giving me an honest interview.

A big thanks to Greg Lynn, the fire chief of Electra, Texas, the real town that Wharton Rock exemplifies. He kindly answered all of a newbie's questions about fires and smoke inhalation treatment.

I found fantastic help, as usual, on the American Christian Fiction Writers (ACFW) online loop, especially for information on postpartum preeclampsia and fires. Two friends who went through chemotherapy for breast cancer, Linda Simco and Carolyn Ballard, offered insight into the mindset and pain of shingles and cancer.

Two faithful beta readers always strengthen my writing. The first is former teacher Sue Watson, who gives me lots of help on point of view, grammar, and pacing. The second is my dear husband, Charles L. Brown, who critiques the male roles. When Katie made him mad, I knew I had hit a nerve.

Thanks, most of all, to my Heavenly Father, who never ceases to amaze me with His blessings. Thank you for allowing me to tell another story of victory in Jesus.

About Janet K. Brown

Even Janet was surprised that she had a penchant for teens and ghosts when she released her debut novel, an inspirational young adult story, *Victoria and the Ghost,* in July 2012. She's been writing ever since. She uses her platform as a recovering compulsive overeater to weave stories of hope for addiction, compulsion, or impossible situations, with an occasional detour into the paranormal.

Worth Forgiving, a work of inspirational women's fiction, is the second in the "Wharton Rock Series," and follows *Worth Her Weight,* published in 2015. The third installment in the Wharton Rock Series is due out in 2017. She also penned an in-depth devotional for healthy living titled *Divine Dining: 365 Devotions to Guide You to Healthier Weight and Abundant Wellness* (2012). An accompanying workbook is due out by the end of 2016.

Janet and her husband, Charles, love to travel with their RV, work in their church, and visit their daughters' families. When not traveling, they live in Wichita Falls, Texas, where she teaches workshops on writing, weight loss, and the historical settings of her teen books.

FIND JANET AT:

www.JanetKBrown.com

Twitter: JanetKBrownTX

Facebook: Janet-K-Brown-Author

E-mail: Janet.hope@att.net

If you enjoy this book, please consider leaving a review on Amazon, Goodreads, or by even word of mouth. It's the best compliment you can give an author.

Special Bonus!

Don't miss Janet's **Worth Her Weight**,
the first Wharton Rock novel,
available at Pen-L.com and your
favorite bookseller in print and ebook.

**How can a woman
who gives to everyone but herself
accept God's love and healing
when she believes she's fat, unworthy, and unfixable?**

PRAISE FOR *WORTH HER WEIGHT*:

"The book was great! And true to the way a food addict deals with their struggles. I know first-hand. Love the book."

~ DEELYNN LOPEZ, Program Director of Behavioral Health
Group & Co-leader for Celebrate Recovery

EXCERPT FROM *WORTH HER WEIGHT*:

Without a word, Mom held out a letter to Lacey.

A cold shiver shook her—the same foreboding she had sensed in the morning. "What's this?"

Her mother shrugged. "Came in today's mail."

Lacey opened it, her Mom watching as she read.

She threw the paper across the room. It bounced halfway back to her. "Well, if that doesn't take the cake." She paced, her heels clicking on the scratched and scarred kitchen tiles. The noise level grew louder when she snatched plates from the cabinet and dropped them to the table.

"Save the dishes." Mom's tone was dry, with no humor.

Something like a growl escaped Lacey's lips. "Katie makes the messes. Lacey cleans them up. Isn't that right, Mom?" She crossed her arms over her chest and glared at her mother. "Did you know about this?" Her fingers began drumming on her opposite forearm. Her jaw got so tight, it hurt.

Her mother shook her head. She glanced at Rachel.

The anger was difficult for Lacey to swallow, but she tried. "Sweetie, go wash your hands before we eat."

The child scooted a chair toward the sink.

Lacey halted her. "Go to the bathroom and use the stool there." Her voice shook from her effort at control.

Rachel looked at the pizza with longing, but she obeyed.

The pepperoni and mozzarella aroma permeated the house. Nausea churned in Lacey's stomach despite how good it smelled.

"Has Katie gone?" Mom asked with a soft tone.

In contrast, Lacey nearly yelled. "Of course, she has!"

The lines in Mom's face seemed to deepen. Her skin paled. Lacey was sure the cane was the only thing that kept Mom from falling as she coped with the pain inflicted by her favorite daughter.

The fight had gone out of Lacey. Her knees wobbled. She eased into a chair and nodded. "She wants me to have custody of Rachel. She doesn't even want her own daughter, Mom. What kind of woman walks away from her flesh and blood?"

A whimper came from the living room.

Heat rushed up Lacey's neck. She jumped up and ran, wishing she could erase her careless words.

Rachel curled into a ball on the sofa, her right thumb inserted firmly in her mouth.

"Aunt Lacey's sorry. I didn't mean what I said."

Rachel sucked harder, pulling it out momentarily to speak. "Is my mama coming to get me today?"

"No, sweetheart, not today. Maybe another day." She patted her niece's bare legs.

The sucking sound grew louder. Lacey sat on the floor patting and wondering what to say or do. A clap of thunder reminded her of the unsettled clouds. "I need to go close my car windows. I'll be right back."

She ran outside, started the car, and raised her driver's side window. Just as she got back inside, the downpour had begun.

Mom still sat at the kitchen table, her head in her hands. She rose, grabbing her cane. Red puffy eyes alerted Lacey to her mother's tears, something that seldom happened.

Compassion knocked at Lacey's heart, but she locked it out, when she realized the tears were all for Katie.

Lacey sat on the floor beside Rachel. "You ready for some pizza?" Lacey wanted kids one day, but she wanted her own with a husband by her side. She couldn't attract a man, but now she had a child to raise.

Mom plopped into her recliner. "Do you think food will fix everything?"

"Works for me." Lacey tried a teasing note. "Whenever things go wrong, food makes it better." She huffed at Mom and grimaced. "Didn't you know that?" Good thing she hadn't planned on the cruise. She crunched up the pamphlet and threw it in the trash along with a few other dreams. She'd stay fat and lonely.

What was she going to do with a four-year-old?

FIND IT AT:

WWW.PEN-L.COM/WORTHHERWEIGHT.HTML

If you'd like to hear more about Janet's upcoming books, free deals, and other great Pen-L authors, sign up for our Pals of Pen-L Newsletter here!

WWW.PEN-L.COM/OPTIN/THANKS.HTML

Special Bonus!

Don't miss Janet's ***Divine Dining: 365 Devotions to Guide You to Healthier Weight and Abundant Wellness,*** available at Pen-L.com or your favorite bookseller in ebook and print.

Daily lessons that are invaluable in helping anyone struggling with weight to find the strength and motivation to reach abundant health.

JANUARY 7

THE PROTECTION OF THE WREN CACTUS

To him who is able to keep you from falling and to present you before his glorious presence without fault and with great joy.
JUDE 24 NIV

If food compulsion is part of our carnal life, danger lurks whenever we leave God's protection.

At a friend's country home, we noticed a cactus bush three to four feet high with a nest of wrens on one side. We commented.

"That's our wren cactus, our sanctuary for birds," our friend told us.

On the other side of the bush, we spotted baby mocking-birds. Instead of flying to high places to be safe from the coyotes and deer, birds make their home here in a small bush. On examination, we noticed birds fly into the cactus without touching the prickly thorns. A larger animal would be unable to do that, so the birds make their nests in perfect safety right under the noses of their enemies.

God is our wren cactus. He protects us from certain defeat and destruction while in the presence of food that would tempt us. His loving arms encircle us. The enemy can't get past His defense.

PRAYER: *When I'm at a restaurant or party, a potluck, or another's home, I'm vulnerable without your hedge. Please protect me today, Lord.*

MAY 14

FORGET ABOUT IT

For I will forgive their wickedness and will remember their sins no more.
HEBREWS 8:12 NIV

When I pull into my garage after going to the grocery store, I love to spot my husband's car at home because I know he can lift my burden of groceries and bring them into the house, relieving me of that weight. Once I told him to pile everything on the sofa so it wouldn't be on the kitchen counter where I needed to start dinner. Unfortunately, he didn't follow my instructions. By habit, he placed every sack on the kitchen counter.

I huffed, puffed, and transferred every item from the counter to the sofa struggling against the weight of five pounds of flour and two milk cartons. When I'd finished, my back ached from the heavy lifting, and my anger fomented against my husband.

"Why didn't you remind me?" he asked. "I meant to lift them for you."

Are we like that with God? Do we ask for our sins to be removed, but then pick them up again to carry?

Satan uses past sins to disable our effectiveness. When I repented and asked Jesus into my heart, He took my burden of sin and cast it as the Bible says, "as far as the east is from the west." Therefore, I can be sure that any condemnation I have over sins from my past comes from the devil.

Leave them with Jesus. Talk to him about any anguish you feel. He means to relieve us of those burdens. Not unlike un-wanted pounds on our bodies, resentment and anger are too heavy for us to bear.

PRAYER: Lord, I leave my sins at Your feet. Help me
to forget about them as You have done.

DECEMBER 31

SET GOALS AND DREAM

But God hath revealed them unto us by his Spirit, for the Spirit searcheth
all things, yea the deep things of God. 1 CORINTHIANS 2:10

Tomorrow we begin a new year. New Year's resolutions may not work, but setting well-thought-out, written, and prayed-over goals do. It's time to evaluate the illness that tied us in knots. Has God brought an emotional healing during this year? Has He started a new work? Have you hit bottom and you're ready to begin?

Wherever you are on the path, it's time to focus. In the New Year, will it be God's Way?

Go through these steps:

Decide if you're ready to submit to God.

Read this daily devotion book in the New Year and everything else that will help, especially the Bible.

Energize through leaving off sugars and fats that drain your vitality.

Admit your powerlessness and ask God to take over your life.

Mentor others as you receive your day-by-day healing.

Discern God's will daily.

Record your progress and reaffirm God's leading.

Eat the Word. Make it part of you.

Associate with friends that pray and encourage.

Maintain contact with God, regardless of what's going on in your world.

PRAYER: *I can't. God can. Lead me in the coming year.*

PRAISE FOR DIVINE DINING:

"*Divine Dining* is one of the best devotional books I've read. Okay, I admit I'm a sugarholic. Anything sweet, especially chocolate, calls to me. I also admit that I've never had a weight or overeating problem. I try to eat healthy foods, except for the sugar, of course. So why does this book appeal to me? First, the author starts each day's devotion with a scripture. These verses from the Bible apply to all aspects of our lives, not just what we eat. Next, the author tells a short story relating to this verse and how she applies it to her life. She closes with a prayer. She does each day of the year this way, with stories and her experiences. And there's something there for everyone.

"But you'll enjoy *Divine Dining* more if you read it for yourself. I think you may see similarities to your life in some of the stories. I have. This would make a great gift for friends and family, especially those struggling with a difficult issue in their lives. The book will help them realize they're not alone and with God's help they will succeed in achieving their goals. Why not pick up a copy for your local library and your church library, as well as for yourself?"

~ BEVERLY'S REVIEWS

FIND IT AT:

WWW.PEN-L.COM/DIVINEDINING.HTML

If you'd like to hear more about Janet's upcoming books, free deals, and other great Pen-L authors, sign up for our Pals of Pen-L Newsletter here!

WWW.PEN-L.COM/OPTIN/THANKS.HTML